When Ivory Towers Fall

VC Sanford

When Ivory Towers Fall

Published in the United States of America
341 Enterprise
Copyright 2021 by VC Sanford
ISBN: 978-1-7370688-9-1

This is a work of fiction. Except for historical and famous characters, all characters, names, places, and events appearing in this work are a product of the author's imagination or used fictitiously. Any resemblance to real persons, living or dead, is entirely coincidental.

Dedication

Peggy Banks Bradley

No words can do her justice.

Chapter One

"You can picture it, can't you?" Mason Reeves asked Robert Wilson as they sat on the edge of the sofa, his body leaning over the large rolled-out plans spread out on the large glass coffee table. "Instead of building a studio outback, we buy one in an older neighborhood they are developing. Take this empty drugstore, for example. He tossed the printout on the table. "It's too small for big companies to want it, but it's double the space that we can afford if we build new. We can section this part of the building off for the studio, right there, see? All state-of-the art. And it's cheaper than rehabbing old stuff I pick up secondhand. It will be fuckin' amazing."

The late afternoon sun reflected the high-lights in his dirty blonde hair and beamed a bright orange glow through the windows of their Druid Hills home. Ace loved this house for the privacy if nothing else. Set in a thickly wooded lot above a winding road and backing up to acres of heavily wooded forest, they had bought it after returning from Mexico as a quiet retreat from the paparazzi that hounded them. Occasionally, an overly enthusiastic fan might climb the fence, and one hiked through the park and climbed a tree, but usually it offered plenty of privacy. The mid-century modern design offered breathtaking views of the hills in the back, as well as overlooking the picturesque lake. No matter how many times he looked, he never grew tired of the view.

Robby followed his long, tapered fingers that eagerly glided across on the blue architect's renderings of what would be their new recording studio. If they all agreed on a location.

"You won't believe what modern technology has done for music, and it gets better all the time," Ace said as his dark brown eyes danced over the designs. "The songs I can record in a studio with equipment like this will be unbelievable.

Robby pulled the ends of his curly blonde hair behind his ears to get a better look at the plans. "It's great, Ace," he said. "All of it. But you know building a studio there will bring a lot of media attention. We won't be able to keep it a secret."

Ace waved a dismissive hand. "We can handle them. Well, if we can't, we can hire someone who can." He looked up and smiled at Robby, then he returned to the drawings, lost in his fantasy.

Robby hoped he wasn't overreaching. He'd hate for him to burn out. He came so close after Diane's involvement with one of Mexico's largest drug dealers came to light six months ago. Much as he'd like to deny it, things had changed between the members of the band. Everyone had looked for places to lie low until the rumor mongers got bored and moved on to a new victim. It wasn't so bad for him; he could design web sites anywhere. But Sant had a new baby on the way and money was getting tight. Unless they got back to playing concerts, the economy might force decisions no one wanted to make.

"We need to make some decisions. You have money put back, but most of us and getting close to the red line and no one wants to cut into their savings."

"You could always take some photos,"

Ace quipped.

Ace was being a snarky prick, but there was some truth in his comment. Reporters had descended on the band like vultures after they realized the potential to make big money for a couple of pictures. For weeks after the scandal broke, photos of America's top musical artists sold for top dollar. Within minutes of word getting out, the alphabet stations had scheduled hours of TV commentary, analyzing every tragic detail about the band's involvement with the Mendoza cartel.

Ace sighed. "I wish Diane could've seen this place. She would've loved it."

"I do, too, Ace. I do too." They exchanged a meaningful look, but Robby could tell he wasn't really feeling it.

ATF had recovered Diane's bruised and battered body after her kidnapping and subsequent murder at the hands of the hardened drug smugglers. Her parents had never gotten over the loss of their youngest child, blaming Ace for letting her get involved with the gang. Ace had blamed himself. He thought her relationship with Bryce would have kept her out of trouble. Once always hungry to reach for his guitar to express his feelings and dispel his bad moods, Ace lost all his will to play at all after the violent death of his kid sister.

The wound healed slowly, and the scars ran deep. The slightest bump could tear it back open. He might think he's got it together, but the old friends saw Ace falling deeper into depression.

Over the last year, everyone drifted apart. They worked hard to live their lives while avoiding the blinding light of an inquiring media. Ace took it to extremes; becoming more and more reclusive, to the point they feared he might never leave the house. Gradually, he'd opened up, especially after Santwan suggested building their own recording studio. They'd all chipped in fifty grand, but they had also assumed Ace would be ready to get back to work. So far, that had been nothing but a pipe dream.

Ever a pessimist, Robby was online searching for a work from home opportunity just in case money became a problem, when the buzzer at the gate announced a visitor.

"You expecting anyone?"

"Nope. It's probably a delivery truck at the wrong address." He hit the button that opened the metal gate. He didn't recognize the vehicle, but only a few people knew where he lived, so he wasn't especially worried about who it was. They would have to come to the door either way.

"Wassup!" Robby said with surprise as Santwan Martin, Ace's oldest friend and Cat Grinning's drummer, walked into the house. It had been a long time since he had showed up out of the blue that way. "What rock did you crawl out from under?"

Santwan looked around the room. "Nice place. Took me a while to remember the code on the bottom gate. I was just about ready to give up when you buzzed me in. You really need to repave that driveway. Car must have hit every pothole, and I didn't bring tools to change a tire."

"I like private," Ace said. "The telephoto lens on the cameras can't see this far from the road."

"Yeah, well, if that's what floats your boat, go for it. I prefer the nightlife. Speaking of which, I think I made a date to meet this girl and I don't know who she is. When I leave, you might have to follow me down to the bottom, coz the brakes in the crappy SUV I'm driving may not stop me from going over the edge into the water."

"You should be okay. You love to swim, and the only thing down there is the fuckin' reservoir."

They all laughed and took a seat in the living room.

"So, what's up with you, man?" Santwan asked, as Rob passed him a beer. "It's been so long since you dropped by, I was expecting a beard and a banjo."

Ace shrugged. "I'm keeping busy?"

Santwan wasn't about to let it go. "Busy doing what? Perfecting the art of being a fuckin" hermit?"

Ace's eyes darkened. "Not funny man. I'm not being a hermit. Just have things on my mind, that's all."

"Well, Belissa misses her favorite tea party partners."

"Is she still playing with that cooking thing we got her for her birthday?" Ace asked.

"That easy bake oven? Hell yeah! But she's got nobody but me to eat what she makes," he said. He nodded toward Ace's midsection. "You going for a Stone's look? Lose much more and you'll be giving ol' Mick a run for his money."

"Jealous, are we, chunky monkey? I'm surprised Tory hasn't got you chowing down on pretend food."

"Fuck you, I might have gained a couple of pounds," Santwan laughed, patting his stomach. "It's from living with a wife who knows how to cook. They ain't nothing like a real southern dinner to make a man feel loved. Besides, this is mutha fuckin' eight pack, brother, not that starve yo' ass, so you look like you got some abs, bull shit you got going." He grinned. "You look like you've been living on a diet of hot air."

"What's that supposed to mean? I eat... sometimes."

"Yeah," Robby said, "when I bitch at you until you order a damn pizza." He looked at Santwan and grinned. "He orders so many they call and check on him when he misses two days in a row. Hell, he's paying one kid's way through college now."

"Har, har, har. You guys are hilarious. But you're right. Maybe we should start practicing again."

Robby tossed a pair of drumsticks at Sant, and he missed one. "Poor ol' Sant done forgot how to twirl his little sticks. When was the last time you really cut loose on your drums? You staying in practice?"

"For what? It's not like we are the road

playing gigs. I mean, I set in with one of the local bands now and then, but it ain't the same." He looked at Ace and got serious. "Are we ever going to get back to work or are you retiring to record the next generation?"

Robby looked away as Ace cut his eyes his way, questioning how Santwan would know what they had been working on.

Rob didn't feel like fighting. "I need to start dinner. Why don't you two go out on the deck to talk? The breeze is great out there."

"Nope," Santwan replied. "I came to take you both out of here for a few hours. How about going down to Little Five Points? We can stop by the Stock House for dinner. Nothing like a medium rare ribeye and double cheese stuffed potato to get your motor running. Chris said they have a killer strawberry pie this week."

Ace paused. "Nah, I don't feel like dealing with fuckin' tourists."

"That excuse sucks," Santwan said. "Come on, fuckface, I haven't seen either of you in months. Besides, I know you are dying to hear about my session work. Alissa is visiting her mama, so we can stay out past curfew and make up for lost time. Unless you'd rather stay home and watch the masked singer with Rob? Or maybe you can sit out on the deck in the rocking chair and tickle the cat."

"Sounds like fun," Robby spoke up. "Come on, Ace, let's go! We haven't been out in ages. Besides, I just looked and there isn't a damn thing in the house worth cooking. I don't know about you, but I'm sick of pizza. Dawn won't be back until Saturday, and this might be the last chance I get to go out for a while."

"Right," Santwan smiled. "We can act like tourists and watch the freaks come out. It will do you both the world of good."

Ace smiled wearily. "You know how to dig that blade in, and twist, don't you? Oh well, you leave me much of a choice. But don't let me get drunk. I want to sleep in my own bed tonight."

Less than a half hour later, they climbed into Santwan's SUV and headed south down Briarcliff. Five Points was about a half hour south of Druid Hills, so it wasn't much later when they pulled into a parking lot in the eclectic urban neighborhood, where five city streets met each other. Unlike their place, where the only thing they heard was an occasional touch football game in the park, they could feel the energy of the city as Santwan swung into a space close to the Junkman's Daughter.

Little Five was in full swing. Locals with tricolor hair, painted faces, tattooed body art, in outlandish clothing or noticeable lack of it intermingled with preppy college students and eager tourists on the sidewalks that snaked throughout the small business district. Occasional families meandered in and out of the eclectic shops with their hands full of shopping bags, while street kids darted in and out of the crowd, on foot or skateboards. Rows of tiny shops crammed together, offering unique or handmade items. There was even an old-fashioned clapboard salesperson, hawking everything from junk food to wiccan soothsayers along the sidewalk.

Santwan pulled a set of bongos out of the back seat. "Come on, I want to show you something."

Ace and Rob looked at each other, but Santwan was always getting involved in something, so it was easier not to ask. He couldn't get into much trouble with bongos.

Even though the sun was not fully down, the music scene was already in full swing as they walked down to the small park. In the space of two blocks, Robby counted two tattoo shops, a body piercing kiosk and a fortune teller among with a head shop, an old-fashioned Vinyl record store, an ice cream parlor and two bars. The sweet smell of incense from an Indian restaurant wafted through the air as young girls in colorful sarongs passed out samples of tandoori chicken. Most of the cafes that peppered the area had set up simple wooden tables along the sidewalk. The place epitomized the true spirit of the sixties–open air, freedom, sunshine, and an atmosphere to let one's creativity go uninhibited.

Santwan made a beeline toward a group of people sitting under some dogwood trees on the grass just off the main street.

"We're here," Santwan said excitedly. "Here's where I've been keeping up my skills. It's a drum circle."

"A drum circle?" Ace asked. "Like the hippies?"

"Yeah. It started way back in the 1950's. They called them beatniks then, but the hippies kept the idea going. The city thought it was a great idea to bring them back and even promote the idea. These are some of the most talented people anywhere."

The drum circle was already underway. Bongos were thumping, whistles were blowing, hands were clapping, and people were having a good time. A small cluster of bare-chested men were pounding out rhythms in the shade, but more were already setting up an assortment of drums. There were wooden African tub drums, Mediterranean steel drums, metal trash cans, and modern takes on old ceramic urns. One-man had brought his entire ten-piece kit, complete with cow bells and chimes.

"They say Janice Joplin used to sit in circles back before she grew famous," Santwan informed them as he removed his bongos from their case. "They bang on everything. You can get be loud as you want. A lot of onlookers stop and watch, too. It makes it even more cool to play for them."

Robby and Ace watched as Santwan joined them. People were banging on everything congas, djembes, water jugs, paint cans, even orange Home Depot buckets filled with sand. One man even had an old wooden washboard. Everyone was welcome to join in. Somehow, the sound evolved into an interesting blend of sound and rhythm. People gathered around the green grassy knoll to hear the rhythms. A few even danced in the center of the circle.

Ace was surprised when two teenage girls approached him for autographs and selfies. Others lingered to talk to him, asking him outright about when a new album would be released. No one made him uncomfortable or acted like he was not welcome.

"Man, this makes me feel great." His eyes scanned the scene. "I miss being among people who love music. It's cool seeing genuine fans talking to them. This energy makes me want to create songs and to perform again."

Thank you, Santwan! Robby thought. He smiled as Ace wrapped an arm around two young women for a group photo. "That's good, Ace."

***

Dinner was as good as he'd hoped. Ace was in a wonderful mood for a change. For once he didn't whine about getting home when Santwan suggested they stop in one the little bars. "I sit in with the band a lot. It's not your usual style of place, but you won't have to worry too much about drunk women falling all over you." He said as he led them into the small bar on the narrow side street.

"What's a matter, the women don't

drink?"

"Nope. No women." Ace's mouth fell open as he looked around the packed bar... the packed bar full of men.

"Well, I can truthfully say, this is a day of firsts." Ace figured what the hell, things had been going better than he'd expected. It would be a novel experience to set and listen to music without the constant interruptions.

They followed Santwan toward the front of the bar, when he introduced them to Pat and James, boyfriends of two of the men in the band. Ace was curious about what Santwan was up to. It didn't surprise him that Sant would sit in with a local band; he loved playing music and would take any opportunity to get behind drums on a stage. He just wondered what the ulterior motive was.

The band was not bad. A typical bar house band. Nothing special. Ace was about to suggest they take off when a lanky blonde rushed in and took over the lead. It was as if a switch was thrown, and the band came alive. He leaned forward, listening to the riffs, paying attention to how the guitarist's fingers caressed the strings instead of playing them. He had heard a lot of guitarists in his time, but this man ranked up there with Stevie

Ray. His music showed hints of Hanneman, Slash, or Dimebag Darrell. Then he changed to the more mellow southern bluesy style of Duane Allman or Randi Rhodes. Ace grew excited. His heart had broken when his sister died. That wound was deepened when Bryce was killed on his motorcycle a few weeks later. He had avoided replacing him in the band, because he didn't want to admit he was gone, too.

His eyes went to Santwan, and he realized this was the ulterior motive. Santwan wanted him to hear this man play his guitar. He leaned back in the chair and listened.

Chapter Two

Less than a month later, the five men were sitting in the living room at Ace's house, caught up with the idea of creating a recording studio, right in the Little Five Points area. They had found an old warehouse a block off the main strip, a perfect place for Ace to work, to write again, and for them to record music. Seeing his enthusiasm was like a r

esurrecting jump start from Diane in heaven. The band needed to get back to work, and Ace needed to get back to the real world, the world where he sang, they played, and people came to listen. The band missed his creativity, the way he could put words to a melody that would speak to millions of hearts and make it seem effortless.

Ace sat cross-legged on the floor of the studio, listening as Robby picked out a melody on the antique Hammond B3 organ he found in the warehouse's basement when they walked around before purchasing it. Renovating the instrument had been a kind of therapy for him, giving him time to think about the past and come to terms with what happened to his brother. The bike wreck had affected him more than any of the others. It was approaching a year now since he had watched them lower Bryce into the ground. The horror of that accident took away any motivation Robby had to write music for a long time. When he started back, he noticed the timbre of his writing had changed, becoming darker and heavier.

Yet, like the villain in a horror movie playing tricks on your mind, the guilt about Bryce's death had gnawed at him from the moment they had returned home. He was obsessed with the idea that he could have done more to save his brother. He blamed himself for getting involved with a woman he'd met in the club, leaving his twin to ride home alone from the gig. No one could have known that Bryce would panic when APD got behind his bike and take off. Or that he would lose on a sharp curve and hit a tree. The bike had to be doing sixty or more. He didn't suffer, the medic said he snapped his neck when he hit. He reaches for his brother, but his grasp is always just inches too short. Then his brother would slowly fade away, like he did every other time.

Ace suffered similar nightmares. During nights of tortured sleep, he would dream about his best friend. The dreams were always the same. He would fall asleep with a woman, then realize he was in bed with a skeleton and wake up screaming. Other times saw Bryce riding toward him. Just before he reached him, a truck would hit him from the side and drag him and the motorcycle away. He would open his eyes, but Bryce would stand there, his leather jacket still torn and ragged from being drug along the pavement. "You know, it always ends this way, Mason," Bryce would say. "I'm still dead. You can't change what happened."

Keith took a deep drag on the joint Ace passed him and closed his eyes. The images of Bryce still came back to haunt his nights, but not as often. It was a moral wound that refused to heal–until he began working with the band again. Getting on with his own life seemed disrespectful, but it opened his mind to new possibilities once more. He was sleeping through the night again. A hand tousling his hair brought him back to the present. Santwan Martin stood over him. "We are waiting."

Keith smiled and passed him the clip. He had been so engrossed in his thoughts; he hadn't heard him approach. He nodded toward the polished wood of the old organ. "Turned out really well, didn't it? It's all done."

"Yeah, looks great. How does it sound?" Keith looked around. "And look at this place. It feels good to be working together again. I'm surprised Alissa isn't nagging you to stay home every night."

Nagging was the last thing Alissa had been doing while Ace and Rob swirled in their private Hells of despair and guilt. In fact, they hadn't spoken in several months, since she had run away with some guy she'd met at work, leaving his daughter Belissa at the sitters for him to pick up. Booze wouldn't let him forget her leaving him, and sleep wouldn't take away the pain of betrayal, either. At least the studio gave him a swell of encouragement and relieved the depression that barreled through him like a freight train.

Robby laughed to himself and struggled back to his feet after sitting so long. "You know how my mind works. I get started on a project and don't want to stop until it is done." He paused as he gazed fondly at the organ. He loved his electric piano, but there was something about organs that tugged at his soul. "Good thing we found this place, isn't it?"

"Yeah. I'm glad Sant drug us to Five Points that day, or we might never would have got the band back together again."

It was during the ride home from Five Points when Ace's idea of buying the old warehouse and convert it to a recording studio was born. They had detoured off Moreland because of a wreck and drove by a decrepit concrete building with a FOR SALE sign glowing under the corner streetlight. It was a sterile, lonely looking structure, with no activity around it and from the appearance of the overgrown lot, no one had bothered with it for a long time. It had taken several coats of white paint to cover up the faded graffiti.

"What a dump," Santwan had muttered as they approached the property.

"Yeah, but it has a kind of charm to it," Ace replied as he surveyed the building from the car window. It was about twice as big as the vacant drugstore he'd looked at, but a much older building. "It's kind of like that little dive place where we recorded our first demo."

"I remember," Robby said, as he recalled the tiny warehouse studio where Cat Grinning recorded its first set of songs. 'Fewer rats though."

"I think we can do something with it," Ace said. He paused. "There's no place to record and mix music out this way and it's only a half hour from downtown."

"Half hour? Maybe at 4:00 a.m.," Robby replied. "But you might have a good idea at that. It's pretty old, but I like it. Theres enough room for a couple of sound rooms. Maybe we can rent out practice space to other bands. We can even lease out stage equipment if we do it right." Robby was thinking ahead. If you went by the national average of 72, they wear all pushing middle age. Only Keith was under thirty.

The building had been dark and chilly, but Ace had felt a connection with the old structure right away. The interior was two stories, but most of it was a wide-open gutted shell, crying out for someone to bring it back to life. Ace inspected every inch of the space and marveled at the remnants of the past inhabitants etched into the brickwork. The electricity would need to be updated, but that would have been needed in any building they bought. And there was excellent internet service in the area.

When they found the old organ in the basement, Keith had considered it a sign. "You are right. It is perfect."

"Do you really think we can make something out of this place?" Robby asked later as they got into the car to leave. Ace nodded. The price on the building was half what the other would have cost. That left enough money to build a state-of-the-art studio, a comfortable musicians lounge, at least two practice studios, and even stock the equipment rental business. They would need the roof updated, but that's common in old buildings.

As they drove off, Ace watched the building in the rear-view mirror until he lost sight of it. His mind was already working. He had called the realtor before they reached the expressway. "We'll take it. They want 100,000. Offer 80,000 cash and see what you can do."

A few days later, they had purchased the warehouse for 90,000. That left 160,000 for repairs and building the studio. He had a contractor lined up before the closing date. The old building was in a small section of older businesses jumbled together, with forgotten spillovers from the trendy business district a block away. The small parking lot contained faded markings for about 10 cars, just enough for what they had in mind. They installed a higher-than-normal chain-link fence around the back and cleared away all the leftover debris from prior homeless settlers. The addition of two trained guard dogs ensured no one would get close enough to bypass the electronic security features they had installed to protect the equipment. The young, trendy realtor had passed them the keys to the heavy glass doors. "Getting a real bargain here. This area is ready to explode. Good time to get in."

The ink wasn't dry on the closing papers before Ace set to work on his vision of a top-notch recording studio. They named it The Litter Box after the band. Over the following weeks, construction crews had built walls and replaced broken fixtures. The building now included a kitchen, administrative offices, an impressive conference room in which to hash over future projects, and a stylish front lobby. Cat Grinning's framed gold records for 'Mary's Final Call' and 'Orange Sunshine Dreams' were the first items to be hung on the lobby wall. Soon they were joined by framed photos of Cat Grinning, taken at various events, like a wall of fame showcasing their past achievements. Ace had ensured photos of Bryce were part of the wall montage, too. The actual studio was a commercial pro-quality setup with the best mixing equipment available and a 40,000 digital audio workstation. Nothing was shortchanged. They got the best on the market.

Over the next few months, the band spent several hours a day at the studio auditioning and rehearsing with Lajoi and the new back-up singers. Keith hated to admit it, but Lajoi was a much better guitarist than Bryce had been. Ace's writing ability came back right away, and the two men had already collaborated on several new songs. It was difficult to believe that, not long ago, Ace had labored to write a single lyric. Even a few bars of music had often taken him days on end. Now the creative juices were flowing, and they were coming up with killer songs.

"It's working out better than we hoped," Santwan agreed, looking around the room. "Except for having to deal with the overzealous fans."

Despite every effort to keep the information from going public, news of Cat Grinning's studio in Five Points had circulated among the fans. Many of the more dedicated fans began regular pilgrimages to the warehouse, hoping to see them.

"Nah, they don't bother me," Keith said, focusing on the organ as he finished working out the chords for the latest song. "They're harmless. Let them drift in and out. Doesn't stop the work we're doing. It's been a while since we have been on tour. Without the fans, our music is worthless."

Santwan turned to Ace and asked, "Isn't it annoying to you, these people coming to hang out every day?"

"No," Ace shook his head, surprising them all "At first it was kind of amusing, seeing them sitting in the sun all day, waiting for one of us to show up, then rushing to the car door to greet us like we are a fuckin' clearance sale on the latest iPhone."

"Yeah, it can be good for my ego," Santwan mused as he gazed off, thinking. Then he turned back to Ace. "But they connect with you, and you connect with them through your music."

"Hey Lajoi, are you ready to take to the road and tour? It won't be long before we release our next album." Ace had been surprised how easy it was to work with Jo. He had never had a gay friend. To be honest, at first, he had been overly cautious around him, unsure of what to say or how to act. Then one day, it finally clicked into his head that Jo's sexual preferences had nothing to do with his personality. The fans seemed to be alright with it. In fact, their fan base grew once word got out that the new lead guitarist was gay.

Just as they had before the drug dealer had kidnapped his sister, the fans fed his creative adrenaline. Ace looked forward to seeing them as they gathered outside the studio every day, waiting for him. He had sat in on a few jam sessions at the bar with Lajoi, singing a song or two off of the old albums, and frankly, it made him yearn for the spotlight again. Most artists avoided direct contact with their fans, preferring to develop a sense of mystery. Fans respected his wish for privacy, except for the hardcore groupies looking to hook up for the night. But his interactions with the parking lot fans were his way of showing them he was also human. It allowed Ace to connect with the ones who appreciated his work and kept his name out there. Over the last few months, he'd noticed many of the same people when he pulled into the lot, almost always the same females. He became pretty good at spotting unfamiliar faces and often stopped to talk, surprised to discover some coming from as far away as Europe. Once the Five Points district manager had come by to talk to them about an upcoming festival. He'd asked to get a picture with them, and they 'd gathered around like he was an old friend. It was an odd arrangement, but Ace didn't care. He needed the fans as much as they needed him.

They would soon realize how much that need would cost them.

Chapter Three

It was the best dream ever.

Shae was at the Omni, and Ace was singing to her. The stadium venue was filled to capacity, an epic night for a rock show by Ace and his band, Cat Grinning. Somehow, she had grabbed a front-row seat. As Ace sang, her body moved with the rhythm of the drummer's staccato beat. The huge speakers that hug the sides of the stage blasted out the song as Lajoi showed off his guitar's massive power and stance in front of his Marshall stack by ripping out well-known fan favorites. As the memorable music experience ended, Ace made a special announcement.

"Let's give it up for my special lady, Shae Warner!" he called out as security hoists her petite frame onto the stage and into his waiting arms. "This is the muse that motivated my return to the stage. The one who saved the music!" Psyched up by the roar of the crowd, he dedicated his encore to her, leaving her gasping for breath when he finished.

Later, between the sheets in a penthouse suite at the Ritz Carlton, she and Ace made love. She could feel his arms around her, the heat from his body as he moved against her... Her dream was interrupted by a banging on the door. Loud. Repetitive. Annoying. The images faded away. No, no, don't! It's just getting to the good part!

Alice shouted and banged on the bathroom door. "Hey in there! You're going to be late for class again! Get moving."

As the dream dissipated into darkness; so, did the hot water.

"You know how to screw up a great wet dream," Shae called back at her sister as she turned off the shower. She reached for her towel, cursing under her breath when she realized she'd forgotten to hang one beside the tub. She hated having to drip as she dashed across the bathroom to the shelf where they stacked the towels.

Alice heard her curse and grinned. One thing about Shae, she was consistent. Shae never remembered the towel. She was still chuckling as she moved down the hall to wake Misty.

"Shit," Misty mumbled as she opened her eyes. I was dead to the world, she thought.

She sniffed, then looked around her tiny bedroom, noticing the air was damp and musty again. The smell happened every time it rained. The basement of the building would flood, and the smell of stagnant water and mold would rise to infiltrate every apartment for days afterward. It had rained two days ago. She opened the door. "Morning Alice. I take it Shae fell asleep on the sofa again?"

"Yep. I told her to get her ass in motion or she would be riding the bus to school."

"Yeah," Shae said as she passed by the door wearing nothing but a towel." "And she ruined a fantastic daydream."

"Don't tell me... another fantasy about you and that singer, Ace Whatchamacallit."

"Watch how you talk about my future husband."

Alice snorted. "If you want to waste your time fawning over a rock over lord, who probably can't get it up after the endless lines of coke and gallons of liquor, nothing I can say will change your mind. I will admit, the new lead guitarist is cute."

"Too bad he's gay." Shea grabbed her jeans out of the laundry basket setting next to the sofa and shimmied into them. Then she dug out a clean bra and tee-shirt. Alice always washed the clothes she left in the apartment, so she always had clean clothes to change into.

Misty rolled her eyes. She shared the tiny three-bedroom apartment with Lois, a woman who ran a small café in the building where she worked.

Then they met Alice and invited her to move in. Alice worked long hours cooking and waiting tables to ensure her sister Shae was able to continue her studies at Emory, often giving up everything except necessities to keep her sister in school. She also worked three nights a week as a cocktail waitress at a local bar. Her life had become a never-ending parade of bleary eyes drunks, overworked hookers and lecherous old men who got off after a quick feel in the bar's bathroom. Over the years, her nights had blended into bleak glimpses of her previous life, memories waxing and waning like the phases of the moon, into the gray reality of her current situation. It had been a fight to keep Shae's stubborn ass in school long enough to get her degree. This was the last semester, so logic would say it should be the easiest. Alice's sister had never been followed the rules of logic.

After her father died, Alice's family had

tried to exist on the monthly SSI check, food stamps and whatever goods or cash their mama could drum up through relief agencies or the local food bank. Reality had quickly shown them that was nowhere near enough money to support one, much less three women, provide a home, make sure all the bills got paid. Her mama had given up the big house, sold everything except one car, and moved to Jonesboro with Shae. Shea hated it and used every excuse she could to hang out at the apartment.

Misty understood her dilemma. She'd done her share of waiting tables over the years. Then she had met Roger and became his assistant. Life would get even easier now that Lois's tiny catering business had taken off. Alice had moved into the third bedroom, taking a third of the expenses.

A few years after graduation, her parents had moved to Tampa, and she had moved in with Lois. They had rented the apartment off Ponce De Leon, in an old established neighborhood that was reasonably safe for two single women. The apartment was nothing special, a living room, galley kitchen, three bedrooms, though one was barely big enough for a bed and chest, and a tiny bathroom. There was a murphy bed in the living room, so Shae never had to sleep on the sofa. Too bad she considered that too much work, and usually crashed on the sofa instead.

Since Lois left for work around five am, three hours before she had to get up, and Alice worked seven days a week, Misty could sleep until eight in relative quiet. The exception was every other Tuesday. Today. Alice was off work and ready to start her weekly cleaning routine. Alice was spotless, and once she finished, the apartment was so clean the floors squeaked.

It was raining outside so the room held a heavy chill, one that the old-fashioned oil heater could not overcome. Misty pulled the covers of her worn chenille bedspread up around her and grabbed her old cell phone, hoping to have enough minutes remaining before the alarm to go online. She opened her messenger service, checking for anything important. As usual, her mailbox was full of spam sales notices and bills. Nothing important.

"Hey, Lois," she typed a message and hit send. It was a strange friendship. She had met Lois in elementary school, and they had not liked each other. It was only after they joined forces to get even with an overbearing cheerleader, that they formed a bond. After graduation they went in different directions. A few years later they found each other on Facebook and had renewed the old friendship, both doubting they would ever get the chance to meet each other face-to-face. Which was fine with Misty. She didn't have many friends and even if she did, she didn't want anyone seeing where she lived. Then they discovered they worked in the same building. It was as if Karma had a sense of humor.

"What's up?" chimed Lois's response.

"Dealing with Shae and one of her beautiful dreams," Misty typed. "She was with her musician again. Then Alice had to wake her up."

Lois laughed for a moment, then her mood darkened. "Shae says she's the ultimate wicked older sister."

Misty sighed. "Sometimes I feel like I'm living in a Disney movie," she confessed, her thumbs flying over the keyboard of her phone. "I do. I can't help it. Alice works like Cinderella, and Shae just takes and takes. It kills me to watch Alice work so hard, and not even get a thank you. All Shae thinks about is this Ace Rivers guy."

"I agree. He's hot. Shae is young, she just got out of high school. There's nothing wrong with crushing. We've all dreamed about un-obtainable men. There's nothing wrong with thinking big."

"It's not impossible, but not likely to happen," Misty replied. "The band bought a warehouse a few blocks from here and made it into a recording studio. There was an announcement in the paper that they were looking for backup singers. Shae was so excited. Her problem is she can't sing. She didn't get a call back."

"Well, tell her to be careful, and not get her hopes up," Lois replied. "I'm sure thousands of other girls have the same goal."

"Yeah, but her crush is different," Misty said. "She thinks he'd love her if he only got to know her. Snippets of conversation with him at the studio parking lot just aren't enough for her anymore. She has to have him. All of him. I'm scared she may do something stupid to get his attention."

"Maybe you can speak to Alice? Let her know the situation. She might be able to let her down easy." There was a pause. "Hate to go, but my boss is calling me. TTYLTR."

Misty sighed and dropped her phone into its charger. Then she lay back on the bed, closed her eyes to let her mind wander a little longer. Ace Rivers. What was it about the singer that made Alice's sisters' head pound and her heart sing? She wished he were with her right now, so she could ask him a few questions. She had to admit he was good looking. A little thinner than she preferred, but most musicians were under weight. It was like they forget to eat. Or maybe they get so wrapped up in the music that food becomes unimportant. She thought about the band that had played at a local bar last week. Only the drummer didn't look like skin stretched over a skeleton. Probably because he was the only member that was married...

***

The buzzing of the alarm prompted Misty back awake with a start. Her face flushed and body trembling, she lay there panting in the dark. She couldn't believe the dream she'd had. There was no way she was telling anyone. She would never hear the end of it if Lois found out. Shae would have a hissy fit. Overcome by guilt, she dragged herself out of bed and headed for the shower. The door was open, so she glanced at the shrine to Ace that Shae had put up in Alice's room. It had to bother Alice that every inch of that wall was covered with his face. One was Ace in concert, screaming into the microphone. Another was Ace looking thoughtful at an interview. Several were of Ace in group pictures with his band. Ace, Ace, Ace...

Many nights Shae would just lay on the floor, gazing up at the various pictures on the walls and ceiling. The many faces of the man Misty'd just dreamed about.

Shae had collected every magazine that ever contained an article about Ace, no matter how small. They were neatly lined up on a bookshelf. On top of a white silk lined tray, she had displayed of all her trinkets and keepsakes pertaining to the band. Autographed items, from books to pictures, sat next to tiny keepsakes she's collected since Ace hit the music scene with Cat Grinning four years ago, all arranged for maximum visual effect. Her favorite was a pen he forgot to take back after signing one of her CDs back when the band was still playing local bars. Lois had brought her a matchbook from a downtown hotel when he'd performed for a cancer fundraiser last year. She had worked the banquet before the concert and snatched it off the table before someone threw it away. Shae kept all these precious memories clean and in perfect condition. Her attitude was pushing psychotic.

The hot shower water beat down on her body as she thought about the strange dream she'd experienced. If Ace was half as seductive in person as he was in her dream, she could almost understand why Shae imagined she was in love. Not that she would ever meet with him in person. Unlike Shae, she preferred little neighborhood bars to concert halls.

***

Tabitha tried to act cool, but her heart was pounding in her chest. She suddenly needed to find a toilet but didn't won't to risk leaving. It was way past her curfew, and she would be grounded for ever, but she had to try. Now here she was; standing here talking to one of the band! He winked at her and took her by the hand. "Come on, I'll give you a tour of the bus."

He guided her through the bustle of people and equipment to a makeshift lane behind the stage, where the buses were parked along the curb. Once they arrived, he winked at the driver standing by the door before pulling it open. Tabitha saw a group of fans standing behind the barricades. Two young women opened the gold blazers they were wearing to display their bare breasts. She hoped he didn't see it. Other fans called out to various band members as they walked by.

He pulled her close and kissed her, then gestured for her to go inside. Tabitha could feel the other girls' jealous glares. It made her feel special when he gave them a casual wave, then guided Tabitha inside the bus, following behind her and locked the door after swinging it shut, closing out the sounds of their excited fangirl squeals.

Tabitha hugged up against him as he fumbled with the key. He wished she would be less obvious about her needs, but she was gorgeous, and he could deal with needy for a while.

The interior of the bus was like other touring coaches, long and extravagant in its décor. Soft recessed lighting highlighted the leather furniture, marble countertops, and hardwood cabinets. The coach boasted the latest in technology, including Wi-Fi, satellite TV, and a top-of-the-line sound system. Six bunks with privacy curtains took up the middle of the coach and a large, closed-off "back room" containing a wall-to-wall sectional couch took up the rear portion.

Underneath the glitz, however, was evidence of a typical rock band's home on wheels—a living space that smelled of smoke and stale beer, with grungy clothes scattered about. The trash can was filled with fast food wrappers and empty beer cans. Open bottles of bourbon and whiskey sat on top of the kitchen counter, along with snack bags in the sink. There was an open baggie of pot sitting on a rolling tray beside a small hemostat.

She took a seat on the soft leather bench-style couch while he pulled the blinds down over the darkened windows.

"Shutting out the rest of the world?" she asked.

"All except ours," he grinned. He went to the refrigerator and removed a pomegranate raspberry wine cooler. He popped the top from the bottle and poured it into a glass before handing it to her. "There are a hundred women out there who'd love to be in here with me right now, you know. Aren't you the lucky one?"

"Of course," Tabitha replied. "You're a bona fide rock star, after all."

She tipped the glass back and took a sip

before drinking almost the entire glass in one nervous swig. "Mmmm, my new favorite," she commented, looking around. "This is exactly what I pictured a band bus would look like."

"We had a slight inkling you were coming, so we cleaned up a bit," he retorted. He was smiling and had a playful gleam in his eye. "I suppose we're not so good at housekeeping. "Want another?"

She nodded.

He chuckled softly, pulled another cooler from the fridge, then selected a beer for himself. He opened it with his thumb and downed half of it. "Make yourself comfortable."

"Bathroom?"

"First door." He watched her cross the room.

She was back in minutes, eager to keep his attention. He waited until she sat down and picked up the wine cooler, then smiled and sat down next to her, openly admiring her garters under her black skirt, which was hiked to mid-thigh from crossing her legs.

"You look stunning. Keep it up and I'll be dead meat for the show."

Tabitha looked up at him and suddenly

felt the need for an intimate connection. She reached out to trail her fingers down his arm, outlining his tattoos with lacy trails of her fingertips. His skin felt warm and smooth under her touch. He had lit a joint, filling the air with the skunky, pine bark scent that almost masked the aroma of his cologne.

"I don't know what dead meat tastes like," she whispered. She meant it to sound playful, but her words came out hungrier than she planned. The two coolers were helping her to relax.

"Well then, maybe you should try it," he said in a low, husky voice. Her heart beat faster. She locked her eyes with his, conveying a primal understanding of wanting him as much as he wanted her. She could get lost in those beautiful eyes.

He moved closer and took the bottle from her hand. Reaching behind her, he placed it, along with his own, on the windowsill behind him. Then he brought his hand around to cup her chin and brought his lips to hers.

She responded eagerly, losing herself in the way his tongue took possession of her. She hummed a quiet sound of pleasure, deep in her throat. God, she wanted to feel that tongue everywhere.

"Slow down, honey. It's not a race to the finish. I have to be able to play in less than an hour."

"I can't guarantee your condition by show time if we keep this up," she whispered, gasping for air, but she burrowed into his neck and wrapped her arms around his neck. "It's been a while since I did this."

He kissed her again, sucking her lips, then her tongue. "Me, too. I can't help myself. Being with you is driving me insane." He pulled her back to him and closed his mouth over hers again, hotter than before, stroking his tongue in a rhythmic motion. Tabitha's body eagerly leaned into his, closing the space between their bodies, enjoying the feel of him, his lips, his hands.

His hand went under her skirt and reached into her panties.

Tabitha cried out softly. She pulled her mouth away from his. "What are you doing? We can't be doing this here right now!"

"Why not?" he said, pulling her panties down to her knees.

She playfully patted his hand. "Stop it! Won't the guys need to get in here to change?

"They already changed," he said with a sly grin. "Escape is futile."

"I bet you say that to all your fans," she teased.

"No, I saved that one just for you."

She couldn't help but giggle. "You're so bad."

"Now that they all say," he said. He buried his face in the crook of her scented neck, leaving light kisses that sent a shiver screaming down her spine. He continued his assault, trailing to the other side, his slight scruff rubbing against her jawline. His fingers trailed down to her cropped silk tee-shirt, sliding it up and over her head, then yanking it free. The air conditioner cooled her fevered skin as it hit the floor. His hands roamed over her skin, pausing on curves and contours as he licked his lips with appreciation. He reached behind her to dispense of her bra and bare more flesh for the eager whisper of his tongue, then caressed and teased her breasts with toying tugs until she was crazed with longing. The layers of his hair felt silky against her neck as his sensitive fingers and lips probed and caressed her hardened nipples. Her fingers pressed into his forest of hair, holding him close to her as she gasped back a moan.

"I can't believe we're doing this," she

whispered.

"I'll make you believe." He slid off the couch and knelt in front of her. He unzipped her boots and socks and peeled them off her legs one at a time, tossing them aside. Now his warm hands were on her smooth skin, caressing her thighs, making goose bumps explode with pleasure. He eased her panties off and tossed them aside, then placed his hands on her knees to spread her legs.

Damn, she shouldn't let him do this, but she could die right there under his touch.

When she raised her hips, he gave a low grumble of satisfaction. Then his hands urged her legs apart a little more. He moved in, dragging his lips over the insides of her thighs. Jolts of sensation shot through her. Her breathing quickened, unable to stop the pulsing of her thigh muscles as he moved his lips higher, higher.

"I want you," he said in a deep, husky voice. "Right now."

"We can't—you have to—" Her voice trailed away with a soft moan as his lips found their mark. She was wet and ready for him.

"Fuck the rules," he murmured. "Forget all that bullshit. Sit back now and let me show you how it's done."

She gave up. Like a puppeteer, he manipulated her strings, taking her however he pleased. She no longer had any will of her own. and gave in to the overwhelming sweet sensation that raced through her body. The heated touch of his lips and tongue playing over the hot center of her body. He took his time, stroking her desire as the inferno in her soul raged. Her hips jerked against his hands as his mouth explored her flesh, licking the delicate knot of nerves in her sweet, sensitive folds. She whimpered with pleasure, gripping his hair while her hips thrust back at him, holding him to her as he nuzzled her in the most intimate way possible.

"Please," she groaned. He continued to torment her with his tongue until she let out a strangled scream as her orgasm washed over her like a waterfall. Silently laughing as she writhed against his mouth while her body pulsed against him. Then he stepped back, tearing at his pants and releasing the hard flesh that was strained against the fabric. He threw off his shirt, letting it drop to the floor, then joined her on the couch. Balancing his weight above her on his knees and elbows, he stretched her arms above her head, grasping her wrists together tight with one hand. He was in control, and she knew it.

He looked down at her and smiled. "Now, this is what I call a nice view," he said with a long, lusty breath. His other hand moved with feathery precision over the moist flesh that was still recovering from his assault. Tabitha groaned, writhing with pleasure as he held her hands above her head. The rasp of his calloused fingers over her sensitive skin was almost too much to manage.

"Oh God, fuck me."

He pulled her to him with a sigh of pleasure. "That I will do. You can be assured of that. He rubbed his face between her breasts and kissed her taut nipples again and again. Then he snapped a set of handcuffs around her wrists.

"Owwww, kinky..." she groaned.

His hands trailed down her back to clench her buttocks. She felt him jolt as her hips ground against his cock and he groaned softly against her breasts. She kissed him again and opened her thighs wide.

"Now," she whispered.

He needed no further invitation. He slid easily inside her in one deep, long push. At that moment, his body was hers, and her body was his. His hips thrust against her, giving her everything he had, and she kissed him again hard, her tongue eagerly mingling with his. Her hands ran over his back, his shoulders, then grasped his hips and pulled him closer, craning to take him deeper as he dove deep with a rapid-fire rhythm. Touching him was like filling her soul with music, pure and magical. She wrapped her legs around him as their bodies rocked together with a rapid, hungry rhythm.

"Move for me, kill me before I kill you," he rasped. He sank deep into her again and again as she bucked against him, clutching his shoulders as her pleasure peaked. Her whole body quivered, glorified in the fullness. He moved with her in a fit that was both sweet and erotic. She pulsed her hips, driving her body against him, until the heat finally overtook her, and she came apart, flying over the edge with pleasure that exploded in colors of the sunset throughout her mind. Through a dreamy haze, she opened her eyes and watched as he threw his head back and convulsed against her.

Afterwards, Tabitha drifted in a blissful sea of contentment as she tried to regain her wits. She felt very sleepy, drained, yet content at the same time.

"Be right back," he said. He got up and walked out of the room, then grinned when he returned and found her sleeping. He wet a rag with liquid from a green bottle, folded it, and placed it over her mouth. Then he used duct tape to hold it there. More duct tape secured her ankles. Moving her from the couch to the upper bunk wasn't easy. Once he had her inside, he zip tied her ankles tight against a metal support in case she woke up and tried to kick. After one had awakened and began kicking the wall, he'd learned the best way to prevent any movement or noise. Then he taped her elbows to her side. Once he was satisfied, she was not going anywhere, he slid her against the back wall, and zip tied her hands to another support. Her body was tight against the wall, so she could barely move. After he covered her with a blanket, and added pillows propped against her body, she was practically invisible. Then he returned to the lounge and removed every trace of her presence. Even the empty wine cooler bottle went into the bag. The bag went into his locker. He needed to hurry and dress. The band they followed was starting the last song of their set. At least he'd be going on stage with a grin on his face.

The bus would be on the road in about two hours and back in Atlanta before dawn. Everyone was ready to get back home. He only took a trophy when it was his turn to clean the bus when they reached the house. He'd almost gotten caught once when Robby returned to the bus after eating breakfast and he'd been placing the trophy in his trunk. He'd slammed it shut, muttering something about forgetting his dirty laundry. Robby was too tired to pay much attention, but it taught him to be extra careful. Now he had the process down pat. He added a beer to his pocket and headed for the stage.

Chapter Four

So, what do you want to do this weekend?

The end of the work week was fast approaching when Lois bounced into Misty's office, a routine Misty knew all too well. That was something she could set her clock by, Lois showing up to plan their weekend activities. It had been a year since they had renewed their elementary school friendship and while it sometimes complicated daily life, she could not imagine life without her bubbly best friend.

"Whats up?" That was Lois. She began with the same question each time, before sinking into the chair across from her desk. Lois pulled open the metal tab on the Dr. Pepper she'd brought with her and took a long drink. Misty smiled to herself. She'd played out this scenario with her best friend hundreds of times over the years. So many, she could visualize Lois comments before she said them. She looked forward to the Friday afternoon gabfests, as it gave the two friends time to catch up.

Misty pointed to the display on her computer monitor. "I was looking through this weekends "Happenings". I can't decide if I want a crazy weekend or a lazy one. That is, if I have time to enjoy it. Wanna help?" Misty's job as the assistant to a commercial builder required her to be on top of the daily changes in materials and the current trends in architecture. She was expected to make financial decisions on her clients' behalf and then present the purchases in the best light possible to the client, who was expected to foot the bill. "Which one do you like?"

Lois leaned forward and tapped her brightly painted fingernail on one photo. "I like that one. Those others look too pretentious for the client's profile."

Misty nodded. "I like that one, too." She scooped up the photos and placed them into the folder on her desk. "I'll have to get these to Roger so he can get these in front of the client by Friday."

"I'll take them for you," Lois offered. "I pass by his office on the way back to my stand."

"Great, thanks," Misty said. "I'm leaving early today. I promised to drop by Alice's mamas on the way home and pick up Shae.

Alice's car is in the shop. She's got a loner, but Shae needs a ride to pick it up.

Lois nodded. "That's typical Shae. Always making Alice's life harder.

"Speaking of life harder, don't you have a wedding coming up?"

"Yeah. Next week. I feel for Alice. I don't know what I'd do without my truck"

You'd figure it out. You always do. I can't imagine having to plan someone's wedding dinner after only talking to them one time. So many things could go wrong. You make it look simple."

"Keeps things interesting." Lois was scanning the weekend happening on her phone now. She usually had a wedding every Saturday at this time of year, so having one off was an unanticipated treat.

"Oh, you thrive on it," Misty replied.

That was true. Lois loved to be involved in the entire fairy tale setup. Misty would hate it. "My life is not hard. I only answer to myself. You have Roger. It's all you can do to get him motivated enough to provide input for your suggestions to the clients."

Misty grinned. "He's not much help. I only let him present them to make him feel important."

Lois laughed. She liked Roger a million times more than her ex-Bruce and enjoyed his company.

Lois's relationship with Misty's previous business partner, and ex-boyfriend, could be considered anything but cordial. Bruce McDonald, the owner of B&D Construction, was a megalomaniac who had insisted on controlling every aspect of Misty's life from day one. She had to get permission and leave him an online schedule of where she would be, and when she would be there, any time she left the office without him. A total control freak, he kept Misty on a strict budget and even chose the clothes she could wear. When he took her car keys and told her she couldn't go to a movie with Lois, Misty decided she'd had enough, and told him it was over. He'd been gone several days before it clicked in that the business was in Misty's name. Lois often wondered if he'd have spent so much time and money on the business, if he'd known their relationship would be history a year later. Her new partner was a gift from heaven in comparison.

"His jealousy wasn't all bad," Misty reminded her. "He could be warm and considerate when he wanted something." Especially sex...

Lois smiled. "Well, if you say so. I still think you made excuses for him too often. I'm just glad he's history."

Misty leaned back in her chair. "So, what are we going to do tonight?" she said, changing the subject. "Black Veil Brides is in town, but I'm not sure if any tickets are available. Or if I can afford the ones that are." She sighed. "Such is my luck. My rent comes due the same week that a show I want to see hits town."

"You love music," Lois giggled. "I could never get into all the groupies. Besides, Alice would kill us if we went to their concert without her." Live events were an integral part of the southern entertainment culture, and Misty attended as many concerts as she could.

"Well, where else can a single girl go without a date in this town?" Misty asked in mock defense. "At least we try to stay away from the bar crowd. Theres not that many options available. Movies are full of teenagers. You meet someone online, you do the endless text conversations, and just when you think you've got a good catch, you find out he's got a fetish for rubber suits and whips, or sleeps on nail beds, or lives in his mommy's basement. Or all three. I seem to attract the control freaks."

Lois smiled. "That's why I love bikers. They are so upfront and in your face. I adore a bad boy. You should try it some time."

"Bruce rode a motorcycle."

"A rice burner. That's not my idea of a motorcycle. Never could understand needing to lie down to ride one. I like to set back and relax." He looked wistful for a moment. "Mr. Right will come along. Just give it time."

"Well, I hope so," Misty lamented. "I've already met Mr.-Right-Now, Mr. I-Need-a-Loan, and Mr.-I'm-Married-but-Its -Open.!"

"And don't forget Mr.-One-Night-Stand." After sharing a laugh, Lois said, "Anyway, I was thinking we could go down to Five Points. I have a friend that can get us on the list for the VIP lounge at The Stardust. Want to try it? You never know who will be there. We haven't been out in ages."

Misty shook her head. "Sure. But don't you need to hang around and help?"

"No. I need a break. Besides, Reba's cooking for a baby shower. She'll have the kitchen tied up all night."

"At least she leaves you free samples in

the freezer. I'm on a first-name basis with my pizza guy."

"And you're always hungry. I'm making Thai shrimp curry, so we can gorge on Sunday after it's all over.

Lois nodded her head in agreement. That was another added benefit. Besides acting as a sounding board whenever she was feeling mixed emotions, Lois was a fantastic chef. Unlike the Pre-wedding dinner, Lois never knew how much food would be needed for the reception. She tended to overcook, and that meant lots of leftover. She kept her and Misty's freezer full. "With your and Reba's schedule these days, I haven't needed to cook in months. It's like the food mysteriously appears."

Misty's secretary tapped on the door. "Misty, you have a call holding for you on line 3. The caller's been waiting for quite a while and refuses to leave a message."

Lois sighed as she rose from her chair, glancing at her watch. "Why do these people always call while I'm here with their emergencies?"

"They know you will fix it." Lois laughed. "We can leave around seven. Dress to Impress."

Misty nodded. "And you say, 'I need to stay out of trouble!'"

Later, Misty drove toward Alice's moms after work. Heading past the downtown connector in heavy traffic, she had time to think. Towering commercial buildings, hotels, convention centers and big businesses fell away behind her as she entered the ramp to I-75.

As usual, traffic was at a snail's pace as she stopped and started on the freeway. The road was jammed with regulars going home for the day and truckers unsure of which lane they needed to be in after a long day of driving. Her mind was on nothing to do with work and everything to do with what she was going to wear that night. She shielded her eyes from the sea of chrome bumpers that reflected the late afternoon sun as the steady stream of traffic slowed to a sluggish crawl. The freeway arteries always became clogged with cars as far as the eye could see at this time of day. She checked her watch. If she didn't start moving soon, Alice's sister would start calling. Over and over again.

Her mind returned to Bruce. Sometimes she missed him terribly. It seemed like an eternity since they'd broken up, even though they spoke by phone occasionally. Still,

Misty wondered if it was him, she missed, or just being part of a couple. Or she missed his touch. Perhaps she was too damn picky, just as Lois liked to say. Temptation to call him whispered in her ear, saying it was just a booty call. It was not like she was making a commitment.

"Arrgh!" She growled out in frustration as she slammed her phone closed.

The traffic thinned as she approached the exit for her mother's place. She got off the freeway and continued along Tara Boulevard, past the commercial businesses and older neighborhoods. A left, a right, and then another left at the stop sign, and she arrived at the house.

The door was open, with only the screen to provide privacy. Pulling it open, she entered and walked to the back of the building. She found Shae in the kitchen.

"Misty!" Shae exclaimed as she rose from the table to greet her. "Is it already time? I got busy working on a class assignment, and it got away from me. Shae could be a bit of an airhead. It amazed her that she could pass any of her classes, much less be graduating in less than 3 weeks.

Marion, their mother, was the exact opposite. She was in her late 50s now. While she wore the latest hairstyle, she preferred the same classic clothing lines she had worn since starting her job at the bank. She had a slight stoop in her posture from years of bending over a typewriter before computers became the norm and gained a few pounds but still retained her slender body. She had been considered a beauty in her youth — and it could still be seen in the fine structure of her perfectly rouged cheekbones, the long lashes over her eyes, and her sculptured chin. She looked good for a woman her age and still had a gentle, southern mother-like kindness that Misty had adored since she'd met her.

Misty inhaled the familiar scent of flowers that permeated the home, taking in the wide variety of greenery in the room. While some homes look cluttered from poor plant upkeep, Marion's green thumb created a flawless forest of greenery that was e an oasis of freshness and harmony. Marion decorated her space with a variety of elaborate indoor plants and flowers, some so exotic that it would be a challenge for an expert to grow, but she managed it herself with ease. Decorative pots perched on every available space with shiny splashes of greenery along with neat, brightly colored blooms she tended to with a water spritzer bottle and a pair of gardening gloves she kept on a nearby shelf. She had an eye for color and design when it came to flowers, and Misty often wondered why she had not been a florist.

She came around to embrace Misty in a hug.

Even though Alice was nearly 30 years old, her mother doted on her as if she were still a young child. She liked to show the same attention to all Alice's friends. Today, she brushed a strand of hair out of her face., and commented that she looked nice, but Misty knew she didn't approve of a job where jean and steel-toed boots were daily attire. Her voice was smooth and charming with the drawl that brought images of mint juleps and fresh peaches cobbler to mind. Everything about her manner breathed southern country gentility.

"Thank you, Marion." Misty smiled.

Marion offered a wan smile and sat down at the round oak table while Misty took a seat across from her. Shae was cleaning up the last of her experiments, putting the modern kitchen back to its usual state of cleanliness and order. Every appliance, the furniture, items of equipment, even the blinds that covered her windows, were perfectly coordinated. A Photographer could pop in unexpectedly and immediately shoot the cover of a home magazine. It was clear where Alice got her habits.

"Marion, I don't know how you do it. These plants are gorgeous! I can't keep a plant alive to save my life."

Marion laughed. "Oh, it's easy," she said, looking around at her collection with pride. "It takes a bit of practice, but after a while, it becomes as natural as breathing. I love carin' for the little sweethearts and tryin' out new plants. Did you know indoor plants remove toxins like molds and bacteria from the air?"

"No, I didn't know that. Maybe I should get some for my office. Not that they would survive. Instead of water, I'd end up spilling coffee all over them."

Shae came back into the kitchen. "Speaking of plants, maybe mom would like to do all the floral arrangements for the wedding Alice is catering?"

Misty grinned. "She would be perfect for it.!"

"Oh, my goodness, do you really think I

could!" Marion said. "I'd be happy to do it, but I'm much better with greenery than cut flower."

Marion pointed to a large pot in the corner of her credenza. Long green leaves surrounded clusters of large, dangling trumpet-shaped flowers that swayed gracefully from sturdy brown stems, perfusing the air with a sweet scent. Two porcelain winged cherubs, masses of golden ringlets surrounding their smiling faces, sat in the potted soil.

"I got the plants from an exotic plant nursery last week," she said. "Angel trumpets. Aren't they just gorgeous?"

Misty admired the large, fragrant flowers. "The flowers are gorgeous. Maybe you can use some of them for the wedding."

"A great idea," Marion said. "These grow tall outdoors, but I keep this pot trimmed. Plants have feelings, you know. I talk to them all the time. Your father would've loved these. Pepper always liked big flowers."

"I remember daddy picking flowers when we'd walk the trails at the park," Shae said.

"He always brought me a bouquet. He would've been a great florist," her mother said. She paused. "We talked about opening a shop. We could have been successful,

I think. I'm so glad you got to experience the life we never could. It makes me feel like both my girls have the most wonderful life, because I know you both love what you do."

Shae felt tears well up. Her father had died 20 years ago, but she remembered the accident like it was yesterday. It was a glorious Saturday that summer, the first sunny day after a week of heavy rains that swamped the city. They had gone for a day of swimming in the Cockran's Mill, a natural swimming hole situated at the outlet of an underwater stream. She loved going to the picturesque gorge. The pool, fondly called the "millpond" by the locals, filled up with swimmers. Many of the braver teenagers would jump into the crisp, cold water from top of the falls, notwithstanding it was both cold and dangerous.

Misty hated this memory since she had seen him fall. Misty and Lois were insepara-ble friends. As soon as they arrived, the two 8-year-olds ran down the trail to swim in the pool. Later, as the sun reached its zenith and lunch was finished, they were re-energized for a healthy game of tag. They took off for the willow-lined path, darting among the rocks and foliage that surrounded the pool.

That day, Lois was "it" and was chasing Alice at full speed to touch her and pass the designation of "it" to her or Misty. Shae was only 6 and could barely swim, so she stayed on shore most of the time. Misty ran to the water's edge and jumped off a large rock into the chilly water, with Alice right behind her. Lois was in hot pursuit. Alice quickly ducked under the water to keep Lois from finding her until the coast was clear. She heard nothing but the peaceful swish of the current in her ears.

Alice soon ran out of breath and popped her head out of the water. When no one trued to tag her, she looked around for Lois, but she was nowhere to be seen. Alice quickly swam to the bank and climbed out of the water; confident she had won the game. Wrapping her arms around her shoulders to keep from shivering, she stood at the pool's edge, calling Shae's name over and over as her eyes scanned the water's edge, but she was gone.

To this day, Misty remembered the tingle of fear that crept into her body as she climbed onto the bank that day. She spotted Marion and mother on their knees near the base of the trail that climbed up to the top of the waterfall but couldn't see Pepper. Lois was trying to comfort the now hysterical Alice. Shae was crying. Misty could hear sirens approaching in the distance. Then she saw two police officers running in their direction. A few minutes later, an ambulance arrived and took their father away. He never woke up after striking his head on a rock. He had been climbing up the waterfall trail when he fell. Later, it was determined that he had lost consciousness almost immediately upon hitting the rock. Knowing he was never in pain helped, but Marion had never been back to that park. The shock that gripped her heart was something she carried to this day.

Since her husband's death, Marion's obsession with plants served as a replacement for the man she lost so tragically years ago. Channeling her grief in such a loving way seemed to be appropriate and touching. That was when she was still at the bank. Then the bank was bought out by a big chain and her branch was closed. She worked a series of part-time jobs, but nothing clicked. Her mother had moved to Florida and Marion had moved to Jonesboro. Now her home teemed with greenery, and all her spare time was spent caring for them when she wasn't visiting her father's grave.

Shae didn't want to tell her she had no intention of being a florist. Her degree was in business, and she intended to find a motel or apartment in Florida or California to manage. Not that she didn't appreciate the techniques her mother had passed on that enabled her to make some money while going to school. She changed the subject. "I saw a mob outside the Litter Box on the way to school this morning. I guess the band is back in town.

"I wish they would go away," Misty muttered darkly. "They all seem like desperate females with no life!" She made no secret of the fact she found the fans that accumulated to see the band humorous. She felt a twinge of guilt when she remembered Shae's pile of fan letter reply's, folded notes and envelopes from the band, as well as gifts—stuffed animals, artwork, and other offerings—stacked on the top of the chest at home. Shae loved reading the letters, even though she realized it was probably a secretary that written them."

"If I had the time, I would be down there with them." Shae sighed and grabbed her bookbag. "We need to run. My class starts in an hour. Kisses." She gave her mom a peck on the cheek.

Misty didn't say anything until they hit Moreland Avenue, heading north." Those women tickle me, the way they treat the band members like they are gods."

"They stare at me when we drive by," Shae stated, "but they are harmless. They look at the car because they hope it's one of the band members arriving."

Misty didn't reply. She'd seen Shae in the crowd several times. While she had to agree that fans being allowed on the lot was a privilege, people took advantage all the time. The land near the studio had turned into a fan mecca, with tents popping up aggravating the people who lived nearby. APD had removed the tent village, but they had no jurisdiction over the parking lot.

To help calm the neighbors, Robby had set up a rudimentary security system for the building, mounting a camera above the doorway that showed the entire parking lot on a small television monitor at his desk. He could view the activity in the lot. If a visitor arrived, he could push a button at his desk, which would unlock the front door to let them in. The setup didn't record anything outside, but the slightest touch to the building without him unlocking the door would alert the police.

Shae could tell it was a battle she could never win. "Oh, enough about them. What are you and Lois up to tonight?"

"She mentioned the Stardust Ballroom."

"Pass." Shae said. I would have to go home and get dressed up. By the time I got there, I would need to leave, or I'd miss the last bus. I've got a lot to do before tomorrow's wedding. We are still going to do the graduation cruise. I can do some research and let you know what I find out about pricing and packages."

"That's fine. Check with Alice and see what her limits are. I can cover yours as a graduation gift, but I can't cover everyone. I imagine it's been a long two weeks for you."

Shae smiled. "Yes, it has, and it seems like this whole wedding been a big rush, even from the time they got engaged to the service tomorrow afternoon." She sighed. "Nothing has been normal. Alice is making the shrimp curry because the husband to be loves spicy food and it's easy enough. But she's also doing baked chicken in case no one else can handle the burn."

"That's smart."

"What if we can't pull it off? This is the biggest wedding we've tried to cater."

"I'm sure you'll do just fine, hon. You get this way every time."

Misty pulled up in front of the auto repair shop and waited while Shae grabbed everything she needed. She was back in minutes with Alice's Honda. "It's running much better."

"I would still take it easy on the way to class. And be careful heading home. Make sure you take the main roads." She watched until Shae was inside the building before pulling off.

As Misty wove through the traffic toward home, she hoped Shae wouldn't get a ticket for driving faster than she should. Alice was right. It took a while to get ready, and she needed to get started, or Lois would bitch about having to wait. She could be worse than some men about wasted time. It's too bad Alice had a catering job tomorrow. It would have been fun to have her with them. She started thinking about what she was going to wear...

Chapter Five

Misty finished her drink and pushed the empty glass to the side and turned to study the room. Lois had been wrong about the Stardust Ballroom. It was not the high-class lounge they'd been expecting. She would have described it as more of a neighborhood tavern.

In the form fitting black sheath she was extremely overdressed; but it obviously bothered her more than the people in the club. Other than a few territorial glares when a man took a second look, no woman one paid that much attention. The men looked and realized she wasn't searching for a hookup and moved on to easier pickings. Misty knew her problem wasn't getting a man's attention. It was his keeping hers. She was what most men called 'high maintenance', expecting to receive as much in return as she put into a relationship. So far, none of the men had been looking for an equal partnership. She seriously doubted she'd run into one here.

When they first arrived, she'd danced

with a few of the more persistent admirers, but after realizing she had no intention of furthering the connection, they had moved on to easier, more intoxicated targets. One man in the band had bought her a drink, but she had no interest in joining the throngs of female fans that followed them like puppy dogs when they took their breaks.

Misty spent the next hour scoping the room and checking out the local version of eye candy. Despite being attracted to the clean-cut business executive types she usually dated, she had to admit there were several extremely handsome men inside the club that would never be caught dead in an office. Instead of suits, most of them were dressed in faded denim jeans and skintight black tee shirts that showed off every inch of their hard-earned muscles. Not one of these hard bodies came from a gym. Some men wore their hair cut short, others wore it down to their shoulders or longer. Beards and five o'clock shadow dominated. So did testosterone.

A slight lift of her lips softened her serious expression. Considering how many alpha males were in the room, it was surprising more fights had not broken out.

Her eyes kept drifting back to a man sitting at the far corner of the bar, back against the wall, sipping on a beer. He was so quiet, you could almost miss him, except for the way people would stare and whisper when they noticed him sitting there. He saw her looking at him and winked. Then he got up and walked her way.

The arrogant ass looked like he could have walked right off the cover of a romance novel. He turned and looked her up and down before he approached a second man sitting two chairs further down the bar. They talked quietly for a few moments; then he returned to his bar stool in the corner, passing by without a second glance.

Her face flamed when she realized he hadn't intended to speak to her at all. She jerked her eyes away, searching the dance floor for Lois. As usual, her bestie was having a great time, dancing with one man after another, not spending much time with anyone in particular. The bartender brought her another drink, her third of the night, and she took a drink. She loved the sweet and sour flavor of the tropical drink, never developing a taste for the beer Lois loved. Usually, she would limit it to two for the night, but tonight she felt the need to relax and let down her barriers. Still, it surprised her when she sucked the last of the liquid through the straw.

Her bladder was screaming out its need for relief, so she stumbled toward the bathroom, leaving her jacket on the chair to hold her place.

***

Ace was camped out in his usual spot in the corner, sipping on a Heineken and doing his best to avoid anyone who recognized him. He'd promised to meet his friends there; but he hated the fans that followed their group. The Stardust Ballroom wasn't as big as some clubs they played. It was extremely noisy, but the employees all knew him by sight, and he never had to fight to get a seat. Even better, it was within walking distance of his house in case he was too drunk to drive. That had only happened once. Tonight, he was on his bike. After band practice that afternoon, instead of going back to the house to shower and change, he'd come straight to the bar. Of course, tonight the club was packed.

He wondered if he'd ever get used to seeing men in expensive three-piece suits sitting next to women wearing jeans and tee shirts. Or women wearing couture, he thought as two gorgeous examples walked past him to vacant seats along the bar. The dresses the pair were wearing probably cost more than most of the people in the bar made in a month. Maybe they were models? The one with blonde hair was a little short, five seven maybe, but the fashion industry had loosened up on the height restrictions. They stuck out in a bar filled with blue collar clientele.

For several years, he'd felt like his life was on a downhill spiral with no way to stop the nose-dive. It was during the last year that things had changed and appeared to be moving in the right direction. That was a good thing. The band was back playing gigs, and he was dating, even though he'd restricted it to one-night stands. Luckily, there was always a new cutie willing to take his mind off everyday aggravations.

Tonight, none of them caught his attention. He was more interested in the blonde in the black dress. Something about her was tugging at his mind, pulling his glances back to her over and over again. He did not know why. She was doing nothing to attract attention. Sipping her drink and listening to the music.

Ace watched her shift her position on the barstool, making sure she had a good view of the people in the room. She was not his usual type. She was probably five years older than most of the women he picked up after his concerts. Closer to thirty than twenty. She was beautiful; at least five-seven, perfect champagne glass breasts, and a firm, athletic build. He's bet anything that hair that fell to her hips in a silken sheath was naturally blonde. Her big blue eyes seemed to shift from sultry to savage without warning. Not to mention that face, an artist's dream, full lips, an aristocratic nose, and a lone freckle high on her right cheek. She was everything he ever wanted in a woman. There was no arguing about that. So... what made him hesitate? Could any woman be as perfect as she seemed? He watched her for a few minutes and decided he had to know.

She was so hot she could make a dead man hard. Several of the guys had made passes at her, but she had brushed them off with some minor excuse. Every limp dick in the bar was twitching as she walked across the room. On the way back from the john, he made it a point to stop at the corner of the bar and grab a cold beer. Of course, he stopped right beside her chair.

"Slumming?" He took a sip, allowing her an opportunity to answer. She looked at him like he was crazy, definitely not the reaction he's hoped for.

"Excuse me?"

"Never mind. Why is a beautiful woman like you sitting all alone?" he asked. He noticed the sadness in her eyes. Amazing eyes... brilliant cornflower blue eyes.

"What makes you think I'm alone?" She could see that the answer had caught him by surprise. She looked up, absorbing every tiny detail of the walking wet dream. He was grinning; showing a set of straight white teeth. Teeth were one of her pet peeves. The idea of kissing a mouth full of rotten teeth was a definite turnoff. If a man took care of his teeth, chances are he took care of the rest of his body, too. Up close, she could see he had dark brown hair, almost black, and gorgeous green eyes. Despite the eyes would risk all the money she had on her that there was Native blood somewhere in his family tree. She could see a scattering of tattoos along his muscled forearms, usually a sign that more were hidden beneath his tight black tee shirt. Despite her aversion to bikers, she was curious about what else he was hiding.

He stood there in silence. Say something! Anything. She's not like the others. "Well shit. That wasn't much of a conversation starter." He looked like a little boy caught with his hand in the proverbial cookie jar.

She could help but laughing at his expression. The man was interesting. She was used to attracting a variety of men, but this one made her squirm her without saying or doing a thing. Maybe it was the green ice in his eyes. They literally made her shiver, and it wasn't from fear.

"Buy you a drink?"

"No, thanks, I'm good". Misty replied.

"I guess a dance off the table?" He held out his hand, expecting her to jump.

"Don't dance to fast songs." And even if I did, it wouldn't be someone like you. Cocky prick. He got the message. She watched as he turned and walked back to his hidden corner.

The band broke into a slow, romantic ballad. It seemed like a good time to get some air. She reached for her jacket, then froze as an unexpected voice whispered directly into her ear, "Are you ready to dance with the devil?" He reached for her hand and pulled her chair away from the table.

"Thanks, but I'm going to sit this one out," she said without looking up.

"Now that would be a waste, considering all the hard work I put into getting them to play this song," he stated.

Misty felt her face flame. It was obvious he wasn't about to take no for an answer. He held his hand out to help her through the tangled chairs, so she allowed him to lead her toward the dance floor. As he pulled her into his arm's, she wondered if she was making a big mistake.

A few minutes later, she knew she was.

Chapter Six

Ace found himself in the unusual position of wanting to impress a woman. He led her into an intricate spin on the dance floor, then slid between the other couples with Misty in his arms. He was a decent dancer, but she had a lot more rhythm than he'd expected. Their bodies matched perfectly, seeming to float across the floor as they moved to the music. The slow ballad ended, and the first beats of a faster song began. He moved into a perfect slide step combination without a faltered step. She giggled like a little girl. His own pulse grew faster as she moved to match the infective rhythm. Watching her move, he was surprised by how sexy it was. The rotation of her hips was in perfect sync with the song, and it helped him to keep his mind off his growing erection. He was turned on in a way he hadn't felt in....

Damn. Why had he let his mind go there?

Misty noticed the change and asked if he was ready to sit down.

He nodded, his throat tight, and escorted her back to her barstool. The chair next to hers was empty, so he sat. The bartender immediately placed their empties with fresh drinks.

"In case you're interested, I'm Mason. Mason Reeves." He picked up his beer and nodded her way.

"Misty Warner. Nice to meet you." Misty's heart was racing. She needed the cocktail more than she needed to know where it came from. She took a long drink, finishing about half of the glass.

Ace cocked an eyebrow but didn't ask. It was clear she did not know who he was, and that was a welcome change. He couldn't remember the last time he'd had to charm a woman and wondered if he remembered how to flirt. He finished his beer as the band began another slow song. This time, instead of asking, he removed her glass from her hand and placed it on the bar's wooden countertop, followed by his own.

"Let's go dance again."

She smiled and picked up her glass.

"What are you doing? Stalling, so the song will be over?"

"You know damn well what we're doing.

You're getting me drunk." She tried to stick to her limits but was finding him harder to resist by the second. She downed the rest of her cocktail, all thoughts of limits forgotten.

"Guilty as charged."

"You're intolerable, you know that?" she murmured, her resistance crumbling as he pulled her back into arms. She melted into his arms, pressing her body against him as he held her lightly.

"As rotten as they come." He shifted so that his head was closer to hers. "You smell so good," he mumbled, running his hands along her back, then her hips, pulling her closer to him. His body clearly wasn't indifferent to hers.

She glanced up through her lashes. "So do you." His scent was mesmerizing, his embrace intoxicating. She relaxed and moved with him, enjoying the way her body reacted to his. Every movement sent shivers down her spine.

He groaned as her nipples grew taut and pressed tight against his chest, easily felt through the thin material of her dress.

She tilted her head up to look at him, her eyes dark and full of repressed longing.

A sexy smile crossed his lips. "Let's get

out of here," he whispered.

She nodded.

Lois was sitting at the bar when they walked off the floor.

The bartender had replaced their drinks, and Misty immediately drank most of the new one, before she reached for her jacket, pulled out a set of keys and dropped them in Lois's hand.

Lois looked from one face to the other, then went to find someone to dance with. There was no way she was going to interfere. This was the first man Misty had been interested in since she broke up with Bryce. That was three years ago.

Mason stopped beside his bike and pulled her into his arms. He pulled her to him, pressing his lips against hers. His tongue slid into her mouth and entwined with hers. Misty moaned softly and leaned into him. Their kissed deepened, tongues tangled, full of pure excitement and the sweet thrill of new possibilities. He felt as nervous as a kid still in high school, his body shaking, his palms wet and clammy.

He covered his nerves by passing her a helmet, for once wishing he'd driven the car.

"Have you ever ridden a bike?"

She shook her head no.

"It's only a few blocks. Just keep your hands on my hips." He passed her a helmet, then checked to make sure the strap was tight.

***

Misty didn't remember much about the ride. It was an upscale neighborhood, and she vaguely remembered a lake. The property was surrounded by a solid, eight-foot-high stone wall, with a gate that opened electronically. There was something about the wall that she felt was important, but her mind was too fuzzy from the alcohol to concentrate. The vibration of the motorcycle between her legs had increased her awareness of the man she was pressed against. All she could think about was the way she he made her feel. She wanted more. Needed more. And she intended to get more.

As soon as the helmets came off, Mason pulled her back into his arms. Somehow, they made it into the house, but she didn't know how. She didn't care. Instead, she surrendered to the overwhelming rush of sensation tearing through her. When he stepped away, she had to fight to keep from dragging him back.

Needing something to distract her from the emotions she'd kept bottled up for so long, her eyes went to the dark framed floor-to-ceiling windows that spanned the back of the house. The glass panes flooded the interior of the house with natural light and offered a spectacular view of the city beyond the trees.

"It's beautiful."

She felt his hands against her shoulders, then his body was there. Pushing her hair aside, he nuzzled her exposed neck and throat, making her tingle with pleasure.

"It pales beside you." He nuzzled her softly, breathing in to enjoy the clean scent of her skin. A shiver wracked her body. The delicious sensation was driving her insane.

As if he heard her thoughts, he turned her to face him, pulling her into his arms. His mouth returned to hers, then he took her face in his hands and left gentle kisses on her forehead, her cheeks, before stopping to nuzzle her neck once more. His kiss was drugging her senses, setting her heart pounding and waves of electricity throughout her body.

She couldn't believe how heated she felt. She shimmied out of her jacket, but it didn't help. As if Mason was feeling the same thing, he slid his leather jacket from his shoulders, where it landed with a thump on the floor.

"We should slow down," she murmured, but it was a hopeless battle.

"I know. I have something else in mind.

She felt his fingers threading through her hair, pulling it loose from the hair clip and letting the pale golden tresses spill down into his hands. He left searing kisses on her neck as he reached behind her and slid the zipper down.

"Let me—" she breathed, trying to gain some control.

Mason placed his finger to her lips. "Shhhh." He reached around her waist and slipped the material down over her hips. It pooled at Misty's feet in a crumpled pile. Then he cupped her face in his hands and silenced her as his lips met hers. She wrapped her arms around his neck and drew his tongue deeper, caught in a rush of desire. It was as if she'd been alone for an eternity, and he'd rescued her. She wanted his clothes off, to feel every inch of him pressed against her body.

Maybe I should go," she teased, knowing he was as aroused as she was.

"The only place you are going is my bed." he murmured into her ear.

He lifted her easily, cradling her in his arm's, as he walked to the bedroom. With gentle hands, he stretched her out atop the mahogany sleigh bed, then straddled her thighs, looking down at her.

"Beautiful isn't enough. I want taste you... devour you," his words husky with desire. He lowered his mouth back down on hers, kissing her, then licking and nibbling over and over.

Ace moved to the sensitive skin of her throat, stopping just long enough to yank his shirt over his head. His fingers made quick work of the clasp of the bra, needing to strip it away, to bare her breasts. While he dealt with the tiny wisps of lace, she ran her hands up under his shirt, caressing the hard muscles of his bare back and exploring his muscular chest. It felt so good, her hands touching him. He needed her to touch every inch of him.

Her aching breasts awakened under his touch, the pale pink nipples spiking into tight rose points. He reached for the lush globes and squeezed while his lips traveled over each one, licking and kissing. Her fingers tightened in his hair, drawing him closer. He covered the tight, hard peak of one and sucked, teasing the tips with the heat of his mouth, evoking moans of pleasure from her. His tongue stroked against the tight bundle of nerve endings, sending fingers of electricity shooting through her body to the apex of her thighs. He felt her squirm beneath him and fought to maintain control as his body responded.

He pushed himself off her and the bed, using the need to remove his clothes to regain some semblance of control.

Through slitted eyes, she watched his fingers at the waistband of his jeans, unfastening the snap of his jeans, then the zipper. He slid them down over her hips, and her body responded with a rush of wet heat. He had an uncomfortable moment while he kicked off his boots, then he slid them down and off, leaving them in a puddle on the floor. The rest of his clothes quickly followed. A sexy, boyish smile curved his lips while his gaze roamed over her.

He could see the banked flames in her eyes. Not the 'fuck-me now' eyes that so many of the bar whores have, but more the 'you've got my attention, now what you gonna do about it' look that only a few women can carry off. The challenge sent his senses racing.

"Get a hold of yourself," he murmured, his voice hoarse. He could feel the heat raging in his body like a blast from a furnace. That he was so incredibly aroused wasn't lost on him. Every part of his body ached for this woman, and he intended to take care of that as soon as possible.

She moved her body under him, straining to get closer. Her slightly parted knees were a clear invitation, urging him to take her into the flames and set them both on fire.

"Mason," she breathed as he lay on the bed beside her. Once again, she took the tip of her tongue and slowly made the circuit of her lips. That one signal was all it took.

He needed no more encouragement. With an urgent groan, his lips came to hers again, his kiss hungrier than before. There was nothing tender in the way their mouths locked, just a raw hunger they both wanted to last forever. He moved his hands over her body, setting fire to every place they touched. Her curves contradicted her slender wiriness, a wonderful combination of softness and strength. When he couldn't stand it any longer, his hands slid to her thighs, his knee gently nudging her knees apart.

"I'm going to take you to heaven, babe," Mason whispered into her ear as his hand slipped between her thighs. His hands grasped her hips, lifting her up to his mouth. He gasped and jerked, making him wonder if she'd never been taken this way. If he was the first, intended to ensure that memory would stay with her. Her soft moans only increased his determination, and he was not satisfied until she lifted her hips and thrashed beneath him, crying out sharply as waves of pleasure swept her away.

Before the final crest had ended, he'd moved forward, pulling her into an intense kiss, as he thrust his hips forward, gliding into the smooth, hot welcome of her body in one effortless motion, blending his heat with hers until their passion grew to a full-fledged fire. He could feel her heart beating against his chest, hard and strong. Then she tightened her muscles, and he had to move, or it would be over before it began. His muscles flexed as he began a slow, steady stroke, pressing deeper with every thrust. When she tried to pull him down, his fingers gripped her hips tightly, holding her in place, as the head of his shaft caressed that hidden source of pleasure lying deep inside her.

"Mason. Oh God." Moans of desire spilled from Misty's lips with each long stroke, every inch piercing her with desire. Consumed by blinding passion, she rolled her hips against his, her body giving and taking as they moved together and apart, racing along the deepening surge that was building in intensity. His hands moved down to her thighs as he pushed his shaft deeper, and harder inside her. Her arms wrapped tighter around him as they moved, hard and desperate, her breath coming in shorter and shorter gasps.

Tides of building pleasure rose like a tidal wave inside her, taking her closer and closer to the crest, then stopping short, making her body fight for release. Holding on to either side of his shoulders, she lifted her hips, writhing against him, and grinding hard. In response, he pressed against her relentlessly, driving shallow thrusts against that sensitive bud as she groaned out her pleasure.

"You're killing me," Ace groaned, his breathing ragged. He gripped the headboard with one arm as he raised her hips, holding her against him as he began thrusting toward her core with a speed that drove her to the crest of the wave, then sent her sliding over the edge, her muscles clenching, squeezing, then releasing in an agonizing assault of pleasure. She tightened and arched, crying out his name when the first wave hit, overwhelming her senses, then shuddered beneath him as she was swept away by a tsunami of sensation.

It was too much for him. Mason cried out his final climatic thrust, then groaned as his body was wracked by an explosion of overwhelming sensations. His release spilled into her in waves of pleasure as he joined her before gradually slowing his strokes. Finally, he shuddered and gasped for air as his muscles quivered with exhaustion.

Misty snuggled close to him. His arms around her felt so warm. So right. She closed her eyes and relaxed, enjoying the feel of his body along hers.

Mason shifted so that her hips curved against his. He could hold her in his arms forever, listening to her soft, satisfied breaths. "So, what would you like for breakfast? When she didn't answer, he realized she was asleep. He smiled and pulled the covers over them and joined her.

***

The shrill ringing of the phone woke Mason from the best sleep he'd had in years. He glanced at the clock next to the bed, surprised to see it was almost noon. Robby must be having a fit, trying to figure out where he was. He'd had a bit to drink last night, but that usually didn't prevent him from working the next day. He had a vague sensation that something was wrong, but he had no what it was. He stretched and rolled over, noticing the other side of the bed was rumpled, and the pillow next to him was indented. Someone had been sleeping next to him.

Misty! She wasn't a dream. But... where was she?

***

The night air was cool, and the rain refused to let up, leaving the streets around the elite neighborhood deserted. The hour was early, even though there were usually a few of the die-hard fans hanging around, each hoping for a glimpse of Ace or the other members of the band. Shae paced back and forth along the edge of the wall, trying to stay warm and reasonably dry. She'd been hanging there since her sister had cooked at five thirty that morning. Lois had been banging around in the kitchen, cooking food for some rich bitches up near Alpharetta's wedding that evening, making it impossible for her to go back to sleep. Instead, she'd got dressed and caught the early morning bus, hoping to catch the eye of Ace as he left for the studio that morning.

A taxi approaching the gate caught her attention, and she stepped into the shadows, using a shrub for cover. The metal gate opened, and a woman slipped out before it closed behind her. She slid into the back seat of the taxi. The cab pulled away, but not before Shae got a glimpse of the woman in the back seat. A face she Shae would not forget.

Chapter Seven

The sun, or lack of it, rose to present a chilly, rainy day when the alarm began clanging at 5:30 that morning

Crap, Lois said to herself as she threw off the covers of her bed. This was a jam-packed wedding day, and she hoped the weather wouldn't ruin it. No, nothing would ruin her mood. She had too much to do. It was going to be a great day.

She sprang out of bed and headed toward the shower.

From your ivory tower, you look down below,

never been on the street,

what the hell would you know...

Lois sang the lyrics of Cat Grinning's latest hit over and over as the water pounded down on her. The loose water pipes made an awful banging noise whenever the hot water was turned on, but it didn't stop her from being on a high, ...a wedding high. She loved catering weddings. The entire happily ever after moment made her feel warm inside. Most of the dishes were prepped and ready to pop into the deluxe commercial forced air oven she's scrimped and saved to purchase.

Well, here goes nothing, she thought.

She reached into a drawer and removed an apron that she'd bought last year at a co-worker's Pampered Chef party. The arms were so long she had to wrap them around and tie it at the front of her waist. Then she got to work. Following the recipe, she had designed, she chopped the bell pepper, carrots and shallots and placed them in neat little piles on the cutting board to use later. Then she started the jasmine rice in the rice cooker.

Now to cook. Taking a deep breath, she turned the stove on to heat the peanut oil in the pan and combined the rest of the ingredients as stated in the recipe. As the mixture simmered, she pulled out all the little extras, fresh coconut milk, and the Indian spices she used to make the meal special.

She was finishing up the curry when she heard someone heading that way. She poured her a cup of coffee and had it ready when Misty walked in. Misty shook her head no and grabbed a bottle of water instead.

"Long night?"

Misty blushed, but only nodded.

It surprised Lois to discover Misty was hesitant to speak about why she was dragging in at ...she looked at her phone...9:30 in the morning. It must have been one hell of a night. Misty stumbled off to bed and she went back to cooking.

Three hours after she stepped from the shower, every shelf was filled, and she was ready to peel and de-vein the partially steamed shrimp. Three dozen eggs were already boiled and setting in cool water, ready to be deviled. Four pans of pecan crusted chicken breasts were cooling and four pans were prepped and ready to go in as soon as the current batch were done. She stepped to the stove and tested a spoonful of pilaf, smiling at the tender grains of rice.

Two hours later, she pulled the last pan of croissants from the oven. It was a little after one and the wedding started at four. She was right on schedule. After adding a final checkmark to the preparation list, she sat down to relax a moment before loading the catering truck. She peeked a glimpse at her cell phone, ensuring there were no last-minute changes in the menu she had to address.

It wouldn't be the first time she had to buy every stem of asparagus in the area in a last-minute dash to change mushroom and bacon stuffed tomatoes to the more traditional steamed sprouts with hollandaise sauce.

Loading the truck took almost an hour. She was especially careful, walking slowly with one pan at a time to prevent accidents. The specially designed covered racks held the trays firmly, minimizing any chance of destruction during the trip to the reception site. Two warmers kept the rolls at the prefect temperature. Every dish had come together exactly as she'd hoped. So far, so good. The wedding cake was already there. The bakery had delivered it and the smaller trays of cookies and Petit fours. She loved the tiny French pastries with the fondant icing and considered them the perfect desert after a wedding.

She took the usual route from her apartment to the Renaissance Event Facility, about an hour north of her apartment, but a peaceful drive up Lavista to 400. Lois loved this road, as it kept her out of the misery of downtown traffic every day. She'd driven it a thousand times while attending the culinary arts school, and then during the year she interned.

This time, however, she had somewhere other than the campus to go. So far, everything had gone perfectly. The ceremony was beautiful. The dinner was served with no one having a plate of food dumped into their lap or having an allergic reaction from the shrimp or the chicken. She had thought ahead and cooked one tray of chicken without the pecan crust, just a simple butter and herb marinade. This worked out well, as seven of the guests could not eat shrimp or nuts. The extra piece was welcomed by the larger man, who claimed it was the best baked chicken he'd ever eaten. Of course, the three cocktails he'd enjoyed prior to the meal probably didn't hurt. Guests were now celebrating with the happy couple, and dancing to the mellow sounds of the eight-piece wedding band. With three singers, they were able to provide a wide variety of cover tunes, enough to please every age group.

The bride and groom came from affluent families. Besides the requisite family associations, both must have invited everyone on the family's friend lists. There were over two hundred tipsy guests in the room, and most had not noticed that the bride and groom had slipped away from the celebration. Perhaps to do a little private celebrating of their own. Or maybe they just wanted to avoid the hour-long goodbye.

Patsy, the wedding planner, had outdone herself this time. She moved among the celebrants, ensuring that the servers never carried an empty tray. This was the elite of the Atlanta Society, and they were both going out of their way to ensure each guest had as good a time as possible. Both women knew how people gossiped and neither wanted to give a guest a reason to disclaim publicly how disappointed they were with the wedding or the reception. With luck, they would give a glowing report and their friends would hire them in the future.

Still, Lois could not explain how happy she was to see the last guest leave a little after midnight. Finally, she could break down the tables and stow the leftovers away in the truck. Not that there was much left to stow. She offered a snack to anyone remaining to clean up; which most were happy to receive. Like her, many had been there since early that afternoon, and it was after midnight now.

Unlike at home, once the leftovers were

stored away, Lois was not expected to clean up behind the guests. There was a crew already at work in the main room and before she pulled out of the lot, there was very little remaining to show that over two hundred revelers had been partying the evening away less than an hour earlier.

When Lois finally pulled into the yard a little after two in the morning, she was surprised by how tired she was. The idea of moving all the leftovers into the house and packaging them for the freezer didn't help. She really wished she could leave it all in the truck and go straight to bed, but that was a ridiculous waste of food. By the time she woke up, most would be past the expiration and need to be tossed. She sighed and reached for the first tray of food, then grinned and added another to the stack. There was no reason to take the extreme measure of caution carrying them back inside. She was going to drop the breasts into freezer bags and dump the asparagus into a quart container. It might take two to hold all the leftover Thai shrimp. It tasted great but was too spicy for most of the diners. The croissants went into the freezer in the same type of baggy as the chicken. There was very little of anything else remaining. She'd snagged herself a dozen cookies and five Petit fours. The cookies went into the glass jar with the others but the French style pastries she kept for herself. Finally, satisfied she had done as much as possible at the moment, she crawled into the bed minutes before the bedside alarm to begin its morning clamor.

Chapter Eight

The sun, or lack of it, rose to present a chilly, rainy Saturday.

Crap, Shae said to herself as she threw off the covers of her bed. Today was a special day. She hoped the weather wouldn't ruin it. No, nothing would ruin what she was about to do. It was going to be a great day.

She sprang out of bed and headed toward the shower. Her mother must have been doing laundry. The water was warm but far from the temperature she preferred. She sang the lyrics of Ace's latest hit over and over as the water pounded down on her. The tepid flow was aggravating, but it didn't stop her from being on a high, an Ace high.

She threw on some clothes, and avoided her mother, easing shut the front door as she headed out in the morning drizzle to catch the bus going to Atlanta. She was on a mission to get the perfect birthday gift for Ace.

The white MARTA bus was rounding the corner as she reached toward the bus stop.

The driver saw her running and hit the air brakes, allowing it to roll to a stop. Shae ignored the rain dripping down her face as she stepped inside the double doors. She swiped her easy pass card and made her way back to an empty seat near the rear of the vehicle. The bus wasn't crowded, so she plopped down by the window and put her backpack in the seat beside her to discourage anyone from sitting next to her. She wasn't one for conversation with strangers, even though someone seemed to hit on her every time she rode this bus. Normally, she was on the way to school, however, today she had somewhere else to go. She transferred at the Airport station, catching the northbound train heading to Buckhead. Less than twenty minutes after she'd left the house, she was walking down the sidewalk that snaked along a two-mile stretch of Peachtree Street. She strolled past the funky souvenir shops and cafes that were just opening for the day until she came to a small tattoo and piercing shop. The door was propped open, and she wandered inside. It wasn't an impressive business. Little bigger than the average bedroom, most of the shop was taken up by two dentist-type chairs at the back of the room. They sat about three feet away from each other, with no type of barrier separating them. There were a couple of stuffed chairs setting beside the entrance. The shop smelled like ammonia and pine cleaner and looked spotless. No one appeared to be inside.

She figured they would not be gone long, so she looked around

The walls were covered with a variety of body art, some stock and some with intricate custom designs. A display case contained charms for piercings and a photo album overstuffed with pictures of tattooed people. She sat down to browse the pages, studying the techniques inside.

"You got an appointment?" The deep voice made her jump. A burly, dark-haired man stood in the shop's doorway. Both of his arms were covered with tattoos. He couldn't have been more than a few years older than her.

She got down to business. "How much is it to get a tattoo?"

"Depends on a lot of things. What tattoo you want. How much time it takes. How much color is involved?" His eyes took in her worn jeans and department store t-shirt, and grinned. "Probably more than you can afford."

His tone told her he didn't take her seriously. "Look, if you're one of those street kids—"

"I'm not," Shae said. "I go to college. Right now, I want to get a tattoo."

"All right. Do you know what you want?" he asked with annoyance. "Because I don't have all day and my regular customers will arrive soon. They're all different prices depending on the size and the design."

"Yeah, I know what I want." She walked over to the wall and pointed to a design. "I want this. I want you to tattoo the name Ace, with a guitar and a heart in it, and I want you to put it on me here." She pointed to her left chest, above the bra line.

"Not asking for much, are you? That design would run about five hundred, including the guitar and the heart."

Shae never had that much money in her life, but one girl at school had told her what to say. "That's a lot of money for me. I want it for sure, but I'm short. Or...er...can I, uh, pay you some other way? Like a trade?"

"A trade? Like what, meth, pot, cocaine?" he could tell the girl did not know what she was getting herself into. He'd bought the business from the widow of the previous owner a few weeks ago. The previous owner had been killed by the boyfriend of a female customer, a fifteen-year-old girl who'd been giving him a blowjob in trade for some work. The young man had followed her to the shop and didn't appreciate how Larry was operating his business.

"No, no drugs." She looked down at the floor.

He smiled. "Sex?"

Shae didn't look up. "Yeah." She signaled to her mouth and licked her finger.

No, she definitely wasn't familiar with the sex trade. "A blow job! You kidding, kid? I can get that for $50. And a very good one, too."

He grabbed her by the shoulders and spun her around. "Now, an ass like that, well, maybe that's worth something." Shae could see the lust reflected in his eyes showing in his groin. He was interested, but she doubted he was five hundred dollars interested.

"How much cash have you got?"

"Hundred-twenty." There was no way he would do a tattoo for her cash and three -hundred and eighty dollars was a lot of money to charge anyone for sex. Even she knew most hookers charged a hundred a pop.

He winced, then asked, "How old are you?"

"Twenty."

"Got any ID?"

She handed him her college ID."

He glanced at it and then pointed toward a door at the back of the shop. "All right., Elizabeth. You got a deal. Pay me, then go in there and sit down. I need to lock the door."

Without waiting for him to change his mind, she passed him the cash. Then she hurried past the curtained doorway into a stark white back room containing a tattoo chair with an accompanying worktable containing various hand tools. It was even cleaner than the cubicles in the front part of the store. The counter gleamed, and it had a sterile smell to it. The chrome instruments glittered under the white recessed lights in the ceiling.

She saw him flip over a sign on the front door and realized she was committed and couldn't escape even if she wanted to.

A minute later, he entered the room. Standing before her, he looked larger than he did out in the store. He pushed her into the chair. Her heart pounded. She realized at any moment, a stranger was going to expect the agreed upon payment, and she would have to follow through. His eyes locked on hers and she realized he wasn't the type of man that played games.

But instead of removing his pants, he sat down on a round stool and rolled a portable table containing his equipment next to the chair. He snapped on medical gloves and flipped a switch, which started the buzzing of the machine.

"You're going to have to remove your shirt if you want this done."

He was grinning as she struggled to remove her tee. "The bra, too."

She glared at him for a second before taking it off.

"Nice tits," he said. Then he folded the tee shirt and placed it over her breasts.

He used a laptop to design the tattoo, then traced the design on her chest above her bra. There was no turning back as the needle touched her chest to trace the outline of Ace's name inside a guitar. Shae didn't take her eyes off the design on the laptop as it came to life under his gun. It hurt for a moment, then the area went numb. After that she didn't feel any pain, just pressure. The vibration of the needle was hypnotizing. After the outline was completed, he switched to a gun with a four-needle configuration and filled in the outline.

In what seemed a very short time, he was done. He wiped the area clean and cleaned up his work area. Shae looked down at his work. A beautiful tattoo honoring Ace, all her own! She just couldn't take her eyes off it.

He removed the gloves. "You're done," he said gruffly. "Keep the tattoo clean for a few weeks to make sure it doesn't get infected. And don't mess with it, either, until it's completely healed."

He handed her a hand-held mirror to inspect his work. She smiled. The tattoo was just right.

Not waiting for an answer, he took the mirror out of her hands. "Glad you like it. Now pay me." His hands reached for his zipper.

"Oh yeah," she breathed. "Okay, sure." A deal was a deal, and she couldn't just return the goods and leave. She turned around and slowly pulled down her shorts and bent over, her heart pounding.

She glanced back at him. "Just don't hurt

me, okay?" she said.

The store owner looked down at her for a long moment. Then he turned and left the room.

"Hey!" Shae stood up, calling after him as she pulled up her shorts and followed him out into the store. "Where are you going?"

The owner stood at the door. "Leave."

"But what about your payment?"

"You can pay me when you get the money. Now get out." He gave her a light shove out the door before turning around and walking toward the back of the store.

Not waiting around to argue the point, she hustled out the door for the bus stop. Her heart didn't stop racing until she boarded and found her seat, headed for Ace's studio near Misty's apartment in Five Points.

The bus dropped her off less than a block from her goal. She was whistling one of his songs as she walked to the studio parking lot to wait for Ace. Just as she expected, the lot was full of young women, most holding some type of gift for his birthday. She was almost giddy with excitement. She couldn't wait to show him what she had done for him, her pledge of love. The skin was tender underneath the bandage, but it looked great. It would look even better once it's healed, she thought.

After about an hour of dodging raindrops while standing beneath a soggy oak tree, she saw Ace's truck make the turn and head toward the studio. He was driving slow on the rain-slick street, as though he didn't trust his tires. Her heart fluttered. She touched the tattoo under her shirt. It was sore, but she didn't care.

Then she noticed he wasn't alone. Shae's jaw dropped. As she stood with the others, a hot flush of anger crept up her neck. She'd expected a chance to talk to Ace alone, and it was spoiled by this woman. It was someone she'd never seen before, but she seemed comfortable. They pulled up and made a run for the door, trying to avoid the rain. Shae waited anyway. It was his birthday, and she would not leave until he did, even if the rain didn't stop. Ace may emerge alone, and she could see him then. She sat under the tree, waiting, along with the other fans.

The minutes seemed to drag by. What were they doing in there? Her imagination filled in the blanks. The thoughts were enough to make her seethe with jealousy. A short time later, the woman emerged from the building, carrying a box.

She headed toward her car, not his truck. Shae knew she had to act fast. No one was paying attention to her. It was going to be close, but she had to try. She ran up the walkway toward the closing door and ducked inside. "Ace!"

Ace turned and smiled down at her. "Hello, darlin'. What brings you here on such a miserable day?"

She just loved it when he called her darling. He was so close, she wanted to reach out to him. She felt his eyes burning into her. She stepped closer, longing to be as near to him as she could, then blushed. "I want to show you something—" and pulled up her shirt, displaying the new tattoo. By now, the dressing on her chest was blood stained and seeping through her shirt.

"A new tat? I' m sure it will be beautiful once it heals. Send me a picture." He smiled, and a winked before walking out the door, heading directly to his truck. The fans swarmed the vehicle, piling gifts into the bed of the truck. He waved and smiled at the fans, slid the guitar case behind the seat, and jumped into the driver's side.

Shae stood in the rain and watched as

the car pulled out from its parking space and drove off.

Chapter Nine

"Hey man, grab me a beer while you're there." He took a bite of the pizza he was holding, not wanting to take his eyes away from the screen. When Robby passed him the beer, he twisted the cap and chugged about half before he realized what he was doing.

Ace, along with Robby, Santwan, and a few other local musicians, were in the studio, partying in what Ace dubbed "the foxhole," a large recreation room he'd built next to the control room. It boasted a complete home theater, a fully stocked bar, plush furniture, a snooker table, and even a dart board. It was a perfect place for musicians to relax while they were not needed in the studio. Ace liked to just to hang out and have some fun at the studio since he hated to rush home to an empty house. It had been a week since the amazing night he'd spent with Misty, but despite his every effort, he'd been unable to locate her. No one at the bar knew her, and the detective he'd hired could not locate a Misty Warner in Atlanta or any of the surrounding counties. It was almost as if his mind had created her to fulfill some unspoken need. After kicking himself for not finding out more about her, he'd finally resigned himself to the idea that he might never see her again. It surprised him how much that bothered him.

Staggering past Robby's office after relieving his bladder of too much booze, his eye glimpsed movement on the drummer's desk monitor. The camera allowed Robby to observe the empty parking lot outside; only now it wasn't empty. He squinted to focus on the image. Someone was standing out there, leaning against the trunk of the ancient oak tree he'd fought the city to maintain. A female, hands thrust into hoodie pockets. Alone. In the rain.

He recognized her right away. She was one of the regulars who showed up at the studio whenever they were in town. A petite-little thing with bright blonde hair and big blue eyes. She would be cute if she fixed herself up. But ...she seemed a little off. Too quiet. Her clothes were faded, and she always wore long sleeves even on the warmest of days. She always stayed back from the others who gathered at the door, waiting until the rest were finished before approaching him, like some lost puppy. Amusing. Definitely dedicated.

He walked to the front door and pushed it open. "Hey, you!" he called to her, the effects of the alcohol making his voice sound a loose southern drawl.

Shae whirled around.

"Whatcha doin' out there in the rain?"

At first, she said nothing, staring at him while he stood at the door, regarding her with curiosity. "I missed the last bus home," she stammered, her weight shifting nervously. "It's Sunday and they don't run as often, so I'm waiting for the next one to come in a few hours. I feel safer staying here than at the train station in Inman Park.

"Well, you can't stay out there by yourself. Come inside before you get yourself killed by a passing ax murderer."

Ace was inviting her inside! Wasting no time, Shae hurried into the building. Ace pulled the heavy glass door shut behind her.

"Follow me," he said as he walked back down the hall toward the lounge. "Your name, again?"

"Shae."

Ace nodded. "That's right. I remember now. You come down here often."

Shae beamed. "I sure do. I told you, I'm your biggest fan."

"Right," he said with amusement. He slid his arm around her waist and led her into the room where the other musicians were hanging out, drinking, smoking weed, and playing darts. Liquor bottles and half-empty tumblers littered the wet bar and end tables. A rather large bag of marijuana lay open on the coffee table, along with a couple of pipes for those who wished to partake.

"Well, what have we here?" Robby asked Ace as he surveyed Shae. "What'd you do, man... order delivery?" He looked at him and winked.

"Nah, found her out in the parking lot. No bus for a few hours, so I figured she'd like to visit with us while she waits."

"Well then, sweetheart, come join us," Robby replied as he handed a red solo cup to Shae. She accepted the cup and took a delicate sip, surprised to discover it wasn't straight coke. "Thank you," she said and then turned her attention back to Ace.

Ace downed the last of his beer and dug

around the bar refrigerator for another before returning to the couch.

"Why don't you go sit next to him?" Mike suggested playfully, gesturing toward the sofa.

Shae wasted no time taking a seat next to Ace. He noticed how close she had positioned herself next to him. He thought of Misty momentarily, then shrugged it off. No harm being done, he thought, bringing the fresh bottle to his lips.

Ace pointed to the group of guys playing darts. "That's Rip, Tyce and Kin."

"From Demon Dreams," Shae said.

"Right!" Rip said. "The girl knows her music!"

Kin nodded toward the parking lot. "She hangs out there all day?" he asked Robby.

"Yeah, the man has his own harem that shows up daily," Robby said. He turned to Shae. "I've seen you plenty of times."

"Really?" Shae said. "I didn't think anybody noticed me."

Tyce walked over to her. He reached out and pulled her off the couch and into his arms. He leaned in to murmur into her ear. "You're more noticed right now than you think." His eyes raked over her. "You wanna hook up? Enjoy some one-on-one action? I guarantee you I can make your little heart go pitter-patter."

"No, I don't think so."

Tyce held her tighter, stroking her hair, her back, her leg. "Come on, sweetheart. Why don't you show me what a little sex demon you are?"

"Hey, hey, hey!" Ace admonished him. "She's not showing you anything. I didn't bring her in to entertain the animals."

"Aww, come on man," Tyce whined. "Having sex with a rock star is what a groupie dreams about, isn't it? I'm just trying to fulfill her fantasy."

"Well, neither your tiny willy nor your massive ego can fulfill her fantasy," Ace answered. "So back off."

Tyce reluctantly released her and slumped into a side chair, dipping into a bowl of peanuts while the others laughed.

Shae leaned back, letting her top fall off her shoulder to reveal the tattoo and a sexy red bra underneath. Robby raised his eyes suggestively from the bar. "Ohhh, look Ace, she's got ink! I think she wore that pretty thing just for you." He opened a bottle of bourbon and poured another round for everyone, including Shae.

"Thank you," she said, taking the glass from him. As she leaned forward to take it, Ace's name was easily seen in the new tattoo.

"You twenty-one?" Ace asked, downing his shot in one gulp. He did not know if she was over 21 and didn't care about Georgia's drinking laws, but he needed to take his mind off how the red bra displayed her luscious breasts.

"If we use horseshoe rules." Shae asked. "Twenty should be close enough." She took a long swig, then grimaced, shaking her head. "Wow, strong."

They all laughed.

"She needs something to go with it," Sant said. He went back to the bar and pulled a can of coke from the refrigerator. He took a swig, then brought it back to fill her glass. "Here, now try it."

She took a sip. "Mmm, much better."

"Never let it be said we're poor hosts," Ace said.

A couple of hours later, after more drinking and smoking, everyone seemed to have forgotten that Shae was supposed to be waiting to catch a bus home while she made herself very comfortable in the studio lounge.

Not that any of the boys minded, but Ace found it amusing to play along and watch them make ass's out of themselves. If he'd been on the road, he might have kept her around for a day or two, but he made a point of never messing with the fans in his home neighborhood. His mind returned to Misty, and he realized he hadn't given the rule a thought. Maybe it was because she only knew him as Mason.

Ace looked at his watch. "Buses should be running. You need to be going now," he told her. "We need to get back to work."

"Hey, let's give her a souvenir of her time. She can look back on it in twenty years and remember how crazy we were tonight," Tyce said. He grinned at the others and raised a brow as if to say, watch this. "Give me your phone, honey, and we'll take some pictures with you."

She handed him her phone. He opened the camera app and pointed it her way. "Here, let me take one of you and Mr. Superstar there."

Ace looked up for the picture and smiled.

"Oh, come on, Ace, you can do better than that. Rock stars have a reputation to uphold!"

Ace rolled his eyes and placed his arm around her shoulders, thinking he would give his biggest fan a thrill. In a flash, Shae turned and pressed her lips against his. She pressed her body against him, teasing him with her tongue before he could stop her. Tyce snapped away. Ace pulled away, but Kin took his place. Then the phone was being passed around and more pictures were being taken by the others—Shae with her arms around Kin, Shae kissing Tyce, Shae in a group selfie, with hands all over her. In all of them, her eyes were fixed on Ace, her cheeks flushed with excitement.

"Time," Ace declared after the guys had their fun. "That's enough pictures."

Tyce handed her phone back to her. "Here," he said.

"You can have the photos as long as you don't kiss and tell." Ace said. His voice became firm. "I mean it. Don't make me regret letting you in here."

"I promise. I won't show anyone," Shae promised.

"Good. Well, time for you to get home, and for us to get back to work."

He walked her to the front door.

Shae gave him one last hug. "Thanks Ace,

for everything. I felt a lot safer in here than I did out there. I hope I wasn't in the way."

"You were fine, Shae," he said with a platonic hug. "Now git, before one of those horny bastards forgets you are only twenty. I'd hate it if I had to shoot one of my friends." He watched as she headed toward the train station. She seemed harmless enough, but he couldn't get the little nagging voice out of his mind, saying he'd made a huge mistake letting the girl through the door. Ignoring it, he walked back toward the lounge.

Robby met him in the hallway. "You think we got too carried away with that one?"

"Naw. The boys got a little wild, but no one got hurt. Those damn pictures bother me, but if she keeps them under wraps, no trouble will come of it."

"How much trouble could a few stupid photos cause?" Robby said as they walked together to the sound room.

***

Shae stood on the sidewalk near some bushes, watching as Ace walked back inside the studio. Her heart pounded, way too fast for safety. She could feel her blood pressure rising faster than the temperature on a sultry August afternoon. She needed to get home and take her medicine. Her vision blurred, and she felt dizzy, but she was high on love and didn't care. Ace had kissed her. And he'd kept the other men away from her. She saw it clearly; he was jealous. His protective behavior confirmed his feelings for her. But she couldn't overlook what she'd seen the previous week. At that moment, eliminating her competition became a spark in her mind. A spark that was fast growing into a raging wildfire.

Ace loved her, and she loved him. But he was a man and men could be tempted by a beautiful woman. She would go to any extent to get what she wanted, especially when it involved Ace Rivers. But it would not be easy. She needed to get rid of the competition in a way that did not point to her being involved. That would take planning. Shae turned on her heels and walked toward the bus station.

Chapter Ten

Misty was working at her desk when the crank calls started.

She picked up the receiver, hearing someone breathing, but nothing else. The same thing happened six more times before she left for the day. She would answer her phone, only to find no one on the line. It was becoming annoying.

There were many logical reasons it might be happening. It could be a fluke. Or a cell phone that dropped a call. Even a wrong number. After five, she realized it was intentional, and began listing the times.

The notes started around the same time, strange threatening messages that never said her name, but made it clear she was the intended recipient. They were always delivered in plain manila envelopes to her work address, each with a fictitious return address and each containing a single sheet of paper with a cryptic, disturbing message. Sometimes the words were cut from magazines and pasted onto the paper. Others contained misspelled words written with a permanent black marker:

YOU CAN'T WIN

YOUR A WHORE

YOU DONT DESURVE TO LIVE

She threw the first one away, then something in her gut told her to retrieve it. She dug through the trash in the wastebasket and saved it, along with the envelope it came in. In case she ever needed them.

A few days later, she'd been out to lunch with Alice and Shae. She'd needed to run some errands before returning to the office. It was the middle of the afternoon by the time she headed back to the office and parked in her space in the secured parking garage area for building employees. She got out of the car. The area was void of people at this time of day.

Except one.

Movement in the dim garage alerted her peripheral vision. The lights near the companies' reserved parking spots were out.

There was a someone standing several cars down, watching her. He stood in the darkness but out in the open, leaning against the trunk of an SUV, with his arms folded. By his appearance, he didn't look like he worked in the professional building. He had a hard, uncared-for look about him that was heightened by the dim light. His clothes looked disheveled, with a white, wrinkled T-shirt that was half tucked into old, faded jeans and a black hoodie. The hood almost covered the pale blonde hair. On his bare feet were a pair of old, rubber-soled mule style loafers. Something about him looked vaguely familiar, but Misty couldn't recall where she'd seen him.

As she walked toward the elevator, Misty glanced back to see that the man was walking too, following her. The bottoms of his rubber-soled work boots made a soft swishy sound on the concrete that grew louder as he drew closer to the elevator. Misty could feel the hair raise on the back of her neck, an almost instinctive, primal warning that something wasn't right. She kept walking, even while the fear increased with every beat of her heart. As she walked, she glanced around, hoping to see someone else in the parking garage, but the area was empty.

She reached the bank of elevators that would take her up to the building lobby, expecting him to turn around. Instead, he stepped up to stand next to her, staring at her in silence. Misty pushed the elevator's call button to summon an elevator car, aware that the man's eyes never lost their focus. She looked up at the digital floor indicator display in the concrete wall, willing the numbers to drop faster. Come on, she silently urged. It seemed to be the slowest elevator in Atlanta.

Her parents had gifted her with self-defense lessons before they moved to Florida. One lesson had stressed the importance of never showing fear. Taking a deep breath, she turned to him and smiled. "These things take forever to come down at this time of day, don't they?" She kept her voice casual and tried to relax.

The man said nothing but continued to stare at her, as if taking in every detail of her to remember later.

So much for idle conversation, Misty thought. She looked away from the man as the elevator doors slid open. A few people stepped out, passing them. Once the car was empty, Misty stepped in. He followed. The door slid shut, leaving them alone. Misty pushed the button that would take her to the building lobby, then took a reflexive step backward against the elevator wall to put as much space between her and the strange man as possible. The elevator began its slow amble upward while they stood in silence.

"Excuse me, but do I know you?" Misty asked.

The man shrugged. "Maybe. Maybe not."

That's it! Recognition slammed into Misty. He was in the bar the other night. He'd offered to buy her a drink. His intense stare had stopped Misty in her tracks, forcing her to maneuver around him on the way to the bathroom. It was the same stare that bore into her now.

Misty noticed that he had positioned himself between her and the elevator doors, blocking the only way out. Up close, he seemed younger, only a year or two older than her, but his unkempt hair and waxy skin made him look years older. He stood defiantly, arms folded in front of his chest, almost begging for a confrontation. Underneath his young street tough persona, he looked sad and dejected. Misty felt a twinge of sympathy, but there was something creepy about the man's disposition that made her nervous.

"Oh yes, I remember you now." Misty tried to keep her tone light and professional as the elevator began its ascent. "What brings you downtown?"

His eyes continued to bore into her with piercing azure eyes filled with malice. She felt her stomach tightening up. Whatever he had in mind, he felt it was the thing to do, and no amount of rational reasoning would convince him otherwise. Her thoughts tumbled wildly, trying to think of something to say that would ease the tension.

Misty felt vulnerable in the enclosed elevator but doubted he would do anything to draw the attention of the security guard monitoring the system. She kept one eye on the digital floor indicator on the panel display. Almost there, almost there. She silently willed the car to move faster. When it finally bumped to a stop and the doors swished open. Misty sidestepped quickly around him and moved into the lobby. There were people walking inside to go back down. The lobby was a large, bustling area with people coming and going. In the center stood an imposing reception desk containing security staff who greeted visitors to the building and made a record of who was coming in to conduct business. When the doors finally slid closed, she almost collapsed.

Sam, the guard, walked over from the security station and asked Misty if she was okay.

She nodded and stepped toward the bank of private service elevators that would take her up to her floor. As she stepped into the next available car and pushed the button for her floor, she looked back into the lobby before the doors closed. There was no sign of him. It was not until she reached her office, shut the door and sat down at her desk that she realized she was trembling.

Her thoughts were racing. This man knew where she worked and what kind of car she drove, even the parking level where she parked. He had been waiting for her, in a place where she would be alone and vulnerable. Is he the one who was calling? Or sending the notes? Suddenly, what she'd considered childish pranks didn't feel so innocent.

She replayed the scenes over and over in her mind, but there was nothing that would constitute a threat to the police. The fear that occupied her mind was now being replaced with anger and doubt. She didn't know if he was involved in the notes, but it was clear his presence was an attempt to intimidate her. The problem was, she had no idea why he was angry. No, the pranks were something someone younger would do. It was some smart-ass teenager's idea of fun. Their mother or father could work in the building. Or she had not hired one of them for an open position. That was the likely answer.

Either way, she had no control over the situation. It would be best to focus on the work at her desk and ask Sam to walk out with her when she left for the day. She became so lost in thought that when her desk phone rang; she jumped in her chair and almost fell out. By the time she grabbed the line, it had stopped ringing.

Chapter Eleven

Misty looked at the stack of threats and sighed. She'd filled one folder and had to start a new one. Now the second one was almost full. It was hard to believe it had been going on for almost two months. She'd finally decided she needed to tell Lois what was going on just in case something happened to her. "I'd hoped that face-to-face encounter would have been the end of my nightmare. If anything, it only got worse"

Lois set down her coffee mug. "Why did you hide this for so long? You could be in real danger."

"I don't know. I spent days trying to figure out why. What had changed? The only thing I can come up with was the night I spent with Mason."

"Could it be him?"

"My gut tells me no. It didn't seem like his style. I think he would be more direct. This seems like something an insecure kid would do. Nothing about him was childish."

She sighed. "Besides, he does not know who I am or where I work. I gave him my mother's maiden name."

"Why?"

"I don't know…. it just popped out. Then I took off while he was asleep. He's probably grateful he didn't have to come up with an excuse not to see me again."

Lois shook her head sadly. "I don't understand you. You finally meet a man you really like, and instead of fighting for him, you run away."

"I don't have time for a relationship. Besides, he was as drunk as I was. Once he sobered up, he probably forgotten I exist."

"Too bad this psycho hasn't…" Lois picked up the letter and read it again. It made her shiver. Whoever was behind this, they needed some serious help….

***

The calls and letters kept coming. Some were simply letters cut from magazines and pasted on paper. Others were lengthier and reminded her of a something a student would put in a book report. Those were typed and printed, but it was never the same printer. Obviously, the sender had access to a variety of equipment.

She picked up the latest and read it again. It was a review of the Sharon Tate murder in 1968. That was strange. Most people did not know who Tate was. It had happened when her mother was in elementary school. Another had contained cut outs from news articles about O.J. Simpson and that murder.

She picked up a longer one. This was all about the BTK murders. Every letter had an implied message: she would die. Easily and whenever he decided to kill her.

Not long after the incident in the parking garage, everything changed. She was sitting at her desk that morning working on the materials purchase order for a house when she received a call.

"Is this Misty?" the man asked.

"Yes, how can I help you?"

"Sweetheart, you can call me...baby. You know why I'm calling."

"I do?" Misty asked, confused.

"You mentioned you were shy and innocent. I've been thinking about you for an hour and I'm hot and ready. Where do I meet you? Do you have a room, or do I get one? And is it included in the price? I'm hard as a rock and ready to fuck."

Misty hung up the phone, shocked. It had

to be a wrong number, but then, how did the caller know her name?

Half an hour later, she got another call.

"Hey sweet girl," breathed a raspy voice. "I've got a new position I want to try with you. When can I come over?"

"Who is this?" Misty demanded. "Why are you calling me?

"Aww, come on, don't play games. You asked for a call ..."

"No, I didn't!" Misty's voice rose. "What are you talking about?"

"Hey, bitch, I don't have time for this." His voice turned harsh. "If you don't want the calls, don't place the ad!"

"What ad?"

"The ad in POF looking for a hookup. Don't post the ad if you don't intend to follow through with it!"

Misty hung up the phone. POF? She'd heard of it but had never cared enough to check it out. The last thing she wanted was an online hookup. She turned to her computer and pulled up the webpage. It turned out to be a free nationwide listing for sexual hookups. Singles, couples, group sex. Straight or kinky After narrowing the ads to the Atlanta area, she started searching for her business number. It didn't take long to find it listed under phone sex.

Hi, I'm Misty. I'm hot and I'm lonely. I've got a lot on my mind and I'm ready to tell you all about it. Give me a call. I'm waiting to hear from you! I may sound innocent but keep pushing. It gets me hot and ready to fuck. Call (999) 555-1234. Hurry, I want to get it on with you.

Shit. Why were they doing this to her? She had to get that ad off now. Roger would not think it was funny

She felt her stomach tighten as she read the words. Someone had placed an ad with her name on it and her work phone number. She studied the site, looking for a way to contact someone, anyone, at POF to get it canceled right away. There was no direct contact number.

She would have to notify the police. They could get the ad removed. She dialed the non- emergency number and asked for a detective who handles harassing threats.

They connected her to a detective Sansom, who listened to her explanation and asked for her office information. He showed up fifteen minutes later.

After reviewing the stack of letters and

observing several phone calls, the officer agreed it had gone past the point of a childish prank. He asked her to make copies of the mail and give him the originals. His forensic team would be able to locate where they were originating.

Several sex calls came in while the officer was making his report. He made a call to someone, and within half an hour, he had a valid contact number to POF home offices. The officer made the call for her. Although they promised to remove the ad, she was informed that the calls may still come in for several more days. Possibly longer if someone had made a record of her number.

Roger surprised her. Instead of being angry, he was upset that she had endured the harassment for as long as she had. He suggested switching the phone system over to the out of office recording, while they worked to remove all traces of her number from the POF system.

The officer turned to Misty and said, "I hate to be the bearer of bad news, but people who pull this kind of prank are rarely happy with the results. They usually look for other ways to upset the victim."

"What do you mean?"

"Have you googled your phone number?"

"No. Oh gawd! Don't tell me..."

She quickly typed in her number, then sat there in shock as listing after listing scrolled by. They must have enrolled her in twenty sex sites. It was going to take days to contact them all.

"You might want to change the number." Detective Smalls picked up the stack of materials he was taking with him.

"I will let you know if anything shows up, but chances are nothing is in the system about the suspect."

Roger took it better than she did. "At least it's not the main office number, just the direct dial number to your office. Just get it changed. Anyone trying to reach you for business knows the office number. It will be okay."

Misty nodded, too angry to talk about it. It was infuriating and delayed business having to screen calls and then return calls to colleagues she hadn't picked up earlier. She'd wasted hours sorting out the dirty calls from the legitimate business calls. The business office of the phone company called a couple of hours later, informing her they had made the transfer. She wrote the new number on a pad, mentally cursing over all the business cards she would need to toss. As soon as she hung up, she called the printer and ordered cards with the new number. Then she began dumping her business cards. Once she had cleaned out her desk, she knew she had to get out of the office and put some space between her and the hellish day.

With trembling fingers, she called Lois's cellphone. "Hey. Wanna go out for lunch?" she asked lightly. Despite her attempt to talk calmly, her voice was high and strained.

"Lunch?" Lois asked. "It's Monday. You never go to lunch on Monday." She paused. "You, okay?"

"Yeah... No...I don't know." Misty tried to keep her misery out of her voice, then gave in to her fear. "No," she whispered, fighting the sob that was forming in her throat.

"Give me five." Then the line went dead.

Misty shook her head. Lois, the epitome of impulsivity, had been hard-wired to function at lightning speed from birth. She'd be halfway from the commercial kitchen she rented to the elevator by now. She wouldn't worry about why she was dropping everything to race up to her office. She wouldn't need a reason. Lois was the kind of friend who cared.

Misty blinked away her tears and stuffed the copies of the crank letters into her desk drawer. Then she headed down to the lobby. It was a bustling place at this time of day, with people coming and going from the building. Lois worked in the building, but she didn't have a key to the bank of service elevators. She'd be waiting on her in the lobby downstairs. When the elevator door opened, she heard Lois pacing back and forth on the marble floor even before she saw her.

No one missed Lois. She loved her friend, even though they were opposites in every way. Lois was sassy, smart, and assertive. She was also drop-dead gorgeous. Next to her model-thin, five-foot ten frame, Misty felt fat and dumpy. She was also curvier, and looked 20 pounds heavier, even if they wore the same size clothes. But that was as close to being a model as Lois got. Lois was more laid back, preferring jeans and a tee shirt. It wouldn't matter if she'd been wearing a potato sack; she would look wild and exotic. And probably start a new style trend. The woman looked sexy in sweats.

Misty was the one who loved dressing in the latest high-fashion clothes. She owned matching heels of every color. Even though at five -seven she'd never be mistaken for a model, she still took pleasure in turning heads. With her healthy girl next door beauty, Misty never felt exotic, no matter what she wore.

Lois rushed over to Misty. "Love the suit, but it doesn't go with your complexion. You look pale. Are you alright?"

"Sure, I'm fine." Her lips barely moved, as she tried to smile

"You're such a lousy liar. I'm glad you don't play poker. You'd be broke all the time."

Misty nodded. "I just need to get out of here for a while. Let's go."

"Okaaay?" Lois hesitated, then decided to wait until they were eating to ask what was bothering her. It was clear something had her best friend upset. Something that had happened since the detective arrived.

They pushed through the revolving glass doors of the building and out onto the sidewalk. It was busy in Atlanta's business district at this time of day. But there were plenty of options to choose from. Somewhere quiet. A place they could talk, would be best.

People bustled by on the sidewalks. Taxis and cars clogged the roadways. Lois flagged down a cab and directed him to a Chinese restaurant they both liked. It was about eight blocks away, too many for Misty to walk on those heels. They offered dim-sum and several lunch specials. It was a favorite amongst downtowners, but by one PM, it usually quieted down. Misty had not argued about taking a cab, and that was significant. Whatever had her upset, it was enough to change her normal behavior.

As they stepped inside the dark, comfortable restaurant, they were greeted by Ms. Kim and escorted to their favorite booth in the back corner. The elderly hostess cocked an eyebrow at Misty's quiet demeanor, but only handed them menus. She waited patiently as they placed their lunch order, nodding as Lois prompted Misty into adding her favorite bacon wrapped scallops. A few minutes later, a server came to their table and set out several small plates.

"They have the best dumplings here, don't they?" Lois said as she popped one into her mouth. "Just the right amount of ginseng and not overpowering." She picked a chunk of chicken out of the soup bowl. "Here, try the soup. It's great!"

Misty shook her head, deep in thought.

Her fingers poked at her grilled scallops. Then she sighed and took a small bite, before laying down the fork.

Lois put her fork down. "Uh-oh. This is worse than I thought. My bestie isn't eating bacon and scallops," she said. "So, what's going on?"

Misty sighed. "I have a problem and I don't know what to do about it."

Lois leaned forward. "Details, woman," she said, jumping in immediately. "What kind of problem? The make you want to scream kind or the oh-shit kind?"

"Neither one. Both. Maybe? I don't know." Misty's said. She told her about the phone prank and gave her the new office number. "I freaked," she continued. "He placed an ad on every personal sex site he could find. I've spent the day screening out the calls of every perv in Atlanta. It's impossible to take care of business and the only way I could stop it was to change the number. Then she told her about the man from the employee parking garage and how he'd followed her up to the lobby. I know it's connected. I don't even know why."

"Mmm hmm," Lois nodded, tapping her chopsticks on the table. "Yup, I know the type. This falls into the rare category of bat-shit crazy."

"Right," Misty agreed, "but the detective is afraid he's set his sights on me and has no intention of stopping until he feels whatever slight he thinks he's received has been paid back."

"I never could understand people like that," Lois said. "One time I accidentally dropped a roll in the lap of a diner at a wedding I was catering. She insisted I'd done it on purpose and blasted my name all over the internet. I asked her point blank why she was doing it, and you know what she told me?"

"No, what?"

"That people like me should never work in a business that required contact with people. She suggested I find a job where I could stand there and look good but didn't need any other qualities. Like modeling.

"Rude bitch. What did you do?"

"Changed the business name and kept going."

"The detective doesn't think this one's a normal prankster. He seems to be fixated on me. His threats are escalating."

"So, what started all this?"

Misty shrugged. "I don't know, but it's

aggravating as hell."

There was the loud crash of metal in the kitchen. Misty jumped and knocked her tea off the table to the floor. She closed her eyes and sighed, her shoulders sagging.

"At least it wasn't full." Lois said as Ms. Kim moved to bring her another glass of tea.

"Thanks," Misty said, taking the tea from her and set it out of danger. She needed to get her nerves under control. She looked at Lois. "I'm a nervous wreck."

"You're not focused, and it's making you jittery."

Misty picked up her fork and speared another scallop. She held it for a moment, thinking. "What if he's just torturing me before the grand finale? I don't know how long he's been watching me. He's clearly infatuated with murders."

Lois took a warm egg roll from the basket on the table and spread duck sauce on it. "He has the psychological part of a classic stalker down to an art form."

"The story would make a great screenplay," Lois chuckled. "But I wouldn't worry too much about that happening."

Misty nodded in agreement and smiled.

"I'm just dreading calling everyone on my

full list of business colleagues. At least half will want to know why I changed numbers, like I did it to make their life more complicated. How do I explain this?"

"Tell them the phone company screwed up. It happens all the time," Lois said. "Besides, you've been working a lot of hours." She straightened in her seat and her face brightened. "Hey! Maybe we should take a break? Go down to Florida or over to Biloxi."

"Oh, I don't know—"

Lois's eyes lit up. "Yes, yes, yes, a weekend away. Just us girls!" Her voice revved with excitement. "You need time off, anyway. Let's get the girls together and we can take a quick flight to Mississippi. Bake on the beach, clubbing. It would be fun, a chance to cut loose, as they say!"

"Well, it would be fun, but it would have to be after your wedding," Misty mused. Knowing Lois, she would already have the hotel's number committed to memory. She'd already know every casino and late-night hot spot for their group to visit before the plane even touched down. A hectic weekend of activity by any stretch of the imagination, but maybe a girl trip out of town would lighten her mood.

"You talk to Alice," Lois said. "I'll check into it and get the ball rolling. A weekend away will take your mind off things."

"We can even take Shae," Misty said. She took a sip of her iced tea. "But to be safe, I'm not going to tell anyone but Roger about our plans."

Chapter Twelve

Shae huddled under her pink chenille bedspread as she sat cross-legged against the bed frame, a heavy purple throw draped around her delicate frame. It was raining again and chilly. The central heat was on, but her sister never liked it as warm as she did. She had her laptop propped atop her knees as she worked her way through the various websites. Music played from her laptop. His music. It was always his music. His raspy voice lulled her into a dreamlike state, allowing her to leave the confines of her bedroom to be with him.

She'd always dreamed about Ace, reliving every moment she ever spent near him, but now her thoughts were consumed with her time spent in the studio with him and his friends. She smiled to herself. That was one fantastic night. Missing that last bus was the best thing that ever happened to her. The kiss had elevated her devotion to a whole new level.

Once, when they'd first moved to Jonesboro, she'd been exploring the houses' basement and found a can of black spray paint lying in a corner, left over from where repairs on a foundation leak were underway. Scarfing it up, she slipped it back into her room. Still bouncing on her adrenaline high, she'd dug it out of the closet.

Now I LOVE ACE was sprayed along one wall in her bedroom. She'd printed out all the photos they'd taken and thumb-tacked them to the wall. When she was finished, she looked over her work and smiled. A remembrance of her special evening. Her mom had not been happy when she saw it, but Shae didn't care. It was her wall, not her mothers.

She leaned her head against the headboard of her bed and gazed at the special group of photos she'd taken that night, her "private collection" as she fondly called them. She could almost feel Ace's arms around her again. Who cared if it was just an arm over her shoulder? It was still his arm, even if Tyce had put it there. She relished the memory of his mouth on hers when she'd kissed him. He tasted sweet, like the bourbon and coca cola she'd drank. The photos were her greatest treasure, like the tattoo, an affirmation of her love for Ace, and his love for her. She knew he wanted her. Otherwise, why would he let her into his private studio to hang with him and his friends? With no other women around?

Ace understood her. They both came from single-parent-households. Knowing she had suffered the safe rough childhood drew him to her like a moth to a flame. They complimented each other perfectly. He might not see it yet, but he will, she vowed, because she had no intention of living without him. She looked at the makeshift stage she'd built in the corner, where she often imagined him performing just for her. That was one of her favorite fantasies, watching him sing only to her —

"Shae!" her mother's quavering voice interrupted her thoughts. Lately, she'd interrupted her much too often.

"What?" she replied angrily. Why can't that woman ever leave me alone?

"Please, turn that music down! I can't hear the television."

Shae sighed. Then she reached over and lowered the volume on her laptop. Once she got comfortable again, she loaded her second favorite daydream—getting rid of her mother. She'd pictured multiple methods, killing her in so many delightful ways... poison, stabbing, drowning, strangling. Lately, her favorite fantasy of putting the bitch out of her misery featured her standing above her mother with a loaded .44 pointed at her head, ready to blow her brains out while she cowered in a corner like a little baby, her eyes wide with fear. "It's time to die, Mama."

"Why?" her mother cries, trembling. "Don't kill me, Shae! I love you."

"Too bad I don't love you." Shae says as she cocks the gun.

"No! Don't do it, please!" Her mother hides her head in her hands from fright as she opens fire, pulling the trigger over and over while her body jerks at every hit like a broken marionette. She fires until there are no bullets left in the gun. Then she grabs the shiny dark hair of her fuckin' mother, drags her to the bedroom window, lifts her up and tosses her out. Gone. Like yesterday's trash.

Will she miss her?

Hell no, she won't miss her. The only reason the bitch was still alive was because she had to be twenty-one to buy a gun. Once she was gone, the other would follow.

Shae rolled over and opened the drawer

on her bedside table. Inside is her favorite possession, a pocketknife with the band's name on it. She kept it hidden under some old envelopes, a small razor-sharp blade stored nearby, for when she needed to relieve her anxiety. The blade was the perfect size to relieve the itch. She'd stolen it from Gordy's Knife Shop at the mall. At the time, she'd only cared about the photo on the handle. Now it was her best friend, her only friend. No matter how stressed she was, it was her first stop when life became more than she could bear. Somehow, the little shiny little blade took away the itch brought on by the bad feelings, the hopeless future, the life she lived without Ace.

She had been cutting since middle school. If a knife wasn't available, she'd learned to improvise...the blade out of a plastic pencil sharpener, the point of her compass, any-thing sharp that cut through skin. Once she'd been stuck in the principal's office when the itch started. She found a plastic ruler and broke it, then used the edge to gouge back and forth across her wrist, although that didn't seem to do much damage. It held off the worst of the itch until the bell rang and she was able to leave the office and get her spare knife from the locker.

That day on the bus, other kids watched her, repulsed by what she was doing. After that, she found a private spot to cut. They thought it was crazy, but to her, it was a natural act. At least she didn't do drugs. Cutting was an escape from what troubled her. It worked every time, but it didn't make her any friends. Everyone thought she was just too weird to talk to. If only they knew about the man, her mother lived with. Not even Alice knew about him. She had been away, visiting their aunt Jackie when it happened. She closed her eyes and put her hands to her ears, willing the movie of her bedroom door opening and the voices in her head to go away. But somehow the movie always played on in her head once it started, as if it were happening in the present, all over again. She watched it again, and cried...

"Shae! Where are you, girl?" a drunken voice called out from the doorway. "Take those blankets off you right now!"

"Yes, Daddy," the girl answered to her mother's the latest boyfriend. All the men who came and went were called "Daddy." They always seemed to pay a lot of attention to the girl on the reel.

He approached her bed and seeing the walk was agonizing. It was like she was outside of her body looking on as the perverted bastard approached her bed. It was a scenario she knew all too well with the men her mother brought home. She couldn't run. All she could do was stay in her bed, feeling helpless and dirty as he shut the bedroom door behind him. She never showed her fear of what was about to go down. He wouldn't have cared, anyway. "There you are," the man said, pulling the blanket away. He climbed into the bed beside her. "Well, let's go. I ain't waitin' all night. You know what you have to do."

Shae closed her eyes tightly and her hands pushed harder on her ears. She hated this part of the movie, but there was no off switch on the player. She didn't want to hear it anymore, but she couldn't make it to stop.

Her body turned over. She lay still while he stripped her nightgown away. Then the rest of it. It didn't take long. It never did.

"That's my good girl," said the voice in the dark, falling asleep in drunken contentment. "You're such a good girl..."

But this time the ending differed from the other times. The good girl padded in silence to her bedroom closet. She retrieved her rescue, a Louisville slugger baseball bat. Calmly, walking back to the sleeping form in her bed, she raised the bat and brought it down hard on the monster's head as hard as she could. The man regained consciousness for just a moment and looked up at her, startled. Before he can react, she hit him again. And through his screaming, she raised and lowered the bat, again and again, until the lump in the bed was finally silent. His head was smashed in, and bits of brain matter sprayed all over her and the walls. Then she sat on the floor, naked and covered with blood, and waited for the police to arrive.

The rest of the night was a blur. First the good girl's mother returned home to the carnage. Then she began screaming. Finally, the police stormed the house. The officers wrapped Shae with a blanket and put her in an ambulance. There, she related her story without a shred of emotion. After a DNA test and physical examination verified her story of sexual assault, the case was determined to be one of self-defense. As a juvenile, she was never charged for a crime. Soon after, she and her mother left Tennessee for Atlanta, leaving that life, and a man's murder, behind.

She ran the knife along her wrist, maybe a little harder than she intended. A wide pool of red liquid burst out of the wound and stained her clothes, but it gave her peace. A smile crossed her face. After that, her mother had started drinking... using the alcohol to expunge her guilt. She never told Alice anything about what happened and never allowed Shea to talk to anyone. It was their dirty little secret, and she wanted no one to know her daughter was a murderer. Shea told no one...

Yup, it's all good, she thought as she watched the blood form a familiar trail down her arm. Over time, it became impossible to wear short sleeves. Or go to the beach. In college she started hanging with some goth kids, but one had noticed she was a cutter and suggested she see a councilor. They still hadn't found her body. She doubted they ever would.

The itch was driving her crazy today. With meticulous care, she rolled up her sleeve, then took the blade in her right hand and found a spot on her wrist among the collection of previous scars that decorated her lower arm. She drew it in a vertical direction, ignoring the pinch of the blade piercing her skin. She did it again. Then one more time. The cuts weren't deep. Just enough to relieve the stress, and she needed some stress relief right now. The thick trail of blood trickled down her wrist toward her elbow before dripping onto the purple throw. She closed her eyes, relishing the intensity of her emotions. It felt so much better.

A psychiatrist once told her mother the act of cutting was to show the world the pain and vulnerability she felt inside. He was so far off; she thought smugly. For her, it was a display of hardness, to show everyone how strong she was, how much pain she could take without breaking. She cradled her injured arm like a kitten, something she could love and nurture while the blood clotted and dried. This was the ultimate form of control. It brought her back into focus. Ace. I'm ready for true love. Just one minor problem to eliminate, the sooner the better. She yawned. She still had a couple of hours to sleep before heading back to their studio to watch and hope he might say a few words. With that comforting thought in mind, she snuggled under the throw and drifted off to sleep.

Chapter Thirteen

Alice's eyes lit up when Misty mentioned a quick trip to Biloxi. "Yes, yes, yes, a woman only junket!" Her voice revved with excitement. "It's a great idea. I can take some time off. I have plenty of vacation time built up. We can take a quick flight down to Mississippi. Beaches, clubbing, hot muscular bodies, and the casinos." Her eyes were gleaming as she anticipated the possibilities.

"Well, I doubt it would be relaxing," Misty mused. Between the two, there would not be a place on the strip they did not try. Lois would have the time scheduled before the plane even touches down in Biloxi. A hectic round of activity by any stretch of the imagination. A four-day weekend out of town would lighten her mood but leave her exhausted and needing a vacation from her vacation.

"Sure, it will be fun," Alice said. "I'll check into room rates and get the ball rolling. A weekend away will take your mind off things." She hesitated, then asked if it was okay to invite Shae.

"We figured you would," Misty said. She took a sip of her iced tea. "I'm not sure if it's something she would enjoy, but she is welcome to join us.

"And it doesn't hurt to have four women. It adds an extra layer of security," Alice said.

Misty looked bewildered. "Like what?"

"We will all have someone to watch our backs, and hopefully, keep us from doing something we will regret later."

Misty laughed. "I thought the idea was to do things we wouldn't do at home."

The conversation turned to other things, and Misty allowed herself the luxury of not giving her stalker a thought, at least for the moment. It felt good to forget her own problems and exchange small talk, the latest shoe fashions, or who's dating who in Hollywood, like her life was normal. Like everyone else's.

***

Shae was out of her seatbelt and on her feet before the pilot announced it was safe to do so. They hit a bump and her slender body catapulted forward and slammed into the back of the next row seat. The man sitting there looked around to make sure she wasn't hurt and then suggested she strap herself back into her seat until the pilot taxied the plane to the hangar area.

Lois sunk into the soft leather seat and stared out the window at the ocean. She'd been pleasantly surprised at the amount of room they had when they'd boarded the private jet plane in Atlanta. She'd expected a short comfortable hop to Biloxi and then an even shorter ride to the hotel. Instead, they stopped in Birmingham and picked up a second group, filling the small plane completely. At least half were teenagers with zero manners.

Now it felt like a prison.

Just as she felt like her head would explode from her tension headache, she heard the pilot's voice on the speaker saying they could prepare to leave the plane. They stopped next to the main building, and someone rolled a mobile staircase up to the door. There was an unceremonious puff of air, and the door's pressurized seal was broken.

The pilot's voice sounded again. "Passengers, you may now exit the craft."

Shae sprang from her seat like a thoroughbred springing from the starting gate. "Finally!". She hefted her backpack and raced down the small staircase. As she stepped onto the tarmac, a woman with black hair tightly gathered at the nape of her neck walked toward the plane. "You need to stay together. Your bus will be here soon."

Shea gave her a drop-dead eye and continued walking toward the main building. She needed to go to the bathroom and had no intention of using the small closet toilet on the plane. The woman reached for her arm, and Shae snapped, "Touch me and you'll never touch anyone again."

Then the woman who had flown with the group rushed over and apologized. "Sorry about the mistake. She thought you were with the group from Birmingham."

Misty was standing at the top of the stairs, and she saw Shae's' response. It gave her cold chills. There was no compassion in Shae's behavior at all. She continued down the stairs, not wanting to say anything that might upset Alice or Lois. They were there to have a good time. Anything else could wait.

"Why is it I'm exhausted when all I did was rest for the last couple of hours?"

"No idea," Shae said, "I feel like I'm wound tight and unless I do something soon, I'm going to pop. Maybe you're just getting old?"

Lois laughed. "How does it feel to be over the hill at twenty- six? Lord knows how you will feel at thirty. You will probably need a wheelchair."

"You probably just need some coffee. In fact, I could use a latte. Theres a barista stand over there." Alice began walking toward the small coffee cart.

Misty shrugged and followed. Coffee would be good, but what she really needed was a shower and some clothes. Like the other three, she was dressed comfortably in blue sweats and a matching hoodie. It was fine for the flight, but now that she was back on the ground, she wanted her normal attire as soon as possible.

Lois laughed at the disappointed expression on Shae's face. "You can go on ahead to the hotel transport. I want to get a latte before going on the bus."

Misty ordered her coffee, and a baked croissant, paid for it, then walked a few feet away to wait on the others to their snack. That's when she spotted him, out of the corner of her eye. There was no mistaking that stringy blonde hair or that surly smirk. He was there! In Biloxi. There was no way it could be a coincidence. He had to be following her. She had to stop herself from running toward the hotel bus stand. Alice gave her a funny look as she walked away without them, but she had no intention of stopping until she reached the transport bus. Misty looked straight ahead, but she couldn't help but wonder if he was following her. She didn't dare look back to find out.

Luckily, the bus was there waiting for them.

As she sat down in the seat behind Shae, a surge of adrenaline hit her—heart thumping, head throbbing, hands shaking. She sank back in the seat and tried to calm her racing pulse. Breathe. Just breathe.

Shae must have told the driver they were on the way, since he shut the door and pulled off as soon as Lois and Alice were inside. Once they were safely on the way, Misty pulled the croissant out of the bag and opened her coffee. The welcoming aroma of the hot brew and homemade pastry calmed her nerves enough to munch away on the flaky roll. Fattening as hell, but who cares, she thought as her trembling fingers slowly went back to normal.

Once Lois saw she had got herself back

to normal, she asked, "What the hell hap-pened? One second you were fine, the next you looked like a ghost and were walked away as fast as you could walk without run-ning."

"I saw him. Here. In the terminal."

"Who?"

"Him."

"Him, him?"

Not him! Misty rolled her eyes. "The stalker!"

"Here? It must have been someone that resembled him. Why would he be in Biloxi? How would he know we were coming here?"

Misty wasn't sure what to say. She had never been in a situation where someone watched her or followed her wherever she went. It made her feel helpless and vulner-able, traits that were not part of her person-ality. "That's true. I can't prove that he's the one behind everything taking place. It's just a feeling I have."

Lois reached for her hand and squeezed. "We can't explain it, but we can't say he's here just because you are. It could be a twist-ed trick of fate. Regardless, we will not let it ruin our vacation."

"Agreed! Nothing and nobody is going

to ruin this vacation." After the long flight, the four women were glad for a break from each other's company. They were all ready to head off to their hotel rooms for a shower and a new outfit. The hotel had put them all in neighboring rooms, with interior doors that they could open to connect them into one enormous suite.

Misty opened the door, only to find a stack of luggage almost blocking the doorway. "Looks like they stuck all our luggage in one room."

Shae laughed. "Let's just hurry and grab our stuff. Alice is talking to someone in transportation, trying to find the best place for us to go and party."

"I need to get into something a lot sexier than my sweats. Just give me time to shower and change clothes. I'll meet ya'll downstairs at the bar."

"Sounds good to me." Alice had the handle to one case and a smaller one by the handle. She followed Shae out the door.

Lois frowned when she couldn't find one of her cases. Then saw it sitting beneath one of Misty's bags. Instead of going around, she used her card key to open the door between the two rooms. Somehow, knowing Lois was in the next room helped Misty to relax.

"Do you have any idea where we are going?"

"No, but I saw the dress Alice pulled out of the bag, and she's not planning on taking any prisoners... She's gonna knock 'em dead." Lois grinned and headed for the shower.

Misty flopped down on the queen-sized bed and smiled. Many hotels had extremely firm mattresses, but this one was about perfect. She let her eyes flow over the room, grinning when she realized there was a balcony outside the glass door. The view from the balcony looked out over the empty beaches. It was too dark to see the length of the shore, but she could imagine spending tomorrow walking the old-fashioned boardwalk that skirted the sand below her. A hurricane had destroyed a lot of the quaint little shops, but many had been built back and now helped connect the newer casinos to the older favorites like Treasure Bay. Not bothering to unpack her bag, she grabbed her favorite sapphire blue lace dress, some fresh undies, and headed for the bathroom.

Fifteen steamy minutes later, she had changed into the now wrinkle free blue dress, happy that once again the hot shower had worked its magic. She took a second to make sure her makeup was perfect, and that she wasn't forgetting anything important, smiled and thought to herself, this is going to be an epic weekend.

She pushed the button for the elevator.
***

The sunlight shining through the balcony door was bright enough to bleed through her eyelids, tinting her world shades of red and gold. Misty grabbed her pillow, trying to adjust her body into a comfortable position, but nothing worked. Her head was pounding, and any way she lay, it was still intensely uncomfortable. With a heartfelt groan, she sat up, realizing she might as well get out of bed. There was no way she could go back to sleep with the intense gulf sun light searing her eyelids. But that was a minor complaint. Right now, she was more worried about how she got to the bed. She struggled to recall what she did the previous night, to recall how much she had drunk. How many shots of tequila does it take to forget the entire night? She'd fallen asleep in the itchy lace dress, and she still had one of her heels on. Where was the other shoe?

She tried to stand, but the pounding in her head was too much. She needed something to take the edge off. Normally she carried analgesic tablets in her purse, but after she'd emptied it on the bed, she had to accept there was nothing inside that would help. Overcome by disgust at the waste of time, she gave up and knocked on the door between the rooms. Lois opened it and knew instantly what she needed.

A glass of orange juice and two acetaminophens helped with the headache but did nothing to fill in the gaps in her memory.

"What the hell did I do last night?"

Lois looked like she was fighting to keep her face straight and lost. Finally, she gave up and started laughing. "The evening started out like any other night out. We went down to the casino. That's when thing got crazy." She paused. "You don't remember any of it"

"I get vague flashes of memory. Nothing fits together."

"Well, it started like this. We walked into the Casino, and everyone was looking around. Alice and Shae headed to the Blackjack tables, but you spotted this one pull for it all game. Before anyone could stop you, you popped in a twenty-dollar bill and pulled the handle. Afterward, you swore you thought it was a penny machine since it was at the entrance to that area. To make a long story short, you hit max bet, so you bet twenty dollars. The wheel spun around and landed on X100. So, you won two thousand dollars within a minute of entering the casino."

"Damn. That's more than the cost of my hotel room and plane ticket in one spin."

"Hun, that covered the cost of all four of us. You insisted on covering all four rooms, and the plane tickets down, and you still had over 100.00 left. You did the smart thing and had the money deposited in your bank account instead of taking cash. Not that it would have mattered. You were on a roll. I've heard people talk about someone being hot at the tables, but it was way cooler watching it happen."

"I won more?"

"You won lots more. You started playing craps on the five-dollar table, although they raised the minimum bet amount on the table after you started winning. It was like you said to hell with the odds. You were on a winning streak and losing was not an option. You were drinking shots, so you got wasted before we realized it."

Misty put her face in her hands. "Please tell me I'm not going to lose my house."

"I don't think that's going to be a problem. You kept saying the only way you can win a lot of money is to bet a lot of money. I had heard the only way to win is to walk away when you are up, because if you keep playing, you go down again because the odds are always in the casino's favor. You never hit the go down part."

"I won again?"

"When you finally got too drunk to sit up in the chair, I was able to convince you to stop. You were still winning. The casino is holding your winnings. You can go down later and cash out."

"How much did I win?"

"I don't know, but it was a giant stack of chips. We all took pictures. I even recorded them, stacking them into trays to take them away." She grinned. "It took three trays."

"We all went dancing since you refused to go back to the room. We stayed there about an hour dancing, when you disappeared."

"Wait, wait! I disappeared?"

"Yep. You vanished. The server said you tipped her and asked her where the elevators were. That you were going to your room.

Alice and I decided we'd had enough excitement for one night, so we headed back upstairs. There was just one problem. You were not in the room."

"Please tell me I didn't..."

"No. At least we don't think so. We called hotel security. They began a search. Half an hour later, we got a knock on the door. There were two security guards at the door. You were passed out in a wheelchair. They both grinned and said, 'I think this is yours!' They helped me get you onto the bed."

"Where did they find me?"

"You were totally sloshed, passed out and sleeping on the floor beside the door. Your keycard was in the slot. It was the right room number, but five floors too high!"

"So... what should I do?"

"I don't know about you, but I'm hungry. Let's go eat."

Chapter Fourteen

After staying out most of the night, everyone was starving. The Hotel had comped Misty enough meal passes they would not have to pay to eat the rest of the trip. The main restaurant was packed, so they pigged out at the enormous buffet. Now they were sitting around the pool, soaking in the sun, and recovering after the craziness of the previous night.

Since she was temporarily rich, Misty indulged a bit and spent the extra fifty dollars each to get lounge chairs at the Private Oasis pool. The palm trees and cabanas made it the perfect place to destress, forget about work and all the crazy threats and appreciate the beautiful early summer weather. Misty took full advantage of the chance to unwind by the pool and recharge her constantly draining emotional battery.

She had brought a new bikini for this trip, and it left little to the imagination. Alice and Lois's were even skimpier. What surprised her the most was that Shae had put on a one-piece swimsuit, even though she kept a long-sleeved lace swimsuit coverup on the entire time. She stayed under an umbrella stretched out in a recliner with her legs out in the sun, reading while the others cooled off in the pool.

Misty figured she was trying to hide the tattoo on her chest from her sister. She didn't have the heart to mention it was still easily seen, and they all knew about it. They had discussed it the day after she came home with the bandage over her breast.

Alice had claimed the newspaper and was scanning the pages, looking for something different to do after dinner. They had already bought tickets to tour the nearby swamp the next day, since they were sold out today.

Then Lois had a brilliant suggestion. "Let's go see a show this evening."

Misty's brow furrowed slightly, contemplating Lois's suggestion. "That might be fun. Maybe one of those comedy shows, like the ventriloquist with the talking dummies." It might have been a smart idea to checkout who was in town before making that statement. Unfortunately, Lois blurted it out and everyone started searching the web to see what show we could go see.

When Shae started screaming and jumping up and down, I got a bad feeling deep in my gut, a premonition of impending doom. Sure enough, I did a quick search and Cats Grinning was playing. To make it even worse, it was a free beach show, so we had no excuse not to go.

***

Although the show was free, the hotel that was putting on the concert offered reserved balcony seating that overlooked the small coliseum where the band would be playing. Thanks to her hot streak the night before, paying the surcharge to rent a room with balcony seating was not an issue. Misty was pleased with her decision. Leasing the balcony was a perfect answer to the 'I feel much too old to be wandering around in a crowd of drunken teenagers,' feeling she and Lois had experienced at the previous concert. To make it even more convenient, the hotel had set up a bar near the elevator bank on the three floors they had reserved for the concert. The restaurant was offering a special selection of concert foods to snack on, and comfortable chairs had been added to the balconies.

Shae didn't feel the same way the others did about the balcony seating. She intended to get as close to the stage as possible. She was certain that Ace would invite her backstage as soon as he spotted her in the crowd. As soon as they arrived at the casino hotel, Shae ditched the others and headed for the beach area, looking for a way to get closer to the band.

"No idea why she's going down there so early. There are two other bands that have to play before Cat Grinning."

Alice shook her head. "Who knows? She is so different from the way she was when I was still living at home. "

"That's sad. When did she start changing?" Misty was really curious. Shae was a hard person to get to know. She was certain the young woman had serious mental issues and needed counseling. At the very least, she was bi-polar.

"She started dressing strangely when she started middle school. That's when I noticed the little differences in her personality. But she really changed when Martin died. She was the one who found him. Mama worked at night, and I was in college. Shae was twelve. She never talked about it but finding him that way had to affect her."

"What do you mean? I thought he had a heart attack." Lois leaned forward, curious.

"He did. But mama said he had been... not sure how to put this... pleasuring himself, when it happened."

"How can they tell something like that?" Lois looked puzzled.

"Supposedly, his hand still had his fluid on it. There were some wet spots on the sheets, too. He must have taken a shower and laid down in bed, then..."

"That's creepy. Yes, can you imagine if it had been her father, instead of your Mama's boyfriend?"

"He was nothing like my father. I never liked him. The only thing Martin was interested in was drinking and playing his guitar. Hell, the only time he worked was when his band was playing at some neighborhood bar."

"That might be the connection!" Lois exclaimed.

"Connection?" Alice looked puzzled.

"Why Shae is so fixated on Ace Rivers. They both played guitar."

Alice shrugged. "It's possible. I guess. She didn't seem to like Marvin. I only met him twice, and she avoided him more than she was around him while I was there. Now that I think back, that's when she started wearing long sleeves all the time. But that could have been because her body was changing so much." She grinned. "Puberty sucks."

"Did you she ever get comfortable with her body?" Lois asked as she stretched her legs out and propped them on the railing.

"I don't think so. I can't remember the last time I saw her without being covered up. I was shocked she uncovered her legs at the pool."

Misty stood up. "Well, I don't know about you, but I could use something on my stomach before I start drinking. I think I'll go down and see what's on the special menu."

"Wings sound great. Maybe nachos." Now that Misty had mentioned food, Lois realized she was starving. "Hell, just order a variety and have it sent up."

"Okay. I'll be right back."
***

"I can't believe you're hungry. You never eat before a show." Robby laughed as Ace added coconut shrimp to the takeout box he was filling.

"I should have eaten lunch. I think my

sugar is low or something. I don't have any energy." Ace grabbed a second box and began filling it.

"We could have ordered and had it brought to the room."

"Yeah, but I don't know what I want. I figured if I looked at everything, something might look good."

"What did you finally decide on?"

"Texas style fajitas with double shrimp. And everything in that box and this one."

"Damn, that sounds good. I wish I'd told you to get me some.

"Relax, I ordered enough for all of us..." Mason stopped talking and stared at the cashier by the restaurant entrance. "Well, fuck a duck. Misty!" He took off running toward the front elevator banks, leaving Robby standing by the other elevators.

"Misty! Hey wait up."

Misty had just pushed the elevator button when she was surprised to hear someone calling her name. Just as the door was closing, she glimpsed a man she never expected to see again. Mason! He was in Biloxi.

Mason watched as the elevator climbed, stopping on the second, fourth and fifth floors, before it began its return trip to the main floor. He waited, hoping she had heard him calling. But when the door opened, the woman who was excited to see him wasn't Misty.

Luckily, Robby realized Ace had been recognized, and he jumped into action. He scanned his express pass and the express elevator door opened. Before the girl could make her way through the press of passengers getting off the elevator, the private elevator door was closing. Without a pass, she could not reach the exclusive suites. The main elevator did not stop on their floor.

"I need to go back down. Misty was just in the restaurant. Maybe they know what room she's in."

"Your gonna go down and ask them to search for a Misty. No last name."

"You got a better idea?"

"No." He looked serious. "You need to stop and think for a minute. We might have a bigger problem. That was the Shae girl that you brought into the studio last month. She's here in Biloxi. At the same hotel we are staying in. We might want to notify security."

"She's just a fan. We can't start calling security every time a fan acts like they are happy to see us."

"You don't think there's anything strange about her showing up here?"

There was a knock at the door. Robby opened it to allow the server to push the cart of food into the room.

"No. I think it's strange you are trying to keep me from finding out what room Misty is in."

Robby locked eyes with Mason. "I have a better idea. Instead of calling the restaurant and hope someone will look for the information, let's bribe the server."

"Bribe the server?"

"Sure. They have access to the entire building. If she is staying here, someone will know where she's staying. It's possible she's just here for the concert. She went up to the balcony floors."

"I just had a horrible thought. What if they know each other?"

"Who? Misty and fangirl? That's a scary thought. But they are both from Atlanta. It's got to be a coincidence. Karma doesn't hate me that much."

"I hope you mean it about taking this seriously," Robby said. He took a sip of his iced tea. "Anyway, I'm taking the steps I can. I've told everyone associated with the tour not to tell anyone about where we are staying in each city."

"I agree. It doesn't hurt to add an extra layer of security," Mason said.

Tyce looked at him, bewildered. "For what?"

"Robby thinks one of our fans is obsessive."

"That Shae girl?"

"She's here in the hotel."

"Shit. Call security. Make sure she can't get backstage."

Mason rolled his eyes. "Not you, too."

Robby laughed. "See, it's not just me. We can file a harassment report right now. Theres a form you can file online without having to go to the police station. It would document what that crazy chick's up to in case it gets any worse, especially if she goes full blown stalker."

"Let's just get through this show and worry about the rest once we get to .... Where are we going next?"

"Boise, Idaho."

"Who books these shows? Do they even listen to Rock music in Idaho?"

"You did. And the show is sold out."

"Oh... We can worry about the details in

Boise." He glanced at the clock on the wall. "You heard anything from that server?"

"Not a word."

"Fuck. I'm stuffed. I'm gonna lie down until we have to go down. Someone wake me if he shows." He headed for the bedroom as the others converged on the remaining food.

***

Misty lay her head back against the chair and closed her eyes. That was the thing she hated about live shows. The crowd made so much noise, it distracted you from the music. The band was good, but like so many others, they were constantly moving. The cameras loved zooming in on the half-naked guitarists' fingers and the cute drummer twirling his sticks. The only thing she knew about the lead guitar player and the singer is that they both had long, dark hair and both wore too much eye makeup. She didn't like the brightly colored blue streaks in their hair. The singer bobbed his head a lot, and held the microphone between both hands, so she never got a decent look at him or the lead guitar player. The bass player wore a floor length leather coat and leather pants. He had to be hot under those bright lights. He had super curly blonde hair that fell in ringlets to his shoulders. A golden chin patch matched the hair color perfectly, making it clear he had not got the color from a bottle.

After the first few songs, she'd zoned out and laid the reclining chair back. They had been playing for over an hour and they had to be getting near to the end of the show. She had a sinus headache and was past ready to head back to the hotel.

Alice didn't seem to be particularly enamored with the heavy metal music, but Lois was really getting into the show. Or maybe it was the tequila she was drinking. Either way, she was having too much fun to cut the night short and head back to their hotel. Shae was somewhere in the crowd below, but they had warned her she was on her own if she was not around when they got ready to leave.

Even though Shae adored the lead singer, there was something about the band that bugged her. She did not know what it was. It could be she just didn't like them. It wouldn't be the first popular band she'd not fallen madly in love with the first time she'd heard them play. They definitely sounded better on a song done in the studio.

Alice surprised her by announcing she was ready to go do something else. "I heard enough live music. Let's go to another casino. Maybe I'll get lucky and win."

"What about Shae?" Lois asked.

"If Ace does see her, we may not hear from her until tomorrow."

Lois tossed down the last of her drink. "You mean she really knows this Ace Rivers guy?"

"Yeah, she sent me a photo of them together. She printed out several and stuck them on the wall beside her shrine. If it floats her boat, who am I to pull the plug?"

Lois rolled her eyes at Alice's mixed-up metaphor. She like to put words together in crazy combinations at times.

They pulled the door shut behind them as the band went into their final song of the evening. As the door was closing, Misty thought she glimpsed a familiar face on the video wall. Her stomach dropped. It couldn't be…

Chapter Fifteen

Misty watched the first flakes of the early December snow melt as they struck the warm window. There was something sad about the advent of winter. Especially when it tried so hard to make a lasting impression, only to lose out to the persistent southern winds. Instead, it just made a mess. One she hated driving through. At least it was Friday. Even if it stuck, it would most likely be gone before time to go back to work Monday.

After shutting down her computer, she grabbed her purse and headed for the elevator. In the parking garage, she walked toward her car, unlocking the front door with the key fob in her hand. As she started the engine, she noticed a piece of colored cardboard stuck under the arm of the windshield wiper.

Why do they insist on putting the advertisements on the car? She groaned as she got back out of the car and plucked it free from the windshield. What she had thought to be an advertisement turned out to be some kind of playing card. It was bigger than the cards found in a standard poker deck. Leaning on the open door, she examined it.

One side looked like standard cardboard. However, when she turned the card over, she recognized the image as one used on an album cover of one of her favorite heavy metal bands. Why would someone put a tarot card on her windshield?

The image on the card showed a skeleton, cloaked in a bright scarlet coat, riding a spirited black horse as it blazed across a dead landscape. The ghoul's raised fleshless arm gripped a curved scythe in its bony fingers. Its gaping mouth screamed out a silent battle cry as broken body parts of those struck down by the scythe lay beneath the horse's thundering hooves. She would have considered it a threat, except whoever had left it obviously didn't know that card meant change or a new beginning, not the literal death of the body. Her grandmother had taught her to read the cards when she was still in middle school. They had cut this out of an album cover, probably destroying someone's treasured album.

Were they still waiting nearby to see how

she might react? She tore her gaze from the card and looked around. Other than another office worker walking toward her car a hundred yards away, there was no one in sight. Was it the same man who'd been stalking her before? It had been a couple of months since she'd seen him around, and she'd let her guard down. Then the screech of car tires from the parking level above her broke through her thoughts. Another car zoomed past her, heading for the exit, leaving for home. It wasn't worth getting upset, especially since whoever did it had no idea what he was doing.

Better to be safe than sorry. She locked the doors, started the Toyota and revved up the engine high, her mind willing the 6-cylinder turbocharged surge of power to scare off anybody who might hide nearby. When no one popped up, she backed out of her space and heading out of the parking garage. The evening rush hour traffic was ugly as usual. The thin coat of snow on the asphalt added to the snarled lanes. The thick gray snow clouds, and the exhaust from the endless lanes of vehicles enveloping the buildings, colored everything with a depressive tinge of gray. On this day, the slog to get out of town seemed endless. She popped in some Drake and cranked his voice up loud enough to calm the fearful thoughts that were blowing through her mind like an invisible gale.

She drove home in a state of hyper-vigilance, which only increased in intensity as she headed down Highland toward her condo in Inman Park. Her eyes constantly scanned the road, moving front and back, from side mirrors to rearview mirror. She changed lanes often, slowing down and speeding up, glancing back to see if any cars did the same to show she was being tailed. She didn't know what car the blonde man drove, or even if he drove a car at all.

Soon she found herself in her familiar Fourth Ward neighborhood. She pulled into the driveway and sped up the hill while activating the garage door opener. Before driving into the open garage, she stopped the car and sat without moving for a minute, looking around cautiously. Nothing moved. Everything seemed to be in their usual places—the potted plants, the mat in front of the door, even the hose that was coiled in a haphazard heap on the side of the porch. She breathed a sigh of relief.

Lois was setting in the living room watching an award show she'd recorded when Misty walked in. She sat forward, wondering why Misty looked so frazzled. "What's got your tail in a twist?

"This. I found it tucked under the wiper on my car." She tossed Lois the card.

"Something is going to change?"

"I think they were taking a more literal line of thought." Misty pulled an imaginary knife across her throat.

"Ohhh, I keep forgetting it's the death card. Was it him again?"

"Who knows? I looked but didn't see anyone. I'm just mad because I thought it was over."

"Me, too. But this kinda creepy, in a weird kind of way. You need to call the police before the situation gets totally out of control."

Feeling a bit foolish about over-reacting, Misty placed a call to the Inman Park Station of the Atlanta Police Department to report the tarot card she'd found on her car. Less than a half hour later, the bell had rung. She'd peeped through the hole, relaxing when she discovered a smiling detective holding up his open badge.

He introduced himself as Detective Tim Sansom and passed her a business card with his contact info. "You called the precinct about someone harassing you?"

"Yes, I did," Misty said. She gestured to the chair across from her couch. "Come in, sit down."

Lois perked up as the handsome young officer entered the room. She had never dated anyone associated with law enforcement but figured there was a first time for everything. He was definitely putting out pheromones, she could feel her body reacting to him and he hadn't even glanced her way. Or if he did, he was hiding it well.

After taking his seat, the detective got down to business. He opened a two-pocket leather portfolio he brought with him that contained a large sized iPad for writing. He scanned a copy of the online report she had filed. "I've read the online police report you filed. Why don't you tell me about what's been going on?"

Misty told the officer about the calls, the notes, and the personal ad. She removed the letters from her desk drawer and handed them to the officer, then related to him all the incidents that had taken place over the past few weeks. He carefully made notes about the mysterious man but made no comment. The detective looked interested while he listened to her story, only turning away to type notes and study the items. At least he appeared to be taking us seriously.

Then she pulled the tarot card from her pocket. "This is my latest problem."

The young patrolman looked at the card. "What is this thing?"

"It's a tarot card," Misty said, becoming impatient. "The Fuckin' death card, no less! I found it on the windshield of my car when I left work."

He handed it back to her. "It's probably some kid who thinks it's funny. Besides the letters, have you' gotten weird stuff like this in the past? It could be considered a threat directed at you, but then it could also be somcone's idea of a warped joke."

"No. In fact, I thought it was over until today. I have no idea what made him start again."

"It could be something external that kept him away. He might have been in jail or in the hospital. Or maybe his job took him out of town." He glanced at his notes. "This grungily dressed man you see all the time," he said. "Do you know his name?"

"No. As far as I know, I have never met

him or spoken to him prior to this harassment." Misty's tone became exasperated. "It feels like it's escalating. Hang-up calls, notes, prank ads placed, all for me. Now this card. Someone is spending an awful lot of their time trying to make my life miserable.

He looked up when she was finished speaking. "Have your doors at home been tampered with?"

"No."

"You're sure?"

"Yes, I'm sure," Misty answered.

"You have locks on the windows?"

"Of course."

"The neighbors. Have you talked to them?"

No, I haven't," Misty said, feeling exasperated by the onslaught of questions. "We live in a gated condo complex. The building is on a private drive at the top of a hill. We have neighbors, but the property is surrounded by trees, so we can't see each other very well."

"Let me make sure I have this straight. You get a couple of strange letters in the mail and a series of annoying pranks here and there. You mention seeing the same man around town more often lately, but other than him going up an elevator with you for less than a minute, he hasn't approached you or spoken to you. Do I have everything correct?"

"Essentially." Misty bristled. He was making the entire situation seem trivial. "Is there anything I can do about it?"

He gave her a patronizing look. "I understand you're frustrated. However, I can't pull men away from high priority investigations to look into pranks. What I can do is start some preliminaries. I'll talk to the property management company for the building and see if there is surveillance footage in the parking garage available and notify the office building security department to be on the lookout for the man you described to me. I'll also check out your company phone records to see if we can trace those calls you were getting."

Detective Sansom shifted uncomfortably. Misty could tell he didn't want to answer her question, but knew he had to do it. "That's the dilemma with things like this. We can't do anything until the person acts in such a way that it puts your life in danger. You said, it's been a while since the previous harassment. Have you seen the man around lately?

"No. I haven't. I take it the police will not be investigating the problem for now."

Did she detect a hint of a chuckle from him? His expression looked dubious. "Therein lies the problem. We have no one to investigate." He typed a few more lines into the report, then closed the tablet. "We can't investigate a person who doesn't have a name or known address or that hasn't broken the law," he reminded her.

"What should I do in the meantime?"

"Ignore it, unless these incidents become a real threat."

Misty sighed. "I've been ignoring it and you can see where it's gotten me."

"It's frustrating. But we are restricted by law. We can't act until a crime has been committed."

"So, until he hits me in the head, or shoots me, I have no protection from the police?" Misty asked, her voice laden with sarcasm.

"I wish I could do more for you right now, but I can't. In the meantime, don't react to the behavior. Reacting only increases the behavior."

"How?"

"Let me give you an example," he said. "You have some unwanted person calling you ten times a day and leaving you notes and being a nuisance. You ignore each instance of the guy reaching out. After a week, you get tired of it, and the next time the phone rings, you pick it up and scream at him to leave you alone, or quit calling, or sending you gifts. Then you hang up." For a moment, he looked exhausted. "The problem is that while it felt good at the time; you just taught the perpetrator that it takes so many days, or so many calls or gifts, to get your attention. Now he it starts over again, and the individual could become even creepier in his pursuit because you raised the bar for him to overcome. You didn't stop the behavior, you reinforced it."

Misty's shoulders slumped. His analogy made perfect sense. There didn't seem to be any way out of her dilemma, at least not yet. Maybe she should buy a gun?

The detective stood and prepared to leave. "I hate we don't have the personnel to check every nuisance call that comes in. You have my card. If anything unexpected shows up, don't touch it. Let me come and take pictures. That way, we can document what's happening. Same for any phone contact. Call me, but don't use your phone to do it. I need it to be the last call to get the best trace results. You have a second phone in the house? For the records?"

Lois smiled. "You can use my number...987-654-3210 if you need anything, you can call me."

Misty noticed that he typed it into his phone.

"Thank you...uh?"

"Lois." She smiled.

He was grinning when he left.

"Well," Misty said after she closed the door behind him, "That was a complete waste of time."

"Not a complete waste." Lois showed her the text she'd just received. Both women laughed.

Chapter Sixteen

After the detective left, Misty returned to her bed and put her pillow over her face, trying to will it all to go away. Her life felt like it was unraveling. No one was taking the problem seriously. Lois convinced her to try a simplistic solve-it-in-a-day view of the whole thing, and now the police detective treated her story with complete indifference. In the meantime, a delusional man was somewhere out there, thinking up new ways to terrorize her, all because he's smart enough to stay ahead of the law. Misty didn't consider his activities very funny.

In the days that followed her initial report to the detective, nothing occurred, and she felt like she had over reacted.

Lois said it was possible that he had been watching her and saw the police officer come to the building to take her report. Maybe he figured the game wasn't worth going to prison.

She figured it was the same as before. He

wasn't around.

Two weeks passed. She had just finished reviewing the blueprints with a new client when she realized she had left a catalog she needed for the afternoon marketing meeting in the trunk of her car. Damn it. Might as well take a quick break and grab some lunch. She told Roger where she was going, then began the long walk back to her car. The main elevator did not connect directly to the garage, so she had to exit in the lobby, then switch to an access elevator that went to the parking garage. She hoped the catalog was in the trunk of the car and not lying on the dining room table at home. Absorbed by her thoughts, she wasn't paying much attention to the concrete structure that surrounded her. Because of the dim lighting, she made a habit of carrying her key remote to unlock the doors as she approached her car. She heard the familiar beep-beep before pulling the driver's door open, then leaned in and popped the trunk. In a matter of seconds, she located the material catalog peeking out from under a how-to magazine and sighed with relief. This company did not have a website, and it was the only company that supplied this specific product. At least she didn't have to drive home through Friday afternoon traffic to get it. She slammed the trunk shut, then stood there staring at the words scratched into the paint of the trunk. What the fuck!

It was all she could do not to cry as she walked around the car, surveying the damage from front to back and on every side. Not happy with one comment, the perpetrator had keyed the words BITCH and SLUT in blocked, childlike letters on every side. Apparently, the security camera and passing cars had not impeded the perpetrator in any way. She had bought the car brand new several years ago as a present to herself after graduating from college. The Supra was an investment in herself, and she had just paid off the loan. There was no touching this up. The cuts were deep, right down to the metal. The paint job was ruined. It was all she could do to stand there and attempt to process the extent of the damage.

"Hey, is that your car?" a male voice called out to her. She turned to see an unfamiliar man coming out from the parking garage elevator. He walked up the ramp toward her. He wore a suit and carried a briefcase in his hand, but there was something about him that made her uncomfortable.

All Misty could do was nod as tears pooled in her eyes.

He whistled as he surveyed the sight. "Man, that's bad," he said. "Someone is really angry at you. Did this happen today? I'm new to the building and I drive the same car. Fowler Law Partners, on the 10th floor. I can go report it to security and then give you a ride somewhere if you need it."

Misty waved her hand weakly. "No, thanks. I can take care of it. I'm heading back upstairs, anyway. I appreciate your offer, though."

The man shrugged. "No problem. That's what I call keying a car. I hope they can get those scratches out. They'll have to sand it all the way down and feather it in at the body shop. I'm surprised a vandal could reach this part of the garage, let alone have time to do this kind of damage."

He reached into his pocket and handed her his card. "I'm Riley Williams. It's nice to meet you, although I wish it were under better circumstances." He extended his hand and grasped hers, perhaps a little longer than a standard handshake. "Let me know if I can help you out. I'm headed to a deposition right now, but I'd be happy to give you a ride home later if you need it. Just call me."

"I will, thank you so much," Misty said wearily, forcing a smile. She wasn't in the mood to deal with being hit on in the parking garage, much less thinking of a clever response.

"Well, good luck to you," he said, and headed up the ramp to his car.

She looked around nervously. New lawyer was right about one thing. How could anyone inflict this much damage on a car with no one noticing him? She felt vulnerable. He could hide behind another car and wait for the right moment to attack her. She felt a shiver run up her spine, and realized she'd been standing there too long. Her heart was pounding as she walked to the elevator and pressed her floor along with the "Door Close" button repeatedly, while willing the doors to close. Only after the elevator began its ascent to the building lobby did she relax.

It had to be him again, she thought, her anger brewing. He knew which car she drove. Somehow, he was able to get into the parking garage without being seen.

She sat down at her desk and searched through her wallet for his card, while willing her hands to stop shaking. Then she picked up the phone and dialed Detective Sanson.

"Hello ma'am, how are you?" Detective Sansom's warm voice came through the receiver. She was surprised he didn't seem annoyed by her call.

"Not good," Misty said, a sob catching in her throat. "I went down to my car and found that someone keyed it."

"Keyed it? Not good. Did you notify the building security?"

"Yes, they took some photos," Misty said glumly. "I need to have the car taken to a body shop to repair and get a rental car delivered. You said to let you know before I did anything?

"I will send a forensic team over to check for prints. They probably won't get any. The perp would have held the key, but he might have put his hand down on the car for balance. Sometimes we get lucky. I'll make a report."

"Thanks. It needs one on the record before I call the insurance company to make a claim."

She sighed and turned to Roger. "This is just what I need right before the meeting. But it's only money. It can be repaired, and no one was hurt."

"How could anyone get into a secure parking garage to do this?" he asked, shocked at the news. He paid a higher-than-average rent to ensure things like this never happened.

"A detective is coming over to talk to me. You may have to handle the client."

First, there was silence. Then she heard him exhale with exasperation. "You know how I hate dealing with women."

"Better hope he gets here before she does or it's all yours."

"So, I don't have a choice in the matter?"

"Not this time. I will take it if I can, but I can't guarantee anything. If I don't get this done, I will not have a way to work. I need the loaner while mine is in the shop."

He sighed. "We'll get all this fixed. The police will find him. I'm sure of it." Roger looked like he could cheerfully take care of the man if he could get his hands on him.

Misty nodded. Roger's faith in a positive outcome always chased away her worries. He always had a happy ending for everything, and right now, Misty needed to hear it. Even if she didn't believe a word of it.

Ten minutes before the client was scheduled to arrive, Detective Sansom arrived with his forensic team. He also introduced her to a Detective Price, a member of the special harassment task force. Once the techs began printing the car, the two detectives joined her in the lobby café over coffee.

Detective Price began the conversation as soon as they sat down. "Our department handles cases of harassment or stalking," he explained. "Because stalking is a very complicated crime to investigate, our department keeps one investigator in charge of the entire case, no matter what incidents occur. In your case, Misty; that would be me." He glanced at both of them. "May I call you by your first names?"

"Yes, of course," Misty replied.

"Thank you," he said. "Now, Misty, tell me what has been going on. I see you've already filed a report."

Misty explained the story to date and showed him the evidence she had collected so far. It had grown to a substantial pile.

"Looks like someone is trying to scare you," Price said. "But you say no one has directly threatened you?"

"They're succeeding," she replied. "But it's more aggravating than life threatening. That might change if they continue to damage my car."

"Any idea why?" he asked. "Do you know of anyone who would want to harm you?

Misty looked frustrated. "I have no idea who it might be, but I can't figure out why anyone would want to do this," she said. "Then there's the blonde man. He seems familiar, but I've racked my memory and can't find a single occasion where we have spoken."

"Usually, this type of stalking is personal, but it also could be someone connected to one of your own clients."

Misty turned back to the detective. "I didn't know why a customer would be mad at me. We build houses and small business buildings. I can't think of anyone that was unhappy. It's very disturbing how random things have been happening. At first, it was just irritating. Now my car was keyed. That makes me mad. But not enough to hurt someone. It's got to be tied to the same man who keeps showing up, watching me."

"It is unusual. Usually, the perp is someone who wants a relationship with their victim, even a negative one. You don't know the man, and that makes it harder to tie the perp to a crime." Price said. "Unfortunately, we can't arrest someone for being in the same place you are."

"But he keyed my car!"

"You don't know that he was the one who keyed your car. You didn't see who did it." He paused and drank some coffee. "I understand it frustrating," the detective replied, "but we need more proof than just a feeling you have in a situation like this." He grinned. "We can't just run out and arrest someone on a whim.

Misty closed her eyes to gather her composure as she leaned back in her chair. "I get that," she replied, her tone calm but edged with tension. "But it seems wrong that until my life is in danger, no one can do anything."

"We can't place anyone in jail without evidence of intent. Although the number of stalking complaints has exploded in recent years, our experience is that in most cases, stalkers can be handled early on, before the situation escalates into a serious crime."

"So, once I'm drawn and quartered and discovered by the garbage detail when the plastic sack tears, it will be considered a serious enough crime to arrest him?" Misty snapped.

Price didn't flinch. "Nope. First, we would

have to find out his name. Then we would try to connect him to you. If we could connect him to the body, then we would build a case."

Misty sighed. "Okay, I get your point." The detective was right, and he knew the law far better than she ever would. She needed to put aside her anger and trust in what he was telling her.

He took out his pen from his shirt pocket and scribbled something into his notebook.

"Many investigators get caught up by focusing on the threat itself, instead of the person and circumstances behind the threat. Each case is unique, only the dynamics vary. We have to evaluate the threat of each case, as well as the context in which it was made. Then factor in the person who made it. Thats the only way to determine how threatening a situation is. Any information you can give is important."

"I'm at my wit's end dealing with all this."

Detective Price nodded.

"No, but you to thank about anything that occurred right before the incidents began. Something outside your normal behavior. To be honest, from the things you have experienced, I would have thought that your stalker was a female, not male." Detective

Price looked directly into her eyes. "Simply stated, we can't provide you protection 24 hours a day, 7 days a week. Decisions about personal safety rest with you."

Chapter Seventeen

"Damn rain," Shae muttered as she walked along the sidewalk. Oh well, like they say, give it an hour and it will be something else...

Even though summer afternoons in the southern mountains were hot and breezy, rainy days could quickly make the air dark and chilly. On days like this, the bus stop seemed miles away. The rain coming down was just heavy enough to soak you through, but not enough to make you stay under a shelter until it passed. Her light hoodie was no match for the drops that permeated the fabric right through to her delicate frame. Her hair was already a stringy mess of wet, tangled curls. She leaned against the trunk of the tree, hoping that Ace would see her and invite her in again.

No one had shown up to the studio in this weather except her, not even the other members of the band, but she had to take a chance. Ace was in town, but the band was ready to leave on tour. They had to be in Seattle in three days. Shae had to see him, even if it was only in passing. Maybe he would let her inside again. Maybe then, all alone, he would...

The sound of a car's engine interrupted her thoughts. A car pulled beside her, crawling along with her walking pace. She froze. She knew the car. It was the Audi. His Audi. She knew the car so well she could pick it out in a sea of identical-looking Audis.

The darkened passenger window came down with a whiny hum and the driver's head leaned forward to peer out at her.

Oh. My. God. It's him!

She stood, frozen in place on the sidewalk. Her brain cells couldn't spin fast enough to take in the information her wide eyes were seeing.

"Shae, right?" he called to her.

She nodded, tongue-tied over seeing him outside the studio parking lot. He glanced up at the gray sky. "It's pretty miserable out there. Not a good day to be out walking, is it?" he asked. His eyes crinkled at the corners as he smiled.

"Yes, well, uh, I'm on my way to the bus stop," she croaked, trying to keep her voice steady. He reached over and pulled on the passenger door latch, the hard muscles of his biceps shifting beneath the short sleeve of his T-shirt. "Here, come inside until the rain lets up."

Her jaw dropped. She couldn't move an inch. She stood there. The rain got heavier, and thunder rolled in the distance. A nasty storm was heading that way.

He nodded to the passenger door. "Hurry, get in before you get sick."

Should she? Her heart was beating wildly. Pasting a smile on her face, she walked over to the car; her legs still weak and shaking. She fought to keep her wits about her, trying not to not look like a crazy groupie. She got in, sinking down into the soft Italian leather interior, and closed the door, unable to believe her good fortune.

Shae looked over at him. She had to force herself to breathe because he took the air out of her lungs every time. Focus, she told herself.

"Thanks for the ride," she said, keeping her voice light. "I guess I would have been dripping wet if you hadn't seen me."

"It's fucking chilly as hell today," he said. Without waiting for an answer, he took off his leather jacket and draped it over her small frame. "Here, put this on. So, where are you headed?"

"Home, I guess. It's too wet to hang around here." She wrapped the jacket as close around her as she could, not only to keep warm but to feel the leather tighter around her body.

"Are you in a hurry?"

"No, I guess not. What do you have in mind?"

"I'm on my way to grab a bite to eat. You hungry?"

She stared at him, wide-eyed. Was he suggesting that they go out to eat together? "Uh..."

"You haven't eaten yet, have yam?" His eyes seemed to drill into her.

"No, I haven't. Sure, why not."

He grinned. "Good. I'm so hungry I could eat a horse." He sped away from the curb, driving away from the studio and down Moreland Avenue toward the expressway.

Her heart thumped wildly. The woodsy scent of the car's leather interior hugged her like a glove. She watched as his fingers grasped the gear shift at his side the same way they grasped his guitar. He tapped his finger against the steering wheel to the beat of the song on the radio.

"You surprised me when you pulled up," she said, trying to make some sort of conversation, like two normal people out for a ride.

"It's a wicked ride, isn't it?" he replied with a grin. He glanced over at her and she felt a chill run up her spine. Her mouth was so dry it felt like it was filled with sand.

"Do you live around here?" he asked.

"No, back the other way," her voice came out in a tight squeal. "It's not that far.". She clutched her icy hands together to keep them from trembling, hoping she didn't sound like a complete idiot. Her mind went blank. She couldn't think of any other thing to say. They drove for about fifteen minutes before he turned off the road. The small family-style restaurant he pulled into surprised her. It was nothing like she expected. She shrugged and followed him inside. It was a nice place, decorated with lots of wood and bright colors. The cashier nodded when he walked in, and she felt herself relax. Apparently, he was a regular customer.

Shae looked around. "What a nice place."

"Yeah, I like it," he replied. "No reporters. No one to hound me." He handed her a menu. "The food's good here. And they have the best fries in town."

"I don't eat out a lot," she confessed.

"No worries. Indulge yourself. It's on me."

The server came to their table and greeted them with a warm smile. "What are we having today?"

He glanced at the menu. "Number 5 for me," he said, "and my friend will have the same."

The server smiled. "Good choice. We make everything here in-house. That one's my favorites, too."

"I'll be right back with your drinks," she promised as she withdrew.

"She's nice," Shae commented after she left.

"Yeah, I like to come here when I need to kick back and chill out.

Shae watched as the server walked by them with two drinks in her hand for a nearby table.

He pointed to the mugs as the two men began drinking their beer. "Yeah. And see the glass bottom on the mug? Legend says it was to let you see who was coming to kill you—back in the day, of course." He winked, and she didn't know whether or not to take him seriously.

She smiled back, but her heart was beating a mile a minute.

"You shouldn't be out there by yourself so late at night."

Shae smiled. "I know."

He took a sip of his beer, and she noticed his eyes through the glass bottom. "So, what do you do with yourself when you're not at the studio?" he asked.

"I'm, uh, a student," she said.

"And what are you studying?"

She paused. She hadn't expected him to ask her to elaborate. "Computer Science," she said. "I, uh, like programming."

"I see," he said. You must be good with numbers."

She prayed he wouldn't ask any more questions, especially about math. She passed her classes but by the skin on her chin. She was saved from answering any more questions when the server arrived at their table and sat two overflowing plates before them.

"I need to ...uh..." Her eyes went to the sign above the door.

He laughed as she scuttled away.

Shae was back in minutes. He was already

eating, so she concentrated on her meal. She relaxed as they ate the food, quietly acknowledging it was as good as he promised. He was down to earth and sincere and gradually she began to feel comfortable

"Are you leaving on tour soon?" she asked.

"Yeah, soon, to promote 'Hypersonic Crash.' We're just finishing up the set list."

She quickly brought her enthusiasm under control. "How do you decide which songs will end up on a set list?"

"Good question," he replied. "There are a lot of factors to consider. You walk a tightrope between promoting your new stuff while keeping your audience happy by playing the familiar favorites. It's difficult to blend all those things together perfectly." He shot her a smile. Even though he sounded sincere, she felt like she was talking from a distance. It was like hearing him through water.

He put down his fork. "About time," he said, his tone changing. "We need to leave while you can still walk."

Shae felt her throat tightening like a vise around her vocal cords. Her heart pounded in her ears. She couldn't think of a thing to say at that moment.

"I'm not feeling so good." Her tongue tried not to stumble over the words.

His expression remained unchanged.

She fought to keep her mind aware., but it was becoming difficult to think. Something was wrong, but she had no idea what it was.

He leaned back in his chair. "Stay here. I need to pay the bill."

He went to the cashier to pay the check. Her eyes fell on his cell phone lying on the table. Without thinking about the consequences if she got caught, she dialed her cell phone number from his. When her phone silently vibrated, she quickly deleted the recent call from his phone. Then she placed his phone back on the table. It was back where he'd left it when he returned to the table a minute later.

He picked up the phone and slid it into his pocket. "Shall we go?" After putting his jacket around her shoulders, he took her arm and guided her through the door, back out into the damp, chilly air. Once they were in the car, he buckled her seatbelt.

"I want you to know I appreciate you showing up today. I often get overlooked, especially by women that come to see the band play. Bitches, every one of them. But you can't make people love you," he said. He reached over and grasped her hand, but she was past hearing anything.

Excitement flowed thru his veins. This is it! She belonged to him now. He closed his eyes and imagined what it would be like making love, the weight of his body sinking into hers, his lips nuzzling her neck, his hands touching her, exploring her. As his erection grew, his lips curved into a full, satisfied grin.

Now he had to pull himself together. He'd succeeded in taking her while raising no eyebrows. Just knowing she was beside him was driving him crazy. He'd have to be more subtle in his future activities if he hoped to keep suspicion away from him. With any luck at all, no one would connect them together. They were leaving on tour tomorrow. His place was not visible from the street. If things go as planned, he'll be able to enjoy her for the rest of the night and still arrive in time to pull out at nine the next morning.

"Please don't hurt me, daddy." Shae mumbled under her breath.

What's that? Daddy?

She slipped in and out of consciousness. "I won't be bad. I'll be a good girl, I promise!"

"That's right Shae. You can call me daddy. And in a few minutes, you can show me how good you can be."

Chapter Eighteen

The sharp chirps of her cell phone pulled Misty away from the budget sheet she'd been staring at for over an hour. She picked up her cellphone from her desk, noticing it was already almost five, the end of the workday. The call was from Alice. This was a surprise. She never called during work hours, and she would not be leaving the restaurant before nine that night.

"What's up?"

"I'm a bit frazzled today. Shae didn't come home last night. I realize it's a long shot, but you haven't heard anything from her, have you?" Alice's voice was taut, and she was speaking faster than normal. Her sister not coming home seemed to bother her more than usual. She was probably at the house in Jonesboro asleep.

"Not a word, not that I would be high on her contact list. She's twenty years old. Maybe she met a guy and is laid up in bed somewhere."

"I would almost prefer her to be with a man, instead of standing outside that recording studio all the time. But she's not there. I drove by and the place was dark. They must be out of town. I vaguely recall hearing Shae telling someone they were leaving on tour again."

"I have nothing I can add. Shae barely tolerates me on a good day. Your mom doesn't have any idea where she might be?"

"She suggested Georgia Regional. Did you know you can't call there and ask if someone is a patient?"

"You didn't!"

"It seemed like a good place to start. I was expecting her to show up at the restaurant hungry and wanting me to feed her. That's the usual way I discover where she's been. But that's after she gets out of class, and they are out for the summer. Lately she somehow locates sufficient sustenance on her own. Not that she doesn't clean out the cabinet and the fridge at the apartment when she's there."

"You mentioned the studio was empty. Is it possible?"

"I don't see how it could be. If she took off, she would have taken at least a change of clothes. She didn't even have her backpack with her. It's still setting by her bed. She's not answering her phone either."

"Sounds likes she met someone. Maybe a real man will take her mind off that singer."

"Your probably right. I was wild as hell at her age." She hesitated. "Do me a favor. Call that cop you know and ask him what he thinks I should do."

"Sure. I call you back after I talk to him." Misty waited until she heard the dial tone before she sighed and reached for her purse. It took her a few minutes to dig through her wallet until she found the card she was look-ing for. She'd never called him except from her office line and the switchboard went off at five PM. The detective might not be avail-able at that time of day. She knew police work strange staggered shifts so someone could be available at almost any hour, but she did not know what his schedule was.

She punched in the number and waited. Of course, the call was diverted to an an-swering machine, so she left a message ask-ing him to call her and hung up. By now, her mind was on anything except purchase orders and spreadsheets, so she saved her work and shut down the computer for the night. If she left now, she might have time to stop at the produce market before it closed.

Misty was about three blocks from her house when Detective Sansom returned her call. She quickly answered. "Hi Tim, you're on Bluetooth. No one else in the car."

"Thanks for the heads up. I got your message to call. How can I help you?"

"How long does someone need to be missing before you can file a missing person alert?" The car in front of her was driving slower than the flow of traffic. She debated going around, then huffed when the woman turned into a driveway. No blinkers of course.

"That depends on who is missing." He asked, curious about the hard exhalation but since she was driving, he didn't ask.

"It's Shae. Alice's sister. She's never been gone overnight. It's been over 24 hours with no contact. That's never happened before."

"Shae. She's not quite twenty-one, right?"

"Right. But Shae isn't ...she isn't ...normal? I guess that's a nice way of putting it. Physically she's fine. Emotionally, she's stuck about twelve or thirteen."

"So, the chance that she'd simply hook up with a friend is not likely?"

"I don't think I've heard her mention a friend. Ever."

"Could that be because she's interested in women?".

"No. She's obsessed with Ace Rivers. The lead singer of Cats Grinning. But they are out of town on tour."

"Could she be with them? Bands always have their fans that travel with them."

"No. I don't think so. She would answer the phone, if for no other reason than to crow about where she was. Alice is freaking out. She can't find anyone to help, they are all scared of the privacy laws."

"I'd give it until dark and then if you really feel there is a reason to look into this, have her sister call me."

"Thanks, I will tell her what you said."

"Uh, this is not exactly protocol, but that roommate of yours...Lois. Is she seeing anyone?"

"No one she's mentioned... you should call her. Or drop by the café she runs in my building. Lolo's."

"Lolo's! That's her place? I had lunch there last week. I didn't notice her.'

"She stays in the kitchen cooking unless there's a reason to go to the front."

"Maybe I can drop by there tomorrow."

"Yeah, tonight she's going to be busy driving around looking for Shae. We all are."

Chapter Nineteen

The next three weeks crept by. No one had seen Shae. The police had opened an active Missing Persons file. They had traced her movements using the camera at the train station near the apartment. She had seemed fine when she left the train station. No one knew where she went after that. She could have headed for the apartment or toward the recording studio. The investigator had contacted the band's manager, but no one had seen or talked to her since a few days before they left on tour. They were in Seattle this week and the hotel detective had verified no one that met Shae's description had been seen with the band. As a standard step in the investigation, the police had traced her cellphone use. They had no luck. The battery was dead, or she no longer had access to the phone. The detective had pulled her call log and found that the last call she'd received was from a disposable phone. There was no listing in her contacts, and no way to identify who had made the call. No one answered that number and it pinged off a cell tower near her house in Jonesboro.

Misty didn't think it had anything to do with Shae's disappearance, but her stalker was back again. The hang-up calls had increased, but they were usually heavy breathing or an occasional deep laugh. Once she came home to find a quart bottle of Jack Daniels whiskey and a plastic bag containing a few white pills on her doorstep. A message was left with the items, written with crayon, in a childlike scrawl: Want it to stop?

Misty could not dampen the dread she felt building inside. The stalker had been on the property, right outside her home. When? For how long? Had he been peeking through the windows? Misty might have thought she was alone, but he could have been just outside, watching her.

Each time she would call Detective Price, but either his activities were ambiguous enough to not be seen as a threat, or detective Price would assure her that his department was working on her case and ask her to be patient. The investigation wasn't producing much information. The calls were untraceable, made from inexpensive disposable cell phones, and he'd avoided any surveillance equipment on the street. Having Detective Sansom popping in and out helped. He had been at the apartment when a call came in, and he had listened to the man's heavy breathing. So now she had actual police documentation of the harassment.

At the back of everyone's mind was the same question. Did the unknown stalker have anything to do with Shae's disappearance?

Alice refused to accept the possibility that something might have happened to her sister. She believed Shae was with the band, and they were hiding her. Misty didn't agree with her theory but didn't want to upset Alice by arguing her point. She couldn't identify one reason a touring band would have to hide an obsessed young woman. Shae was over eighteen and old enough to follow the band if that was what she wanted.

The stalker escalated to physical threats one evening while she was having dinner at The Fresh Catch, a quaint downtown seafood spot famous for the fresh shellfish and charcoal-grilled whole fish. It was one of Lois's favorite places to eat. They had a sophisticated wine list and served her favorite entrée the New England Grille. Misty had to admit the combination of broiled bacon wrapped scallops, chunked lobster in white wine sauce, and grilled stuffed shrimp was addictive. Having dinner together had become a way for the three friends to unwind and decompress from the stress caused by Shae going missing.

Not this time.

Her cell phone went off twice in succession. Misty frowned and put down her wine and reached down to retrieve it from her purse. The number contained a local area code, but the number was not on her contact list. The text messages jumped out at her, a quick one-two punch that left her reeling:

I SAW YOU.

Then;

MASON SAYS YOU'RE A CHEAP WHORE IN BED. BUT BORING.

Misty slammed the phone down on the table and reached for her Margarita, taking a sip to keep from crying out. She felt her pulse take off like a rocket, climbing until she could hear it throbbing in her ears. Without doubt, it was him, and now he had her cell phone number. The squeezing sensation around her throat threatened to choke the breath out of her.

Alice looked at her curiously. "You okay, hun?"

Misty passed her the cellphone so she could see the messages. "No, I'm not okay," she said, her voice tightening.

Lois read the message. "Any idea who sent these?"

"None. But he's getting personal now."

"Who is this Mason he mentions?" Tim asked.

"A drunken memory? I didn't exactly spend a lot of quality time with him. Hell, I don't even know Mason's last name," Misty said, blinking back tears. She put her phone down. "Why do I have a feeling this has something to do with my stalker, and from these messages, he seems to know a lot about my life!"

"Could it be a kid? This sounds like something a kid might send to a girl who liked the same boy. Does Mason have a son?"

"No idea. I met him that night. I was totally wasted, to go home with a stranger."

"Maybe you should go talk to him?'

"I'm not sure I could find his house again, Misty said. "It was still dark when I took off, and I walked quite a way, before the cab came by. I was only interested in getting home, and it was a random flag down, so there was most likely no record of the fare. I can't remember what company it was, much less the cab number."

"Change the cell phone number," Alice said.

"I appreciate the thought, but I can't just change it on a whim. I have hundreds of business contacts who use this number to call me."

"At least block the number. He will tire of having it changed."

Alice laughed. "I don't think you can change the number on a disposable phone."

"The question is how he got your cell number. He could be a client."

Suddenly, Misty didn't feel hungry anymore. She put her napkin on the table. "Damn. I never thought about that. I'm sorry. I'm not feeling well. I'm going to pay my check and go home."

No one said anything as Misty but got the server's attention for her bill. Instead, they asked for theirs, too. Tim was on the phone with Price, relaying what he had just seen. Misty's cell phone dinged again as they waited for the bill. Another volley:

YOU CAN'T ESCAPE ME. I KNOW WHERE YOU ARE. HOWS THE FISH?

Misty turned pale as Tim took the cell phone from her and read the message. "What am I supposed to do? Everywhere I go, I'm being watched. Now my phone's been hacked!"

She sighed and placed her hands on the table and steepled them so tightly her fingers trembled, betraying her tension. She rested her forehead on them, avoiding their gaze. "This is too much for me to deal with right now," she said, her voice quiet.

Lois reached across the table and took her hands. "Let Tim deal with it. He'll sort this out and stop the harassment."

Another text came in as they were walking out of the restaurant.

DON'T IGNORE ME YOU SPINELESS BITCH.

Misty made a frustrated noise as her lips tightened. "Him again."

Alice was riding with her, and Lois was riding with Tim. The silence between them lasted as they got on the freeway until they pulled into the gated community. Even then, she checked her rearview mirror before sliding the car into the garage and killing the engine. She was frightened over the texts but also angry that her dinner with her friends was ruined. Like everyone else, her nerves were still coiled over Shae's disappearance. She felt like she could snap at any moment.

She looked around the illuminated area near the condo. Her eyes scanned the walkway, the shrubbery, the front yard, everything within the glow of the light. No one jumped from the shadows. Other than the wind rustling thru the grass and plants, all was quiet. She walked back into the garage and pressed the remote to close the door behind her. Alice had already keyed in the access code to the house. She stepped inside and locked it behind her. The living room, the stairs, and the kitchen all appeared in order. Vigilance was becoming a habit.

"Why don't you go soak for a while? It might help you relax." Alice was already on the phone with Lois, letting them know about the new message.

In the bedroom, Misty looked at her reflection in the dresser mirror. She hadn't slept well in weeks, and it was showing in her features. The woman in the mirror looked tired and pale. A hot bath in the deep, clawfoot tub sounded great. Misty never took a bath to get clean, preferring a shower. But it was her number one go to when she wanted a peaceful, roomy place to relax and think. She turned on the tub spigot and felt the gushing water warm up as it ran over her open palm. While it was filling, she went to the wood bath cabinet and removed a jar of scented bath salts and sprinkled the sparkling nuggets into the hot water. The lavender scent rose as it mixed with the steam, permeating the room. Then she lit a few tea candles, which she placed in rose frosted cups beside the book she intended to read.

When the tub was full, she stripped off her clothes and stepped in. Goose bumps erupted on her legs as the hot water surrounded them, but it felt great. She lowered herself into the water and slid down until her head rested comfortably on the bath pillow, closed her eyes and her mind faded into dullness as her muscles relaxed.

"Misty!"

Her eyes popped open. She was certain Alice had called her name. It was loud, forceful, and—scared? Then she heard a loud thump downstairs, like something falling on the floor. Then the sound of the front door slamming shut.

She sat straight up in the tub. Was someone in the house? Was Alice alright?

Her breath quickened and her pulse pounded as she grabbed the curved edge of the tub and hauled herself up and out. Misty grabbed a towel and wrapped it around her as she ran downstairs. Someone had turned the light out. She flipped on the light switch and spotted Alice lying on the floor. She was moving, but she was bleeding from a cut on her head. Call the police. She looked around for her cell phone, then remembered it was in her purse on the table next to her bed. Damn it! She didn't want to leave her, but she had to get to her phone to call for help. There was a baseball bat by the bed. It wasn't much of a weapon, but it was all she had.

She removed the towel, folding it and pressing it to the wound on Alice's head. Then she made her way back to the bedroom.

Once she grabbed her phone, she threw on her bathrobe and dialed 911.

"911, what's your emergency?"

"My friend hurt. She is bleeding and barely conscious. She needs an ambulance now."

"How did she get hurt?"

"I don't know. I was soaking in the bathtub upstairs. I heard her call out and came to see what was wrong. I found her this way."

"Help is on the way. Stay calm. Is your friend able to talk?"

"I will have to go back downstairs to check." Her heart was beating in her chest like a bass drum. Building courage, she slowly slipped down the stairs. Her trembling fingers clutched the bat tightly. When she reached the foot of the staircase, she took a deep breath and flipped on the rest of the lower-level lights. It took a second for her eyes to adjust, then she surveyed the area. The living room, the dining room and the kitchen were empty. As far as she could tell, no one was there. After checking Lois, she answered the dispatcher. "No. She opened her eyes once but didn't say anything."

Misty could hear sirens in the distance, and someone was knocking on the door.

"Who is it?"

"Tim. Lois called me. She was on the phone with Alice when she heard something, and the phone went dead."

Misty opened the door just as the ambulance was pulling up outside. Lois pulled up right behind them. She beat them to the door.

"What's going on?" she said as she kneeled by Alice.

"Someone hurt her." She turned toward where Lois was kneeling on the carpet.

Tim reacted immediately. He kneeled by Lois and did a cursory check. Once he was sure she was alive, he signaled to the ambulance it was safe to come in. Lois moved aside to let the paramedic take over. As the medic worked, Tim asked Misty what happened. "So, you do not know who attacked her?"

"No idea. I was soaking and half asleep. Her voice woke me, but I can't tell you if she called out before or after she was attacked."

He left Misty and Lois sitting in the living room and checked the house. Once he was certain there was no one hiding inside, he returned to talk to Misty. "I'm going to ride to the hospital and make sure Alice is treated immediately. Lois will stay with you. I'll let you know if anything changes."

Tim followed the gurney out to the ambulance, then got in his car to follow them to the hospital.

Misty locked the door, then she walked around the house and double checked every lock. She missed Alice already. Her imagination was not making it any easier to remain in the house and Lois had to be at work at five am. She saw a mysterious shadow near a window. Frightened, she closed her eyes tight, then opened them again. The shadow was gone. She sighed and snuggled her body further into the sofa cushions. Exhaustion caught up with her as the clock on the mantle struck three, and she fell asleep there in front of the fireplace.

Chapter Twenty

The next torpedo came at home two weeks later. It was a Sunday morning, the one day she could relax. Misty eased out of bed after fighting a tension headache that had been bothering her all night. Whether it was from having too many drinks with Lois at the comedy club the night before or the oppressive weight of Alice's injuries, she wasn't sure. Alice was home, but she was still dealing with the effects of her head injury. Bright lights and loud noises bothered her. She'd given her ticket to Lois and insisted they take Tim with them to the show. It was a sold-out show. Since they had purchased the tickets months earlier, on the day it was announced, they gave them great stage side seating.

The sunny day dawned warmer than normal and would get hotter as the morning passed. Misty dreaded leaving the house. She'd changed into a pair of jogging pants, a loose-fitting tank top and sneakers and tied her hair back into a ponytail.

In the kitchen, she started the coffeepot and popped a bagel in the toaster. Then, with her coffee in hand, went to the check the morning temperature outside before leaving for her morning jog around the park tracks. As soon as she opened the door, something lying on the stoop caught her eye. She looked down and froze.

A bouquet of store-bought flowers wrapped in clear plastic wrap lay at her feet, except these blooms weren't bright and fragrant but dead, brown and dry. She sighed, no longer affected by the near weekly attempts to break her. Instead of getting upset, she picked up the wilted bundle. As usual, there was no sign of where they had come from. She dropped the dead flowers into the trash can by her door, then got aggravated when she saw there was a card attached. She carefully removed the card from the wilted bundle. The message: For your funeral.

Damn. So much for her morning jog.

She looked around, moving her eyes back and forth, looking for any movement. Nothing...nor was there any sign that someone might be watching her. Nothing looked out of place. Sighing, she went back into the house and called Detective Price.

Even though it was Sunday, he returned her call a few minutes later.

"Detective Price, how can I help you?

"I hated having to call you on a Sunday."

"Not a problem," he said. "What's wrong?"

She stared at the wilted pedals on the entryway table. "I found something on my doorstep this morning." She glanced at her watch. It was just past eight. "Dead flowers. They weren't there last night when I came home."

"You found them today? This early?"

Her voice sounded shaky. "Yes. There was a card. It said, "For your Funeral."."

"All right. Don't handle it any more than you have to. I also have some information about Shae I can discuss with you at the same time. Is Lois there?

"Yes, she's sleeping."

His voice deepened. "You might want to wake her."

Misty hung up and went to the kitchen. There would be no running today, another sacrifice in her lifestyle. She set the coffee cup down on the counter, a little harder than she intended, and broke the handle off. Now exasperated and venting, she dumped the last bit of coffee in the sink and slammed the broken mug in the trash can. Then she went to wake Lois, wishing she had never walked out the door.

She sat alone, fuming with anger that the stalker was continuing to cause an upheaval in their lives. Calls and notes at the office and following her around were a nuisance and easy to dismiss. But now it was her home. He could be outside at that very moment. Watching. Lurking. Frustration stung her eyes.

About fifteen minutes later, there was a knock at her door. It was Detective Price.

While she went upstairs to tell Lois he was there, he examined the brown bundle of blooms lying on the coffee table. Then he opened a grocery size brown paper bag he'd brought with him. It was a police evidence bag, printed with evidence labels for recording case information and chain of custody. He reached into his pocket for a pair of rubber gloves and put them on. He placed the flowers and card inside the bag, then folded the bag over and sealed it shut with tape. Then he removed the gloves and placed the bag by the front door.

"I'll take this to the lab and see if they can pick up any fingerprints from the wrapping."

"Have some coffee," Misty offered. "We can sit at the kitchen table." She poured three cups from the freshly brewed pot, then brought them to the table with her. Once Lois was sitting with them, he gave them the bad news.

"A body was recovered from an abandoned house down in Henry County," he began. "It's Shae. She was positively identified last night by her sister, Alice."

"Shae. Damn. I knew she didn't run off," Misty said, her brows furrowing.

Price nodded. "This information changes things. We can't overlook the possibility that your stalker is the same person who killed her."

"Great, and today I get a death threat," Misty said dully. "I feel horrible that she's dead. I realize it's only been three months, but it feels much longer.

"That is to be expected," the detective continued. "Misty had issues you didn't know about. The mother is dysfunctional, a long time alcoholic. When we advised her of her daughter's death, she seemed worn out and weary, not upset about her death. It was almost as if she was pleased that she no longer had to deal with her mentally unstable daughter. We didn't get a lot of cooperation out of her. He paused for a second as if gathering his thoughts. "Did you know Shae was a cutter?"

Misty shook her head no. "I'm not sure what that means. You mean she was missing classes?"

Lois looked up. "A cutter? That explains the long sleeves."

Price nodded. "There was a lot we found out about the victim once we investigated her death. A cutter slices open her own body. Some doctors believe it's a way of punishing themselves for something that happened in the past."

"So..., Shae had mental problems. She was always talking about Ace Rivers. Would him not returning the affection cause her to cut herself?"

"Not usually. Celebrity stalking falls into the category of someone with erotomania. A stalker doesn't seek to be close to someone who loves them. They seek to be close to someone who doesn't want them, so it becomes a game for them after a while."

"Erotomania?" Misty asked, her interest

piqued. "What the devil is that?"

"It is a delusional disorder in which a person believes another person is in love with him or her, even if there is no evidence that it's true," Price explained. "Social media encourages fans to embrace the people they are following to where some, in their own mind, believe they have a personal relationship with a celebrity and will go to great lengths to protect that fixation."

"That sounds like Shae. But what about this cutting stuff?"

"You should talk to Alice about that. We didn't find anything to tie it to her death. The incident that caused it wasn't closed, since there was no danger remaining." He looked Misty directly in the eye. "The important thing for you is the timing. We considered it but this shows it couldn't have been Shae. She was most likely killed within a day or two of when she went missing. So, she could not be your stalker. But this is important. Your stalker could be her killer."

Chapter Twenty-One

The dreary day of Shae's funeral exemplified how wretched Misty felt about the young woman's death. The afternoon sky was overcast, and the dark gray rain clouds overhead only added the gloom. She was surprised by how much she wished she had an excuse not to attend the service. Instead, she turned off the computer, gathered her things and walked down the hall with several employees who were leaving for lunch about the same time. Since they discovered Shea's body, she felt safer in a group. There were only a few people still inside the car by the time the elevator doors opened on her main parking garage level. In an attempt to discourage the ongoing mischief, building security had assigned her a space next to the attendant's booth. The parking area was brightly lit and completely covered by cameras.

Acting nonchalant, Misty bid the others a casual good afternoon and walked toward the car alone. She was feeling embarrassed and slightly paranoid about being afraid in the middle of the day. Even so, her eyes were constantly moving, darting everywhere at the tiniest sound. No one was in sight. She walked across the parking deck to her car and checked the back seat through the windows before unlocking her door and getting in. As soon as the car engine had smoothed out, she exited the garage and began the drive south of the city, to the funeral home, glancing in her rearview mirror the entire way.

She pulled into the parking lot a few minutes after one and was surprised to see Lois's car wasn't there. A small group of strangers lingering around outside, but most had already entered and spoken to Shae's mother. She got out and began walking toward the front door, listening for the buzz of conversation when she saw Lois drive up.

"Hey!" she heard a voice from behind her. She whirled around to see Alice walking toward her. The last thing Misty wanted to do was chat with Alice about her late sister, let alone deal with a parking lot filled with distant family. She gestured toward Lois's car, and mouthed, will be right in.

Misty started walking toward Lois, when

a heavyset girl stopped her forward movement with a few muttered words, "I know who did it."

Misty stopped in her tracks and turned around. "Did what?"

"Killed Shae. She told me all about it. Well, not about killing her, but I know who she was with." She turned to Misty and nodded sagely, like she had a secret that could change everything. "She told a couple people, and it got around." The small group of girls all nodded in agreement.

Misty felt her temperature rising. Forgetting all about what Lois had told her about not engaging anyone at the funeral, she turned to talk with the young woman.

The girl was about Shae's age, but that was the only similarity. Shae had been socially awkward. This woman showed no hesitation as she sauntered over to Misty. She stood with her arms folded in front of her. Misty faced her potential adversary, ready to do battle. "What makes you think you know the killer?"

"Well, I don't know him. But I know who she took off with. She sent me a text."

The group gathered around to listen to what she had to say. Cell phones appeared out of nowhere, recording the confrontation. Misty swallowed the wave of high school bitchiness that rose to the ready in her throat. She had to stay calm and remain professional in front of a group of girls, barely out of high school. As usual, she was finding it harder to maintain control by the second.

Lois walked over and addressed the group. "Put those things down or I'll have security throw all of you out of here right now!" She hoped they would take her seriously, even though she knew her authoritative voice couldn't stop them from recording the event even if she wanted to. Amazingly, arms lowered, and cell phones disappeared.

Misty turned her attention back to the first young woman. "How do we know what you are saying is not a sick joke?" Was this girl another of the band's crazy fans? She had read that it is almost impossible to talk mentally ill people out of their delusions. Was she seeing this concept play out right in front of her now?

"Why would I joke about my friend's death? I know who she was with, and I can prove it."

Misty felt her pulse pounding in her temples." Okay. Let's see this proof. "

The big girls' ice-blue eyes narrowed to angry slits. Misty felt as if she were looking at a lighted keg of dynamite; one that was about to blow. The young woman reached for her phone, opened her camera app, and scrolled through her camera roll. She stopped at one photo and held it up to Misty's face.

"Here!" she said. "Take a good look! It's her and Ace."

Misty gasped. The image hit her like a speeding freight train. It was a photo of Shae and Mason setting on a sofa, his arm around her. She caught her breath in stunned shock, taking it all in. The information made her head spin. Mason and Ace were the same person! Was Mason her stalker? She heard shocked whispers from the people behind her.

Before she could recover, the girl stepped up her assault. "You want more proof? Huh?" She scrolled through her picture collection. "Here, how about this photo? And this one, and this one." The parade of incriminating photos seemed to never end. Mason and Shae, Shae with his musician friends, Shae obviously drunk and partying in various self-ies. And worse yet, one with Mason and Shae kissing. All Misty could do was stand there and stare in utter shock at the photos displayed in front of her.

Misty swallowed hard before finding her voice. Her eyes narrowed. "Could the photos be photoshopped pictures? Have you ever seen them together?"

"I've seen her going into the recording studio with him. That's not why I think he killed her. It was the text I got. The day she disappeared."

Misty couldn't breathe. She was lightheaded, on the brink of passing out. Somewhere in the distance, she thought she heard a car door open. Then Lois and Tim were standing there. Detective Sansom was talking to the gregarious woman who had the photos, the one the others called Rikki.

"Thank you," Misty gasped to Lois, as she helped her sit down in the front seat of the car. She held onto her arm while she caught her breath and regained her balance. Her voice trembled. "She has proof. Actual proof of how Shae died."

Lois could only nod her head while she shook the dirt from her pants.

Misty nodded and smiled weakly. "Mason is Ace Rivers." Her voice held a hitch of fear. "She said she had a text from Shae."

"Tim is talking to her now. Let him handle it. We need to go sit with Alice. We can tell her the news, after the service."

Misty allowed Lois to walk her into the building without saying a word. She headed for the row behind Alice and sank down into it. Then Lois sat down beside her. The service was starting. Misty covered her face with her hands while tears fell in a torrent from her eyes. With every breath she took, they were expelled in a series of minute sobs that didn't want to stop. All the while, Lois stroked her hair and patted her back in a comforting motion, making soft hushing noises. She had her other hand on Alice's shoulder the entire time.

Shortly before the end of the service, Tim slipped into the pew beside her. His face reflected none of the consternation he was experiencing. His associate, Detective Price, had bundled Rikki into his car and they left for the station. He needed to ensure the evidence was in her possession until the forensic team made copies of the images and the texts. The evidence Rikki had provided changed everything. They would get copies printed and have a judge sign off on a warrant. Within twenty-four hours, the suspect would be picked up regardless of what state they were currently in. He would be extradited back to Atlanta for the inquiry. If he could not provide an airtight alibi, he would be charged with Shae's murder.

Lois's tone darkened as she put a protective arm around Misty. "Misty just had a shock. She needs to get some rest and come to grips with what she just learned. Maybe you should skip the graveside ceremony."

"No," Misty said, recovering her emotions. "I will be okay. I need to stay with you and Alice."

After the service, Lois convinced Misty to ride to the gravesite with her. They could pick up her car on the way back. The procession pulled out, and fifteen minutes later, they arrived at the cemetery.

Greenwood Garden's was one of the older graveyards in the city. It looked rather regal compared to newer cemeteries with its tall, mature oak trees growing in strategic places. Tall gas lights provided muted lighting along the walkways for visitors when dusk approached. The landscaping was manicured to perfection like a city park, yet like all cemeteries, it seemed to be a solemn place, burdened with the sadness of those who came to grieve the loss of their loved ones. Many people choose to forgo the cost of a funeral, opting for cremation instead. Because of the horrible way in which Shae died, donations to the family had taken care of all expenses, including the cost of the plot, casket and vault. Hundreds had sent flowers. This made it sad to see so few actually show up.

The rain had stopped, but there were still remnants of the recent deluge that dampened the grass. Misty followed the hearse through the wide, gated entrance and along the curving road that passed sloping hills dotted with grave markers on either side. White crosses were placed on many of them. Nondescript tombstones stood alongside carved marble statues and ornate, ivy-covered mausoleums that housed the rich in their repose. The more opulent had concrete benches beside them for visitors who came to visit and talk with their deceased loved ones.

The hearse took a left and parked beside a bright red awning and a recently dug grave. Misty took a minute to compose herself, then got out and removed a bundle of exotic flowers from the back seat. With the colorful blooms in hand, she began walking, her heels sinking into the turf as she headed toward the awning. Lois followed a few paces behind her as she walked, more out of respect for this special time than not being able to keep up.

Alice was standing near a small bridge that spanned a brook that wound its way between graves and crypts under the canopy of the majestic oaks. Seeing the two friends sitting beneath the awning, she started wandering that way, aimlessly looking at the military style gravestones as she passed. The special markers stood in silent rows, all perfectly lined up and identical except for the name inscribed on them. Right and left, front and behind, row upon row in the manicured grass, the granite headstones served as historical markers of the dead, pointing the way to the one she sought.

It was sad that most of the people attending the service had not known Shae. That was made clear at the graveside. Other than her mother and Alice, Lois and Misty were the only attendees. The minister said a few words, then the cemetery employees lowered the casket into the waiting vault.

In less than ten minutes, it was done. Shae was at rest, and their lives were changed forever.

Tim had arrived at the cemetery as the casket was being lowered. He spoke to Lois for a minute and then asked Alice if she would join him for a cup of coffee, once they got back to the funeral home. Lois planned to go with them. She asked Misty, "You don't mind being alone?"

"No. You stay with Tim. Someone needs to be with Alice when she learns about the photos. It's going to hit her hard. I'll head home. We can talk later. My mind is having difficulty relating the man I met to the cold-blooded killer he seems to be. Maybe I will feel better after I sleep on it." If she could fall asleep. She intended to try, even if she had to take something to make it happen.

***

The pills she took when she got home let her sleep for a few hours, but the sun was just going down when they wore off. The night was long and lonely, allowing her too much time to think. Her imagination kept her awake. She didn't want to fall asleep and dream about all the things that will never be. Not only was Shae gone, and she had slept with the man that killed her. Misty wasn't sure she would ever come to accept every-thing that had happened. She lay in bed staring up at the ceiling, weighing her future options. She had no obvious answers. It ate at her soul that had she had sexual relations with a possible murderer. And enjoyed it. At one time, she'd actually wondered if she should hunt him down and see if the relationship could go forward. For now, just knowing he'd been seeing Shae at the same time left a void in her heart that she couldn't bear.

Misty lay there, fighting the wave of emotion until the dam she'd created was washed away by her tears, letting her pent-up feelings tumble free. She felt physically and emotionally beaten, like she'd run a gauntlet of psychic whips. It would be great if she could pull the cover over her head and hide out from the world. Instead, she had to get ready for the confrontation with Alice. She wasn't looking forward to it. Would Alice blame her for Shae's death? Would it have happened if she had never met Mason? Logic said Shae had developed her crush before she ever met Mason. Not that logic was going to make Alice feel better. Fuck. The whole thing sucked.

Misty covered her face with her hands to hide her tears and stared out the window through the cracks between her fingers. A beautiful full moon shone through the tall windows, illuminating the room in a dull glow. Misty loved the moon. She always felt a special connection to the glowing orb, even more so when things weren't right in her life. When she was younger, she would gaze at it, and it would always comfort her. She loved to sit on the beach at night and watch it hanging high in the sky, bathing the sea and the hills in silvery light. Now it seemed to watch her.

The tumbling thoughts and emotions continued to distress her until she finally fell into a troubled sleep. Misty knew she might accept the evidence, but she would ever be the same.

Chapter Twenty-Two

The media wasted no time releasing the information they had available. Headlines flowed across the television screen. Ace Rivers Arrested! Come Die for Me! Lead Singer Perp Walk! This Cat's not Grinning Anymore!

Holy shit.

Ace stood alone in the tiny 5 x 8 cell, too stunned to move off the metal bunk after what had just occurred. He'd just been crushed to pieces by a pile driver and couldn't think clearly at the moment. Shae was dead, and the photos they had taken that afternoon it rained so hard were the primary links to her killer. Him! At least, that's what the detective said when they arrested him. His mind churned a mile a minute, trying to figure a way out of this disaster. The popular theory was that he was sneaking around, sleeping with Shae while the band was in town. Then he killed her in a jealous rage before they left to go on tour. It was ridiculous. However, people went to jail all the time for crimes they didn't commit.

Once again, he kicked himself for allowing Tyce to take those photos. That they were all drunk was not a legal defense. He couldn't turn back time. Isn't that what his friend Bryce told him in his dreams time and time again? The damage was done, all you can is live with it. For the millionth time, he wished his best friend had survived. Bryce always had the answers to his problems. The crazy part was now he could understand why someone would kill Shae. The woman could be infuriating. He wished he could choke the life out of her right now. Or take her to some dark alley downtown and use a gun with a silencer to splat her sorry ass all over the pavement. He lay back on the narrow cot and closed his eyes, wishing he could wake up and discover it was all a nightmare. Now he understood why it was so easy to dream about something once it was too late to do anything. Who was he trying to fool? He'd seen death, but he wasn't a killer then and he wasn't one now. Somehow, he had to get the police to believe him.

Mason didn't know how much time went

by as he lay on the molded steel bunk, but somewhere in his consciousness, he felt his body shiver from the cold. Damn cold. Goosebumps raced up and down his skin, pulling him with icy fingers out of his contented fugue. He forced his heavy eyelids to open. The flat light in the ceiling came into focus. Then he rolled his head to the right. That's when he saw someone sitting beside him, watching him.

It was Bryce.

Ace sat straight up, not believing the sight before him. His head felt like it was stuffed with cotton batting. He blinked his eyes a few times, but the image before him remained the same.

"Bryce?" Ace stammered, staring at him in shock. "You're dead. Why are you here?"

"The answer is right in front of you, you just need to look." His voice became exasperated. "Fuckin' hell, man. Why can't you see it?"

"See what?" Ace trembled inside. He was feeling afraid, but he didn't know why.

"The proof man! The shit's all around you. You'll know what to do when you finally look and understand. Save yourself it's too late!" Then he faded away.

Mason sat back on the bunk, concentrating on regulating his breathing and allowing his heart rate to fall back to normal. Did that just happen? Or was it just a crazy dream? The entire encounter lasted a few seconds, but it seemed like time had stood still.

The sun was just rising over the horizon. They would come to transfer him back to Georgia soon. Somehow, he had to find a way to show he was innocent, despite the incriminating photos and the strange text message Shae had sent her friends. He was a thousand percent sure he wasn't within miles of the dead girl during the weeks before they left on tour, and definitely not since the tour started.

Somehow, he had to prove it.

But how?

He began going over the day before they left for the tour. Step by step, he recreated everything he had done. He wished he had something to write with, while everything was fresh in his mind. By the time he reached Atlanta and talked to the detective in charge, he would be exhausted. He was afraid he might overlook so important detail. A detail that might save his life.

He looked up as two guards approached

his cell. It was time....

Chapter Twenty-Two

Detective Price sat across from the scared young musician, studying his behavior. Much as he hated to admit it, Mason did not fit his profile. The man could get any woman he wanted. He was the crush of women all over the country, possibly the world. Even if he wasn't famous, he was what most women consider 'Hot'. Why would Mason Reeves risk everything for a twenty-year-old head case? Could he have fallen in love with her? Stranger things have happened.

Finally, he leaned forward. "Talk to me about the photos. Our experts have looked at them. They are not photoshopped. What happened that night? Be honest with me."

Ace sighed. "It's not what you think, detective. I was in the studio with the guys from Demon Dreams laying down tracks. The storm was getting bad outside, and the power kept flickering on and off. We decided to order pizza and wait out the storm and then finish recording once the storm passed by."

Detective Price nodded. "Okay. There were how many people there?"

Besides me and Robby, there was Tyce, Kin, Rip, Bo and Mike.

"So... there were six witnesses? How did the victim join you?"

"I had to piss. We were all there in the lounge, taking a break and horsing around," Ace continued. "It was late. We were already pretty sloshed. We were drinking beer and eating pizza. Tyce was shooting pool with Kin. It was about 2:30 in the morning. I had to piss, and Mike was camped out in the bathroom. So, I walked down to use the spare in Robby's office. He has a camera set up that shows him views of the parking lot connected to the monitor on his desk. I glanced at the monitor and there was Shae, standing outside in the pouring rain under the oak tree. I don't know why I did it. I guess I didn't want her to be alone out there in the middle of the night. It wasn't safe. My intention was to be kind to her. You've got to believe that."

Detective Price nodded again. He was making notes as he listened, and Mason hoped he believed him. He took a sip of water and continued. "I opened the door and called her over, asking her why she was outside in that weather. She said she missed the last bus home and didn't want to hang around the train station alone. Since it was Sunday bus, the buses wouldn't start running again until six thirty. That was still a few hours away. I felt sorry for her out there alone in the storm and was trying to help. I don't know why I did it, but I did. I took her to the back, where the guys were drinking."

He looked like he was thinking, so Price waited.

"Despite being wet, she wouldn't take off the hoodie. After a few failed attempts, the guys started playing around, trying to get her to relax. Tyce grabbed her cell phone and began taking pictures. It was harmless fun, really, but I can see how it could be misconstrued. She had stars in her eyes and she kind of scooted up close to me a few times, as all fans try to do, but I didn't lead her on. I swear to you, nothing untoward happened. Finally, they gave her camera back. That's when she surprised us and took that photo of her kissing me. I never intended to kiss her and had no intention of it ever happening again."

He raised his face to Detective Price and

peered directly into his eyes. "I made a terrible decision, for good reasons. But I swear I never hurt that little girl. She left as soon as the buses began running about a quarter after six. Robby watched her get on the bus at the corner. Then he came back, and we started recording again. We never gave it another thought."

The door opened, and another man entered. I'm Detective Tim Sansom. I work with Detective Price from the Threat Management Unit, on all homicide investigations. The report I take here will be made a part of your file. Once again, I need to inform you of your right to have an attorney present. That anything you say can and will be used against you."

Mason nodded. "Got it. No need for an attorney. I have nothing to hide."

"Okay. As long as you understand your rights. Do you have any questions? If not, we can begin." Tim hated it that Mason did not ask for an attorney. But he could not force anyone into taking advantage of the law.

"No. I'm fine for now."

"Good. My first question. Have you ever allowed another young woman into the studio?

"Yes. We have hired female backup singers in the past to work during recording sessions."

"Other than for a professional reason?"

"No."

"I have some photos. I would like you to look through them and see if any of them look familiar."

Mason leaned forward and looked at each image as the detective flipped them over. None of the women looked familiar. But he paid attention just in case. Once they reached the end of the stack, he shook his head. "No. None of them look like anyone I recall meeting."

"You're positive you have seen none of these women?

"100% never talked to or met any of them. I can't swear I've never seen one in passing. I have no memory of seeing any of them."

"How about taking someone to your home? Have you ever invited a woman there?"

"Yes. One. Her name is Misty. I met her at the Stardust Ballroom, and we hit it off. I wish I could tell you her last name, but she never told me. She disappeared while I was sleeping." He grinned. "I actually hunted for her. Went back to the Ballroom, but no one knew her. She did not know me by my stage name. She only knew me as Mason Reese. It was great knowing someone wanted me, not my musical persona."

Tim was startled when he mentioned Misty, because he had once asked Lois if she ever dated, and she had mentioned a mysterious man named Mason. Then he'd seen how she reacted when she saw the photos and put two and two together.

He made a note to check out this band, Demon Dreams. There was a lot of information the public didn't know about this case. Shae wasn't the only body they recovered on the property. None of the witnesses to the disappearance of the other women mentioned Mason Reese or anyone looking anything like him. It could be a coincidence that he picked that property to murder the young woman, or they could have the wrong man in custody. For now, they would continue with the investigation with the information they have.

He hated he couldn't tell Lois what he suspected about Mason Reese, aka Ace Rivers. Until he was certain the man was not guilty, it would remain his secret. Right now, it didn't look good for the charismatic singer, or for the future of Cats Grinning. But his gut told him there was a lot of information he needed to check out before they pressed for a hearing.

"Let's move forward to the last time anyone saw the deceased. I need to ask a few more questions. You say left on your tour the morning after the last contact was made with the deceased. What did you do in the twenty-four hours before you left? I woke Saturday morning and had breakfast at the diner on Ponce de Leon with Robby. Then we headed to the studio. We got there about ten that morning. We worked in the studio until three Saturday afternoon. Then Robby followed me down to Tyce's house. He wanted to borrow my car. He had a date and wanted to impress her. We sat at Tyce's for about an hour after we got there and then we started back home. Stopped at the Longhorn and ate. It was about five-thirty when we arrived, and it was about a quarter after seven when we left. You could pull the charge ticket and get the exact time. Then we headed north toward the house. But Robby wanted to play some pool, so we stopped at the Oyster bar and shot a few games. You can talk to Gene.

He was tending bar. It was close to eleven when we left, heading toward Robby's place in Buckhead. We watched a rerun of John Wick, the second one. By then it was after two, so we crashed. Got up at seven-thirty, showered and made it to the bus by nine. We pulled out about nine-thirty."

"So... you stayed at Robby's place Saturday night? Can anyone verify that besides Robby?"

"Sure. His wife, Karen, three kids and his mother-in-law, Diane. They all live there. I shared a room with his son, Alex. He's fourteen, before you ask, and has twin beds."

"What about the new man in the band.... Jo?" He looked down at his laptop. "Lajoi."

"Lajoi? What about him?"

"Would he be the type to hit on young fans?"

"Joi's in a relationship, but even if he was single, he's not the type to hit on young women. He'd gay."

"People can fool you. He may live two lives, one at home, and another secret one that no one knows about?"

"Naw. Even if he and Luke broke up, I can't see him ever hitting on any of the fans. He fought too hard to get out publicly; there was no way he would never be involved in a secret relationship... especially with a female."

"Let me make sure I have this right, you're saying he's...uh...gay?"

"A thousand percent homosexual. And happy with his boyfriend. They live together"

"What about the base player, Keith?"

"Keith had back surgery and didn't go on tour with us. Tyce has been filling in."

"Tyce is the one who borrowed your car?"

"Yes. Demon Dreams is not touring, so he had time to fill for Mikey."

"Okay, I appreciate you talking to me. Are you sure you do not want an attorney?

"I'm certain. But thanks for asking. Think of it this way. I want you to find the sonovabitch that killed Shae. I need my name cleared. Not live with the idea that a lawyer got me off. Cleared. Unless that happens, Cats Grinning is dead. Too many people's lives are riding on this to risk it."

A lot more than you know...

When Mason once again declined the offer of representation, Sansom nodded to Price, then gestured for the officer to take Mason back to his cell. The two men walked back toward the office area together, mentally going over what they had just learned.

Finally, Price turned and said, "You think what I'm thinking?"

"If you're thinking we got the wrong man. Yeah. The theory is dead on. I'm glad you caught that connection. But I don't think Mason is the killer. "

"If his story is enough to give us doubt, there's no way a jury will buy it. Either there's something we don't know, or the killer is still out there."

"I will dig into the other band. Their manager must have a listing of the shows they played. We can correlate the list with missing persons. You need to get the forensics team in on the car. It's still setting in the garage at the studio."

"You think someone might have a key that Mason doesn't know about?"

"That's my first guess. The question is... who?"

Chapter Twenty-Four

Misty stepped on the scale and frowned. She'd lost another pound. That was twelve pounds gone since this nightmare had started. Now that they had Mason in jail, maybe things would get back to normal. She was looking forward to her morning run. It was wonderful to relax and not be on constant alert for anything out of the ordinary. Happy to have her music back, she grabbed her cell phone, scrolled through her playlist, started a beat, and then shoved the device back into its sheath. At the bottom of the driveway, she'd had cement poured to make a flat surface. She pushed her ear buds in and began her warm-up portion of her run with some dynamic stretching. Today she concentrated on leg raises and worked in a few exercises to strengthen her core. Despite the weight loss, her tummy was pooched, most likely the result of too many croissants from Lois's leftovers these past few months. Once she was sufficiently warmed up, she hit the road. The sweet aroma of manicured grass filled the morning air as she jogged down the main path from the house. Years earlier, the state had intended to build a highway connector from I-75 to I-285 through Dekalb County. They used eminent domain laws to conscript the property and destroy all the buildings. Then the state changed their mind. The city of Atlanta had had bought the property and turned it into green space, called Freedom Park. Eventually, Jimmy Carter had built his Presidential Library there. She followed the winding trails, starting out slowly to stretch her calves before heading for her turnaround destination, the children's playground in Chandler Park.

Foot traffic was sparse at this hour of the morning, and she saw no one along her route except for a woman walking her dogs. She exchanged a jaunty wave with her as she passed the two massive rottweilers. The park was about two miles away, a decent jog in her current condition. She struggled to believe she'd allowed herself to get this far out of shape. As if to reinforce that mental rebuke, she was winded and cramping when she reached her turnaround point. Sitting on top of a concrete table to rest, she placed her feet on the bench seat and took a swig from her water bottle. It was working. She was feeling calmer. Her pulse had steadied, and her breathing came in short bursts. After her usual ten minutes, she began walking through the picnic tables and barbecue grills to warm up before heading toward the side paths in the back that circled back to the main running trail.

Misty tried to ignore the random thoughts about Shae racing around in her head, but they came flooding in. The police felt they had a straightforward case against Mason for Shae's murder, but she still had her doubts. She was certain her stalker was connected in some manner. The man she had seen so many times was shorter than Mason, and at least thirty pounds lighter. Mason was more muscular and looked healthy. Her stalker had grungy light blonde hair and was ghostly pale. Like he was ill...or an addict.

She began jogging along the trail that led back to the main path. She had just begun the section that passed between the tall pampas grass banks when she caught a flash of movement from the corner of her eye. Then she felt a blow from something hard. Pain exploded in the back of her head. Her hands seemed to move in slow motion as stretched them in front of her to stop her forward fall, before hitting the ground face first. She vaguely noticed a loud, high-pitched tone that sounded similar to the one emitted in a hearing test. There was the sound of approaching footsteps, then they stopped. She forced herself to lie still as his hands touched her body, removing her fanny pack and cell phone. Finally, he moved away. She lay crumpled on the ground and watched as the dark shape ran away from her until he disappeared into the distance. Then she closed her eyes and fell into the darkness.

***

Sounds came out of the darkness. Squeaky wheels in the distance. Hushed voices. A monotonous beep... beep... beep... She slowly opened her eyes, blinking as her eyes adjusted to the bright fluorescent light around her. Where was she? There was a funny smell, like antiseptic, which told her she wasn't at the park anymore, or even at home. She turned her head, noticing there was someone asleep in a leather pull-out sleeper chair. Then she saw the paintings on the blue and gray walls. A large picture window allowed in the late afternoon sun. A television near the ceiling flashed images of The Weather Channel, but someone had the sound turned off.

She moved her hand, searching for a controller, and felt a pinch. It was from an IV taped to her wrist. Her eyes traced along the tube attached via the needle in her vein to a stack of equipment just behind her. Digital numbers displayed on the machines that clicked and dinged in a repeated rhythm. Two clear bags hung from a polished pole next to the bed. Fluids dripped through the tubing into her body.

Okay. It's a hospital. She tried to sit up, but each movement sent a wave of dizziness washing over her. There was a loose, bulky wrap around her head, some type of bandages. Moving her head even the smallest amount, sent microscopic knives stabbing at the back of her skull. Something stiff was preventing her from turning her head; most likely, a cervical collar encased her neck. She reached for her cup, and missed, but the movement alerted the sleeper she was awake. Her hand looked pale against the blue hospital gown, but Lois's grasp was reassuring and made her feel safe.

"Welcome back. You scared the shit out

of me." Lois wasn't bothering to hide the aggravation in her voice. For a moment, Misty thought the terrible strain on her face meant she was angry with her, but then she saw the pain in her eyes and realized Lois was afraid.

"What happened? Ohhhh—" She tried to sit up again, but the pain pushed her back onto the pillows.

Lois gently pressed her head back down. "Don't move." Her voice sounded tense. "You got banged up. He obviously wanted you dead... Just relax. Don't give him the win."

Her statement triggered fleeting images that began flashing like a slide show into her memory—jogging along the trail near home, the woman with the dogs, the park, then nothing. She reached up again to touch her head, but the bandages were too thick. "What happened?"

"Someone attacked you. You're in hospital. Been out for hours."

"The hospital? How?"

"You were found in the park. If people hadn't noticed you lying there alone on the ground—" She stopped short, overcome with emotion. "They aren't sure how long you lay there bleeding before someone called for an ambulance."

"What time is it?"

"After seven. The sun just went down."

"I looked at my phone around 7:30 this morning. Then I started back toward the house. That's all I remember."

"Damn, you must have laid there longer than we thought. You didn't get to the hospital until almost three.

Lois glanced toward the door as the sound of squeaky sneakers against the hospital floor tiles approached. A dusky, middle-aged doctor entered the room. He was wearing a white coat with his name stitched above his pocket in a blue script. A stethoscope hung around his neck, with the end coiled up in his pocket. He greeted them both and extended his hand to Lois.

"I'm Dr. Obaigbo. I'm the neurologist in charge of Misty's care."

He looked down at Misty. "So, how's my patient?" he asked, sitting down on the bed.

"I've had better days," Misty said. "How bad is it?"

"Oh, there are worse hospitals in this state to die in. I like to think we're not that bad compared to most of them."

Misty smiled. "Nothing like a doctor with

a sense of humor."

"Part of the job description," he replied with a grin. He began a cursory examination, first checking the constriction of her pupils with a penlight. "So, how do you feel?" he asked while he worked.

"My head is pounding, I hear a high-pitched noise and the light as too bright," she said. "I don't remember coming here. Is this the first time you have been in?"

"That's a good question. It looks like you mind is active. You got a nasty wallop. The blow left you with a hairline fracture at the back of your skull, according to the X-ray." Dr. Obaigbo held up two fingers. "How many do you see?"

"Two."

"Good." He then ran a feather along her face, the insides of her arms, and the soles of her feet. "Feel that?"

Misty's foot jerked. "Yes. It tickles."

"Excellent." Then he touched a sewing needle to her arms and thighs, ensuring she still had sensation to light touch and pin-prick. "Everything's good so far." Carefully, he adjusted the bed to a sitting position, then eased her back against the pillows.

After a few more bedside examinations,

he removed his stethoscope from his ears, letting it rest around his neck. "Well, objectively, you are doing better than when you first came in. Your CT scan was normal except for a small hairline fracture above the C1, which is the first vertebra in your neck and the one on the back of your skull. I don't see any neurologic deficits. You will be here a few days while we monitor your symptoms. That way, we can address any changes to your condition. Do you remember what happened?"

Misty closed her eyes and tried to remember what happened. She could only remember bits and pieces. "I remember going running and stopping to rest when I got to the park. I remember starting the return leg. Then nothing. I must have fallen."

The doctor shook his head. "This was no fall. A fall wouldn't have caused the blunt trauma you sustained."

"But ... I was alone? It had to be an accident."

"It appears you were struck in the back of the head with something. Something heavy, like a tire iron or a metal pipe. It's a good thing whoever did this didn't watch a lot of television. If he did, he would have known where the brain stem is at the back of the head. That's the part of the brain that signals your body's autonomic functions, like breathing. A hit there is deadly, but it usually takes over one blow to get thru the thicker portion of the skull. There were two blows. One hit the C1 of your spine, so you have two fractures."

Lois's eyes darkened. "I fuckin' well knew it. This was not an accident!"

The doctor grinned. "That may be true, but I can only address what I know. I see evidence of a blow with the blunt end of a heavy instrument. Nothing I see indicates a hard fall. You didn't even sprain your wrist."

He laid his hand on Misty's. "You're stable and getting stronger," he said. "You lost some blood from that blow to the head, but a hairline fracture of this type usually heals on its own. Given time, I think you will recover fully."

"Well, that's good news," Tim said as he entered the room. "Glad to see you are back with us."

"Evening, detective. We're getting some blood work to see if there are any electrolyte abnormalities, a routine procedure. The imaging studies so far are negative. I think if all goes well, she can be released the day after tomorrow. But she will need to remain in bed for at least two weeks."

Misty stared at him as if he'd grown a second head. "Two weeks?" She groaned. "Roger can't handle me being gone for two weeks. I can get no work done staying home!"

"Your body needs time to heal, and the brain has to recover," Dr. Obaigbo admonished her. "You'll be discharged with a cervical collar to keep your neck immobilized as much as possible. No heavy lifting, no strenuous activity. I'll give you a prescription for any residual pain."

"I'll take good care of her," Lois said. "If she doesn't listen, I will handcuff her to the bed."

"But the cafe—" Misty began.

"The café can handle me not being there. I subbed out the Thomas's wedding to Tamika Taylor. She'll do a great job."

Misty closed her eyes. "I hate that you did that," she moaned. "You need to get back to your business."

"And leave you alone? Not a chance," Lois said. "I'll be here with you. Every morning when you wake up and every night before you go to sleep, my voice will be the sound you hear. All you need to think about is getting better."

She smiled weakly. "I guess I'm not in a position to argue, am I?"

"No, and I intend to keep it that way."

Dr. Obaigbo smiled. He rose from the bed. "The detective is waiting to question you. Do you feel up to talking to him?"

"Sure," Misty said. "Lois will clobber him if he makes my head hurt."

"I bet she would," he said as he was leaving. "Don't let yourself get too tired. Rest and let your body recover."

Tim left and returned with two police officers. One of them was Detective Price. The other was a stranger, and he was in uniform.

"How are you feeling, Misty?"

"Feeling better." She answered Detective Price with a weak smile.

"Are you responding well to treatment?"

She shrugged, "So far, so good."

The detective nodded and collected a notepad from the other officer, who stood back, looking around the room.

"Do you think you can tell us what happened?"

"I don't know," Misty said. "I was running on the trail, and then—I'm here."

"Not sure about your timing," Lois said, her voice showing her annoyance. "Must you do this now?"

"It's okay, Lolo," Misty whispered weakly.

Detective Price addressed her. "It's important. From our investigation so far, this appears to be an intentional act. We have a witness who was in the park and saw someone come up behind her, hit her with some type of weapon, then escape into the tree line along the trail."

"Then why did it take until three that afternoon to report it?"

"He was on his way to school. The witness is twelve."

"Damn. I feel bad now. Did he see enough to identify him?"

"No, but we have a general description. The suspect had on a hoodie with a mask to cover his face. He ran into the tree line and disappeared."

"We don't have all the facts yet, but we have a person of interest in this case."

"I thought Mason was in jail, "Misty asked.

"He is," Price responded. "Mr. Reese is not a suspect in this incident."

"Then who hit me?"

"There are two possibilities. One is a mugger hit you. Your waist bag was taken. The other is our suspect. He might have taken the bag to make it look like a random mugging with robbery." Price looked at Tim and Tim shook his head no. Lois wondered what that meant and intended to unravel the mystery. As soon as she got Tim alone."

"For now, we are just investigating all possibilities." Price's voice softened. "Truth be told, we have a person at the top of our suspect list, but we are still gathering enough evidence to charge him with a crime. Try to rest. We will let you know if anything changes."

After he left, they were alone. The officer remained.

Lois gave Tim a long, searching look.

"Is there something you're not telling us?"

"Yes."

Lois arched an eyebrow. "Come on now. You can't keep secrets like that."

Tim sighed. "I can and I will. Not that I like it, it's necessary."

"Necessary? Hmmm. Necessary like the man sitting by the door you have not introduced?"

"Yep." He crossed his arms over his chest and looked her in the eyes.

Lois nodded, trying to ignore the angry tears forming in her eyes. He leaned over her and pressed his lips to hers. It was a comforting kiss, but it did not answer the question. She knew it would upset Misty if she continued to ask questions. She walked back to the chair beside the bed and sat down. "Try not to worry, okay? You're safe now. I'm here with you."

Tim sighed. "I have to go back to work. Officer Daniels will be right outside the room. If I get a chance, I'll come back and take you to late dinner. In the meantime, try to get Misty to rest."

Lois cut her eyes his way, but she didn't comment as he left. She just squeezed Misty's hand.

***

The meeting was already in progress when Tim arrived at the station. Detective Price was going over the upcoming operation with the team Tim had selected. None of the officers were married or over thirty. Several had been borrowed from Vice and the Drug Task Force, especially for their ability to look nothing like a police officer. It was important that they could blend in with the crowd at the show. All it would take is one slip up and they could lose any chance of identifying the killer. That meant an innocent man might spend the rest of his life in jail.

"One thing we have never addressed before today was how he was moving the body. The assumption was that the killer was using a van or truck. History has shown that the only way to pull off a successful kidnapping and subsequent murder was with an enclosed vehicle to transport the body. We've been trying to locate the vehicle. Now we think we are wrong. We think he could be a roadie or a member of the band."

"Wouldn't someone notice a stranger on a crowded bus?"

"Not necessarily. Women come and go all the time when a band is touring. Some last an hour, others to the next stop on the tour. And don't assume that someone in a relationship is not the killer. Although, I'd being willing to say that Lajoi is most likely not our man. He's gay and in a long-term relationship. Very few active homosexual men voluntarily seek a woman for sex."

"What about the roadies? Fans don't usually go for the hired help."

"And that could be the trigger. Rejection is one of the prime motivators in sexual abduction. And an equipment case could easily hold a human."

"It's possible. Those boxes are pretty big. Some of those speakers weigh a quarter ton or more. And they have to move them, so they have access to vans or trucks."

Price passed out a stack of printed sheets. "These are images of our primary suspects. We want to connect one of them to the missing women. We are also moving forward with an undercover sting attempt."

"Are you sure setting up a sting of this type will work?"

"No. It's a long shot, but the only one we have. We have our suspect. Now we need proof." His eyes went to the female officer setting at the right side of the table. She was definitely attractive enough to tempt any straight man. What was even better, she bore an amazing resemblance to Misty. Not identical, but they could be sisters.

One of the younger undercover officers laughed. "At least you're using the right bait. Hell, If I was a killer, I'd go for her."

Officer Nelson winked at him, and he

blushed.

"Donna is one of our best vice detectives. With her baby face and petite frame, she looks like an older teenager or college coed. His targets all seem to be pretty, but socially awkward. So far as we can tell, all of his victims have been between 17 and twenty-two."

"Older than the age of consent, but still young enough to fall for his pickup lines." One of the swat team slapped the man on his back as three others laughed.

Sansom made a mental note to find out what was so funny. "He may not need a line. Fangirls flock to concerts, hoping to catch the attention of their musical idol. They may pick him up."

"I can't believe he took one inside his home territory. That doesn't fit the usual pattern."

"She obviously did something to draw his attention. It could be she flirted with him, or even that she rejected him." He glanced at the info sheet, made a notation, and then added, "He may not have considered the studio his home territory. There's a lot of traffic in and out of the studio when they are recording. Some are regulars, others come one day and leave. Sometimes they have cattle calls to find backup singers and there could be a thousand applicants."

"Donna, do you have any idea how you plan to approach the suspect?" Price asked.

"The band is playing at the Sleeping Lizard, so getting noticed won't be a problem. Cutting him away from the others might be. Theres always a crowd of college age groupies hanging around the club."

The only other female on the team looked up at her comment. "So... do you go in by yourself?"

"One of the undercover officers who works DTF hangs out there. He will be there before I arrive. No one will pay him any attention. He's there enough that he's considered a regular. And even if I'm alone in the bar, I have backup. My shoes are tagged, and so are my earrings. Several of the bodies were found with earrings intact, so he hasn't bothered removing them in the past. That's means he's not as careful as he seems to be."

Detective Price nodded. "We will send Ariel in with one of the team. Franky looks like he would fit in. You can go in early and sit somewhere off to the side. Watch the first two bands play, so no one will pay any attention to you being there. You will maintain cover unless someone signals a problem."

Price glanced at a paper on the podium. "We will also have two unmarked cars set up with trackers parked nearby. If he takes the bait, we will make sure she is covered at all times." He paused and looked through the stack of printed photos, then pulled one out and placed it on top of the stack. "Everyone, make sure you are familiar with the men in both bands and all their road crew members. We want to tag the vehicles they may be driving. It might not be their usual transportation. We may only get one shot at this, so everyone needs to be well rested and ready tomorrow night."

Tim waited until everyone had cleared the room, then he approached Price. "Sorry I was late Ben. Got caught in traffic leaving the hospital."

Ben gave him a weak shrug. "I knew something had come up. How's she doing?"

"The doctors say she should be able to go home in a couple of days. But he ordered her to stay in bed two more weeks after that."

"I bet she hates that."

"You have no idea. It would be easier to paint an ostrich's toenails than trying to keep that woman in bed."

"Paint an ostrich's toenails? That's what I love about working with you. I never what's gonna come out of your mouth."

"I am unique. See ya tomorrow." Tim picked up his stack of printouts and headed for the door, ready for his dinner with Lois. The invitation had popped out before he realized it might step across a few fine lines, then decided he was being paranoid. There was nothing in the books about dating a friend of a victim.

Chapter Twenty-Five

Bo pulled on the green hospital scrubs he'd pulled out of the laundry cart in the basement of the main tower, pulled his hair back with elastic ties, and shoved it up under a scrub cap. Then he strolled casually along the passageway in front of the room Misty was occupying. He had already checked out the hospital security system, verifying there was only one guard on duty by each entrance door. A friendly clerk had verified there were actually six men, one for each entrance and one that floated around each of the twin towers. They had two monitor rooms, but the man in the front building had left on a break earlier. He did not know where the other monitor room was, but believed it was in the second tower of the hospital. Chances are the systems did not overlap, but he could not risk what might happen if he was wrong.

The friendly employee had forgotten to mention the APD officer stationed outside her room. There was no way he could get past a guard assigned to keep Misty safe. He would need to come up with a different plan.

Bo was working his way back down the hall toward the staff elevator when he heard the distinctive sound of boots approaching. He quickly changed his plans. Spotting a small offset with a couple of vending machines and an ice dispenser, he stepped up to the farthest one, dug through his pockets and prepared to drop a coin. He offered a brief thanks to heaven and the girl at the station who had to give him a couple of dollars in change because she had run out of ones. In the green scrubs and cap, he looked like any of a hundred employees wandering around the building. With any luck, the approaching officer wouldn't notice him.

Luck was a fickle bitch.

Daniels stopped beside the alcove and watched as Bo pulled two drinks from the machine, and then he walked over to talk to him. Shit.

"Hey man," he asked, "You got change for a dollar?" Bo noticed the bill in his hand.

"Yeah, he said, I think so. "He pulled a hand full of change out, counted out four quarters and pocketed the bill with what was left of his change.

"Thanks, bro. The machines won't take bills, and I didn't bring enough coins."

"No problem." Bo nodded and then walked down the hall in the opposite direction from the room. When he reached the corner, he ducked out of sight and waited until he'd ensured the man had returned to his post before taking the staircase down.

When he reached the ground floor, he left the hospital and walked directly to a second man waiting in a blue ford pickup nearby.

"They have a cop stationed outside the room."

"Thanks," the man said, snatching one of the cold cokes from his hand, popped the top and chugged half the can.

Bo waited until he tipped his head back for another swig and tipped the can up, spilling the sweet, sticky soft drink over his face.

"Quit fucking around," his cousin snapped." Sometimes I wonder how the fuck you survived childhood." He cranked the truck and pulled away. "The pig got a good look at you. He won't know you, but he will remember you if he sees you again. We need to go now. There's no way to know how long they will keep a guard on her. Our reunion will have to wait."

Bo nodded. He did not know why his cousin was so crazy about this woman. He was always showing up with a new woman, even though he never kept them around long. She wouldn't put up with that and would make his life hell. But he'd been following this one for months, like a lovesick puppy.

"We need to get back to the warehouse. The band is playing tonight, and Rip is still pissed about Tyce filling in with Cats Grinning. I don't blame him. He makes more fucking money is three months than I make in three years playing the dives Demon Dreams has booked."

"Where are you guys playing tonight?"

"The Sleeping Lizard. You can come, its 18 and older, but as long as you come in with the band, no one will ask for ID."

"Cool. Theres always a lot of drunk chicks hanging out there. I might get lucky again."

Chapter Twenty-Six

The sacred back room, or the "entertainer's lounge" as it was jokingly called, had a metal door separating it from the rest of the venue. The back room had several uses, depending on the band. Many lead singers claimed it as their own private haven, while most bands used it as a staging area for their equipment. Other bands used it as a safe place to smoke a joint or do lines of coke before and after a show. Since the bar didn't monitor the back room, it was left to the musician's discretion.

Donna had shown up around an hour before Demon Dreams was scheduled to take the stage. Just as everyone expected, she stood out in a room full of college age partiers. Besides being a walking, talking barbie doll, she knew how to play the vapid fangirl so well, every half-assed musician in the building was drooling. She had time to talk to every member of the band at least once and several, including her primary target, at least twice.

The electricity in the room grew as the show began. All the lights went out, and the musicians bounded up to the stage in the darkness over the rising noise of the crowd. The drummer kicked off a hypnotic beat. There was a long, drawn-out squeal from a guitar. Then the stage lights flashed on.

The lead guitarist stood in front, his hands wrapped around his guitar, while the rest of the band stood in their places behind him. They kicked the show into high gear with "Ivory Tower," the album's raw and punchy title track, while the crowd yelled, and fist pumped with hundreds of heads bobbing up and down in unison.

From their Ivory towers
They look down below
Never been on the streets
What the hell would you know?

Rip's rhythm guitar and Tyce's thumping bass kept time with Kin's pounding on the drums. The Reverend teased the crowd up front with antics that made the girls shriek while he showed off his energy and musical proficiency throughout the set. He loved playing up to them like that. He once told Mason how the vibe from all that unadulterated adoration from his fans gave him a powerful connection to them. It was obvious to Donna that they loved it as much as he did.

"Are we having fun yet, Atlanta?" Rip called out to them.

The crowd roared their approval.

"It's great to be back home. Let's burn the buildings down!" Rip fingered his vintage Fender Strat with a raw squeal, launching into their next song, Acid Disaster. It highlighted Kin's talent as a drummer, with a hypnotic beat that brought to mind the old Tarzan movies.

The Right Reverend played a solid set of new tracks and pumping fan favorites that kept them singing along and moving in an undulating wave of heads and arms to the funky beats. For some songs, he would slip out of his guitar strap, setting the instrument down against one of the amplifiers. Grabbing a microphone, he would start singing while Rip played lead on a pearl white Les Paul. The bar would get quiet as he crooned out a ballad to the women along the edge of the stage. A wave of murmurs would intensify as he flashed a wry smile down to the audience who lined the front. He had to step back to avoid the hands reaching out to him. Rev couldn't distinguish one face from another as bright stage lights blinded him from seeing anything past the edge of the stage, but they didn't seem to care. The screaming women were a boost to his ego. They wanted him; to be near him. They wanted to be the one who held his arm when he left the stage and headed home. He enjoyed teasing them, lightly caressing the sea of outstretched fingers before returning to the middle of the stage.

In between a series of songs, Tyce would walk back and forth on the stage and chat with the crowd as if he were hanging out with friends at the pub, even answering back to them if he heard someone call out to him. At one point, The Reverend slowed down things and played an acoustic set of covers of some of his favorite artists—Fall Out Boy, Green Day and Nickelback.

Donna kept her eyes on The Reverend. She enjoyed listening to his sultry voice. Captivating and sexy, it could fill even the hollowest of hearts with an intense desire to be close to him that could take your common sense away and sent the girls in the crowd into spin screaming fits. It was too bad he wasn't the target. She might have enjoyed getting to know him.

The band always played one song, "Tomorrow is Too Far Gone," for Bryce. Tyce had written it when he was in a dark place over his twins' death. Tyce used it to openly share with his audience the hopelessness and pain he'd felt when he lost his brother. The stark lyrics talked about dying and drew attention to how much Bryce's death still affected him. He was surprised the message seemed to strike a chord with the critics as well, since it was acclaimed as one of the best tracks on their last album.

"Music kept us sane," he told his fans. "Bryce loved life and did his best to live it to the fullest. I can't explain the bond between twins, but part of him is in me and will not die until I do." Without fail, hundreds of lights from cell phones and lighters glowed in the dark room, making it seem like a sky full of stars. People rose to sway in unison as a heartfelt tribute to his twin. The fans still felt connected to Bryce, even though Kin was doing a great job on drums.

Rev wrapped up the set with a few songs off the first album, ending the show to a roar of screams and cheers. Then the band took their bows and said goodbye with raised fists and blown kisses before stepping off the stage.

Roadies went to work taking the band's equipment down, while the next band's crew was unloading equipment and setting it up for the late show. Donna waited outside, mingling with the other fans. After a show was a time when the band would come down from the high-charged energy of a show and clean up to socialize or pack up to travel to the next show.

The band runner took advantage of the free time to pass out a few backstage passes. Donna smiled and accepted hers when it was offered. The scene backstage was exactly what she expected to see. One young girl, maybe eighteen, but she wouldn't stake any money on it, was sitting on the drummer's lap while his hand clutched her generous buttocks under her mini skirt. Another one in a black stretch-dress and stilettos was pinned against the stage scaffolding, sucking face long and hard with The Reverend. 'Pass-around packs,' Tyce called them as he walked over to hand her a cup with what tasted like jack and coke. Although the band was used to the groupies who lingered around the backstage area or the hung by the door to "introduce" themselves at every show, Tyce didn't often take them up on their offer to hang out with the band all night.

At least she hoped he didn't. Their plan revolved around him wanting a higher class offering than the usual fangirl who care less who she fucked, as long as they were with the band.

Nodding and waving to the various people lingering behind the stage who applauded them as they passed, the band moved through the dim light to the lounge to change and clean up while the crew packed the equipment in the vans.

Though many bands left a venue right after a show, Demon Dreams was a local band and loved doing meet and greets and preferred doing them inside the bar, which would allow for a quick exit when it was over. Event security was used to it and paid little attention when the band came out to meet fans who would linger after a show whenever they could. Whether the show was organized by the promoter or not, the diehards showed up every time. Some fans were bedazzled children, who watched but were too shy to say anything to the band members.

They would stand to the side and giggle like children behind their parents. Others were hardcore fangirls, their faces aged by heavy makeup, looking to hook up with anyone they could in order to spend more time near the band. Some were longtime followers who appreciated the DD's music and wanted to comment on the show. The Reverend loved talking with every person who approached him until the fans were gone, or until the venue security staff kicked them all out so the next show could begin.

Tyce glanced over at Donna, where she stood with a group of people, sipping a can of Coke. She raised an eyebrow. He grinned and winked at her, communicating silently that he was eager for the event to be over so they could talk and get to know each other. She smiled back. He still wore his dark eyeliner, making his eyes look even more striking and, to Donna, hot as hell. He did not come off as a killer. She usually had a sixth sense about men, and he didn't raise any red flags. Another woman stepped in front of him, forcing him to turn back to the fans.

Soon the last band was preparing to take the stage and Demon Dreams after show activity was winding down. The road crew had finished taking down the equipment and was scooping up all the leftover food and liquor to load into the vans before they departed.

Suddenly, Donna heard a voice calling Tyce's name. The girl must have stayed in the shadows until the end, hidden among the crowd until the line dwindled, then appeared out of nowhere to get time with Tyce.

"Tyce!" she called to him. She strode forward, keeping her eyes on Donna.

"Tyce!" she called again. She was close now, and it was clear she was pregnant. Very pregnant.

Tyce turned around to see her only a few feet away. She dropped the soft drink can she was holding and made a beeline toward him.

"Mel? I thought you were in jail." Donna heard Tyce talking to the young woman.

"My mom bailed me out," she said. "I heard you were intown and needed to see you."

"You shouldn't be here in your condition." Tyce gave her a stern glare. "There's a restraining order for you to stay away from me. You're already in trouble with the police. Leave now before they arrive. You'll just make everything worse for yourself!"

"Fuck the police. I'm in labor with your

baby. You need to be there for the birth of your son."

People were gathering around as they heard the disturbance. The rest of the band edged closer to them. Cell phones rose out of nowhere, taking video of what was happening.

Damn phones, Donna cursed to herself. She looked around anxiously, but no one was paying her any attention. She doubted there was any way she could save this sting.

"That's not my baby. We have never fucked. You need to get going before the cops come and take you away!" he replied sharply.

Donna took a chance and tugged at his arm. "Come on, Tyce, let's go grab some breakfast. Don't engage her, it will only make it worse.

"Okay, Tyce, I'll leave," Melinda said, her tone becoming dangerously calm. Her ice-cold eyes danced back and forth between him and Donna. "But first I have something for you."

"Whatever it is, take the fuckin' thing back. I don't want it."

"Oh, you'll love this, Tyce."

She reached into her pocket. Panic welled in Donna's throat, and her intuition kicked in too late. A flash of silver suddenly appeared before her as Melinda let out a primal yell and fired, the bullet hitting Tyce in the stomach.

Tyce let out a cry as he staggered back against the van. People began running. A few muted screams filled the air as Donna watched the scene unfold like a slow-motion cartoon.

Yelling and screaming incoherently, Melinda kicked and fought against the security guard's hold on her. She sent a vicious kick to his shin as he wrenched the small pistol out of her hand.

The guard screamed in pain, "Don't you fuckin' move!"

He grabbed her right arm and pulled it behind her back, then the left. The click of the handcuffs around her wrists was loud in the silence of the few remaining witnesses. Her eyes darted around, her face contorted like an angry animal, but whether from the tight handcuffs or the contractions, no one knew.

She kicked the guard again. The guard yelled out but held on to her. Donna watched him drag her away while she struggled in his hold, thrashing and screaming. She heard the sirens of police cars in the distance.

Donna grabbed Tyce by the arm and pulled him toward the bar. Rip saw what she was doing and pushed Tyce up the steps ahead of him. Then pulled the door shut behind them. Tyce collapsed onto the couch, his shirt wet with blood. His tense expression reflected his pain. He began to shake, and his breathing grew strained and ragged.

Donna sat down next to him. "Lie back. My God, someone hand me a towel!"

"I'm okay," he mumbled. He took a deep breath, then leaned back, closing his eyes. Blood trickled in rivulets from the wounds on his lower belly.

"We wanted headlines, but not this kind," Rip joked, but his voice trembled.

"Rip, this isn't funny," Kin said. "He could have been killed out there!"

"It'll be all right," Rip said, his voice weary. "Just tell them to get the fucking ambulance here."

Tears ran down Donna's cheeks as she surveyed his wound. "We have to get you to a hospital. You could be seriously hurt!"

Tyce struggled to sit up. "No." he said firmly. "Really, it's not that bad. I hate hospitals and we don't need any adverse publicity."

There was a siren growing closer and louder. Then it went silent. Seconds later, the door flew open, and paramedics rushed into the room. They urged everyone out of the immediate area.

"Can't you patch me up here?" Tyce asked as they prepared the gurney to take him out.

"Fuckin' that! They are taking you to get that bullet out!" Kin exclaimed as the medics rolled the stretcher toward the waiting ambulance. He was mad they wouldn't let anyone ride to the hospital. Everyone was milling around the room, so he said, "Fuck it" and pulled a beer out of the refrigerator. Then he sat down in one of the captain's chairs. "Man, that was a close call!"

"Too close." He looked at Donna. "Sorry we can't get to that breakfast. But ...." He shrugged and followed the paramedics.

Donna sighed and reached for her cup.

"Here. Let me get a fresh one for you." Kin took her cup and walked to the cooler. He pulled out a coke, popped the top and poured about half into the cup. He passed it to Donna and then he finished the rest. "The last band is packing up. You might as well sit here until the crowd thins out."

"You're right. Theres no way I'm fighting that traffic." She took another drink and sat back against the sofa. Kin wasn't on her target list, but there was no way Tyce was kidnapping anyone. They sat there in silence, sipping their drinks while the last band did the backstage routine. They were almost ready to leave when Kin looked at her with a smirky grin.

"I'm looking forward to this. I need to grab a few things before we go." Kin asked.

Go? Donna stood up and swayed. Sonovabitch. He drugged the coke...

Chapter Twenty-Six

Misty thrashed around on the bed, struggling in her sleep. She could hear Shae's voice screaming at her. You're not looking! He's right there. The words floated throughout her skull, repeating it over and over. Then she saw a shadowy figure. It was her, lying on a bed. There was a shadowy figure beside her. Then it moved. She felt weight on top of her, reaching for her. She tried to pull away, to get the crushing weight off of her, but the hands clutched her shirt, then wrapped around her neck. "No, please!" she heard herself screaming, but her voice just was too soft, getting fainter and fainter as the distant noise of people talking, scuffling feet, and muffled cries drowned her out. She called out for help, but no sound emerged from her throat.

"Misty!"

Someone was calling her in the distance. Her arms flailed in the darkness while fingers tightened around her throat. She tried to get away, but something was holding her in place.

"Help!" she cried out in the darkness, clawing at the hand that gripped her arm, keeping her still.

"Misty!" the voice called to her again, closer now.

The picture changed. An obviously dead Shae standing was in front of her, bloody knife in hand. Misty fought back against the knife that plunged into her chest, over and over. It was getting hard for her to breathe. Somehow, she knew if she knew if she stopped fighting, she would die.

Fighting, fighting, fighting...

She writhed in the grip of a grasping hand.

"Misty!" She heard a man's voice, then a feeling of being shaken. Gasping, she opened her eyes with a jerk. She looked into Tim's concerned eyes as he stared back at her.

"Misty, wake up! You were having a nightmare."

Tim? Lois? A nightmare? It felt so real.

"It was Shae," she said, her throat dry and raspy. Her breathing was heavy. "She was trying to tell me something, to look again. But when I didn't look, she got mad and began stabbing me. I couldn't breathe—"

The gauze on his shoulder made a wrinkling sound as Lois reached over to stroke her face with smooth fingers. "Don't worry. It was just a nightmare."

She lay still, gathering her wits. "No. My grandmother always said listen to your dreams." She looked up at them. "This one was so real. I need to take another look at something. There's something I missed."

"Look at what?" Lois asked.

"I'm not sure. Something I looked at lately. Do you still have those pictures you showed me of Shae and Mason?"

"Not the originals, but I have printed copies."

He opened his briefcase and pulled out a file. It only took a moment to shuffle through the images and pull out the three she had seen.

Misty look at the pictures. All three showed Shae and Mason. There was nothing else in the photo. Then she noticed a man's legs in the corner of one image. He was sitting in a chair, but all you could see is from his knees down.

"Look. I didn't see this before. Theres someone in the chair in the corner. That's got to be what my mind saw and wanted me to see. Are there any more photos? Ones that may not show Mason?"

Several. Tim began flipping over the stack of printed photos. The first ten got no reaction from Misty. But the eleventh photo made her gasp.

"Oh. God. It's him. That's my stalker. "

"This guy?" He looked at the identification on the back. "Kindrick Rogers. Does that sound familiar?""

"No. I never heard his name. But he's the man who followed me. The one who broke into my house. I bet he's the one who tried to kill me."

"Well, he's the drummer with Demon Dreams. And the only married member of the group."

"He's also a crazy stalker. You need to tell them who to watch."

"Your right. I'll call Price right now."

Lois reached around and gave him a hug. "Thanks for understanding," she said, snuggling closer to him. She nuzzled into his neck, responding both to his soothing touch and the concern in his dark eyes. She sighed. "This wasn't how we were supposed to be spending your night off.

"Its fine. I'm with you. The call won't take

but a minute." He dialed Ben's number but got his voice mail. "Ben. Got some new information. The man who's been stalking Misty is Kindrick Rogers. Not Tyce. You may have the wrong target." He heard the second beep and sighed. The recorder was full. He circled his arms around Lois, pulling her close, spooning her back against his muscular chest. It was like heaven holding her next to him. They wrapped their arms around each other and shared a sense of rightness, of being where they belonged, of being together. He kissed her neck and buried his nose in the silk of her hair before turning and picking up the photo, then walking toward the door.

"Where are you going" Lois asked.

"Gonna go talk to the officer on duty. Be right back." He walked up the hall to the nursing station where Gene, the officer on duty, was eating a sandwich and talking to a nurse.

"Hey Gene, I need you to look at some photos. People of interest. Just in case one comes by." Tim handed him the stack of printouts.

He stopped on second photo. "Too late. This guy's already been here." He pointed at Bo; one of the roadies.

"You sure it was him?"

"One hundred percent solid. He was wearing hospital scrubs. I saw him over by the soda machines. He gave me change for a dollar."

"He's cocky for a teenager. But something tells me it wasn't his idea. My note says he's the drummer's cousin. Our killer thinks he's smarter than then we are. I doubt he would risk sending him back, but you never can tell."

"Yeah. I clocked him right away. This is not a surgical floor. He didn't appear interested in anything but grabbing a drink. He went toward the opposite end of the hall and turned right. Then came back a minute later and ducked down the stairs. It's in my report."

Tim nodded. "I appreciate you taking this shift. Make sure whoever relieves you knows about him and his cousin. One of them may try to get in tonight by claiming to be her doctor."

"Yeah. I met his doctor earlier. There's no way anyone could mistake a slender, white, male, for a heavyset, black, balding male, mid-forties. I will make sure he knows to keep an eye open."

"Thanks. We are about to take off." He turned to the nurse. "Misty had an awful nightmare. Did the doctor leave anything to help her sleep?"

"Let me look at her chart." She tapped a few keys on the computer and pulled up the record. Then she read through the doctor's notes and a list of medications. "You're in luck. The doctor prescribed a sleep aid. I will take it to her now."

Tim thanked her and returned to the room. Lois tensed as he came through the door, then relaxed when she saw it was Tim.

"Ready to take off? Misty needs to rest." He smiled and Lois felt her heat speed up.

"Yes. Was just saying good night." Lois turned to Misty. "Try to get some sleep. There's an officer on duty. I'll be back before I go to the café in the morning."

They all looked up as the nurse walked in. "The doctor left something to help you get that sleep, your friend mentioned. Do you have water?"

Lois poured some in her cup and slid it toward her. "She does now."

"Great. This should take care of any bad dreams. It will help you move right to the wonderful deep sleep stage of the sleep cycle." She watched Lois take the pill, made a notation of the time on the chart and left.

Lois and Tim sat there about fifteen minutes until they noticed Misty had closed her eyes. Then they slipped away.

Chapter Twenty-Eight

Detective Price hated the idea of leaving Donna with only one man to back her up. The primary target was in the ambulance that was about to pull away. The other two guitarists had left in a van, and he'd sent a team to shadow them. The road crew had finished loading the second van, but the man who drove it off was a low priority target. No one had seen Donna since she went backstage about an hour earlier. It was not protocol to split the team, but he had to cover all the options with the people he had.

Her signal was weaker than he liked, but that was most likely because of it being inside a concrete block building. She had to be in the room at the back that the band used. The last band was playing. He wondered why she was still inside.

He glanced at his phone, noticing he had a voice mail from Tim Sansom. That was odd. Tim was off work and mentioned nothing would drag him away from his new woman on his day off. After looking at her photo, he understood.

He nodded for Trapper to move in and keyed in his voice mail code. His eyes remained on his breach team at all times.

There was no way to know how many people would still be in the room. Or if Donna was in there at all. But everyone agreed it was time to hit the room. Guns in hand, they walked directly through the back door, waiting as Trapper peeped in the narrow opening between the frame and the doorjamb.

As far as he could see, the room appeared empty. Using military hand signals, he warned them to be ready as the manager slipped the key into the slot. Immediately, the door swung open.

Holding the black leather pistol grip tightly, he stepped inside. The other men rushed in behind him. There was no sign of Donna. The room was empty.

The door to the bathroom was shut and someone had jammed a metal chair up under the doorknob to keep it from being opened.

"Donna? Are you in there?" Trapper listened but did not hear anyone inside the room.

"Hold up." Ben ordered the breach team.

His hands were shaking as he moved to join his men after listening to the message Tim had left. If he had only listened to it half an hour earlier. He took a deep breath to steady his nerves.

"Our primary has shifted. It isn't the lead guitarist. It's now the drummer and his cousin, one of the roadies."

"Shit! They moved all those boxes to the van right in front of us. And we let him drive away."

Ben looked sad. "I'm more worried about Donna."

"Just open the fucking door," Tune said as he turned the handle. The room was dark, and the light was blown. Even in the dark, he could make out the battered naked body lying on the floor. He moved to position himself in front of the door, knowing how the others were going to react when he saw her.

"Shit, get the fuck out of my way." Trapper shoved past his partner, falling to his knees by the body. Tears ran down his face as he took in her swollen, bruised face, the dried blood from multiple cuts and the duct tape the bastard had placed over her mouth to keep her from screaming as he tortured her. Then Trapper stood up. His voice was tight, but it was easy to hear the anger. "It's not Donna. This girl's cold, so she's been dead awhile. Someone call in the cleanup crew. I'm going to find the sonovabitch who has Donna."

Detective Price had little more to add. "Get an APB out on that second van. We need to find Donna now."

He dialed his department commander and informed him of the current situation. He also updated him on the change in primary targets. "We need you to notify Henry County we are heading that way. Ten to one, he's going back to his home turf."

The radio beeped, and a dispatcher said the van was spotted sitting inside the fence at Cat Grinning's studio.

"Alright men. It's a long shot, but we have to check out the studio in Little 5 Points. Not that I believe Cats Grinning has anything to do with this clusterfuck. It's just a check.

***

Robby looked at the text message that flashed across his phone and frowned.

"Sorry baby, I have to leave." He started getting dressed, pulling on his clothes and shoving his feet into shoes without bothering to put on socks.

Why? What's going on?" his wife asked, confused.

"Police. They're at the studio."

"The police? Why? What happened?"

"I don't know; but I have to go." He gave a quick peck and ran out the door.

Robby rode in silence as he sped back down the freeway toward Atlanta. His hands were clasped tight around the steering wheel. His jaw was clamped tight. He wondered if this had something to do with Mason's arrest. He was still coming to grips with the idea that his best friend could be a killer. It didn't make sense.

Stopping at the traffic signal at the end of the block, they could already see red and blue flashing police lights reflecting off buildings up and down the street.

Just before the light changed, someone tapped on the driver's side window. It was a uniformed police officer. Ace lowered the glass. "Sorry, sir, you have to turn around. We're blocking the road here for police business."

"Police business?" Robby asked, his voice tense. "That's my property, that they are tramping over!"

"You own that building? Stay here a minute." The officer stepped away from the car and spoke into his radio.

A minute later, he returned. "Okay, go on through," he said as he pointed his flashlight toward the road. "Detective Price wants to talk to you."

"Wait, can you tell me what happened?"

"They found a dead body," he said curtly. He stepped back and waved them through.

A dead body. His jaw fell open. Robby had never liked the word dead, or any of its variant forms of death like died, especially since Bryce had been killed. His mind visualized images of bloody corpses stiff with rigor mortis while crime scene photographers snapped pictures—the kind he'd always seen in movies and television shows. But this was real. He had been shocked by the news, but was better at concealing it than most people, maybe a residual emotion from his drug and alcohol days of the past. His eyes were locked on the road ahead; the only outward sign of his overwrought emotions were his clenched jaw and the narrowing of his eyebrows.

He made the turn into the fenced in studio lot and proceeded toward the trio of police cruisers. Several heads turned to look as he climbed out of the car.

From where they stood, he could already see a sizeable group of people gathered behind the police barricade across the street from the studio. The property was swarming with cops and official-looking people. Reports and spectators were confined to the sidewalk area, watching the activity buzzing around the property. The entire area was roped off by yellow crime tape. A fire truck and an EMS vehicle were parked on site with all the police cars. There was another cruiser at the other end of the block, rerouting traffic.

The press had already converged on the scene, smelling a big story as the news broke on the police scanner. A TV satellite truck was parked on the roadway, with people setting up cameras on tripods around it. Other reporters were leaning across the tape, calling questions out to anyone for information. The reporter from XYZ news, anchor Rachel Madder, was walking through the crowd interviewing anyone who would stop to talk to her.

Robby got out of the car and headed toward the chaos. He picked the man who appeared to be in charge and asked, "What's going on here?"

"You the owner?" Price asked.

Robby nodded.

"Our dog hit on the possibility of a body in the blue van. Forensics have checked, and the blood is human. The van is empty, so anything that was inside has already been removed."

Human blood? In our van? Robby was stumped. "I didn't know the van was here. We loaned it to another band. They needed it to carry equipment for a show they were playing tonight." He opened the door and led them down the hall about twenty feet. "This is their storage locker." He opened the roll-up door and showed them the speakers and other equipment boxes stacked inside. The dog walked around but did not hit on anything. If the body had been here, it wasn't now.

"If he drove the van, how did he leave?" Price knew there was no other vehicle in the yard. The blood could have been from the body they found at the Sleeping Lizard. The dog was tracking Donna's scent, and she had been inside the building.

"Kin left his truck here when he borrowed the van. Bo was with him. It's gone, so he's probably on his way home."

Damn... "Roll it up. Fast! We are in the wrong place."

He turned to Robby. "Do not notify him or anyone we were here. If you do, I will personally guarantee you are charged as a co-conspirator in the girl's murder."

He signaled for the street officer to push everyone back until the crime scene techs arrived to take the van in to be processed. They were now working against a clock, and they did not know how much time remained. They were playing games and Donna's life was the coin they were gambling with. Right now, the killer held a better hand.

Chapter Twenty-Nine

Sargent Thomas had been with the Henry County Sheriff's Department for almost twenty years. He was a wealth of information on the suspect. The feisty sheriff was familiar with the suspect's family and mentioned he had answered a few disturbance calls to his house. "You know it's crazy. If anyone had asked me about abuse, I would have put him down as the victim. That wife of his is bat shit crazy. She outweighs him by at least a hundred pounds. Mean as hell, she orders him around like a pet dog."

Ben sighed. That behavior didn't fit the profile the specialist had come up with. The woman in the bathroom had been raped and strangled a few hours before they found the body. The killer that they had been tracing was a collector. He held onto the victims for days, sometimes weeks, before the victim was killed and dumped. "Could he have snapped? Or transferred his anger at his wife to other women?"

"I guess it's possible, but I just can't see it. He's subservient to his wife and lets her take charge of everything."

He pointed to a small frame house sitting back away from the road. "Looks like he's home. Theres his van and her little white chevy."

"He was driving a pickup when he left the studio."

"Most likely at Gopher's place. They've been practicing there since he died last year."

"Gopher was his father?"

"His uncle. His father died years ago. He has two cousins."

"How far away is the uncle's place?"

"Maybe fifteen minutes. But don't you want to check if he's here?"

"Lights are all out. Most likely they're in bed. I'll leave a man here to watch, but I doubt anyone will go anywhere before we get back."

He radioed a pull back to vehicles and by the time they'd walked back to the SUV everyone else was waiting for them.

Sargent Thomas noticed how well his men worked as a team and vowed to see what he could do to get a similar unit together and trained. Possibly he could borrow their trainer. Now he was looking forward to watching them in action. His guys were great on patrol, but nothing like this unit. Other than the two members of the multi county Drug Task Force, none had SWAT training. There wasn't enough in the budgets to cover the expensive training.

Detective Price noticed his curiosity and answered his unspoken question. 'Every man and woman on the team are ex-special forces, Army, Marine, some Navy. I even have one from the Israeli Special Army. My trainer is a retired seal trainer, who spent a few years working at the Whitehouse. He's probably the best at putting a team together I've ever met."

Thomas nodded. "Once this is over, I'd like a chance to discuss some additional training for a few of my men. We have a multi-county drug task force team that would benefit from some expert advice."

They parked the vehicles down the road from the warehouse and moved through a lightly forested patch toward the former garage. There were two cars, and a truck parked outside the building. The sheriff said the truck didn't look like the one he'd seen the primary perpetrator driving, but he thought it belonged to the secondary perp.

The two men crouched down and watched as the team moved into position and then began their approach to the building.

Trapper signaled for the team to move forward as he slithered closer to the pile of lumber. He figured he could use the wood for cover if the suspect noticed him, and it would allow him to get closer if he didn't. He could see moving shadows through the window, but he did not know if Donna was inside the building. A familiar sound made him freeze, afraid that any sudden move could bring disaster. He turned his head slowly, spotting a timber rattler, about six feet long and as big around as a man's upper arm. It was coiled beneath the canvas awning, lying up against an old tire, staying out of the misty rain. From the sound it was making, it wasn't happy to be disturbed. Trapper knew he had two choices, and neither of them was very appealing. He mentally crossed his fingers and began inching his way backward, away from the tarp. He had only the roughest idea of a plan, and a half-assed chance it would work. It all depended on the damn snake. Somehow, he eased his way out with getting bit.

Trapper exhaled the breath he hadn't realized he was holding and muttered, "guess it didn't want to get wet."

Once he reached the open ground, he carefully made his way around the obstruction, making sure he kept something physical between him and the snake at all times. The ground was moist and soggy, the thick leaf coverage prevented any tracks but also made travel difficult. After he reached the coverage of the trees, he made better time weaving between the dense undergrowth and the scattered trunks until he reached an open space that enabled him to run to a nearby oak tree, using the trunk for cover. Once he was comfortable with his position, he radioed permission for the others to advance.

Crossing his fingers that the man inside was not watching for unexpected visitors, he ran for the corner of the building. No one appeared to have noticed his less than stealthy approach. He looked around, hoping to spot Tree before he worked his way into a position that allowed him to see what was going on inside the room. When he finally spotted Tree lying behind an evergreen shrub growing just beyond the door, he could tell from the expression on the lanky officer face it was too late. Tree had already seen more than enough. Something had him on edge. That usually meant one way or another, the man inside was going down.

Tune and Tarp were in position against the back side of the building. Officer Thomas had mentioned there was an access door that Gopher had kept locked while he was alive. It was swinging in the breeze; a soft katap, katap, katap that was perfect to cover any footsteps.

Just out of sight of the building, Trapper kept his eye on his watch. As the minute hand hit fifteen, he adjusted the setting on his night goggles a few times and then he began his run into the yard. His job was to get the attention of the target and lure him outside, if possible, to give the others a chance to get inside and free Donna.

Trapper had on his vest, as well as an extra tactical mesh shirt he had brought just in case anyone needed it. The full-face helmet would help deflect anything moving toward his head and the vest had him covered coming and going. He stopped outside the door to the shop, took a deep breath and then shouted for Kindrick to come outside. He knew the man would have to open the door to see who was outside yelling.

Just as they expected, the door opened a heavily tattooed man with long black hair came out, carrying a sawed-off shotgun. This was not Kindrick. He was at least three inches taller, and no one would ever describe him as a skinny blond punk.

Trapper winced at the sight of the shotgun. He was protected from a direct hit, but they had not counted on the possibility of scattered pellets. Luckily, the young first in officer recognized the inherent danger and put as much distance as possible between them before the gun went off. He felt the sting as one or two of the lead pellets hit his arms and legs, but most of the shells load was wasted. Before he had time to get off a second shot, Tree pulled the trigger on his 45 ACP Shield and the tattooed assailant fell flat on his face and lay still.

Bo heard the shotgun go off and made a grab for the pistol lying on the table with the cards. He ran toward the door, arriving in time to see DJ fall as the man in camouflage returned fire. He ducked to the side of the doorway, using the frame to shield him as he tried to line his gun up on the man who had just shot DJ. A noise from the back made him turn. Tune hit him like he used to hit the quarterback, knocking him through the open doorway onto the cement outside.

The perp pulled the trigger as he fell. The bullet struck his body armor at close range, with the force of a kicking mule. Disabled but do not critically injured, Tune rolled to the side, gasping for breath. Tree immediately surged forward, landing a blow to the man's side that doubled him over. They struggled for a moment, until the larger man slapped Bo across the temple with the butt of the pistol, dropping him to the floor. The tactical officer finished the job with a hard stomp to the back of his hand. A crackling sound erupted around his wrist as the bone gave way.

Tree grinned. The crazy bastard wasn't dead, but he has some serious finger damage. He won't be playing the guitar anymore.

Tarp was securing the interior of the building when he heard the bathroom door opening. The man in the bathroom ducked back inside, returning in seconds with a gun in his hand. He pointed it at Tarp and pulled the trigger.

Tarp was already turning as the gun went

off, his unexpected move causing the bullet to miss. The man didn't get another chance before Trapper put a bullet into his shoulder. Then Tarp slammed him backward. They rolled a few feet before the perp slammed the injured shoulder into a tool chest. The pain made him wince. Tarp knocked the gun from his hand, and forced him backward, using his knee against his shoulders to keep him down. The crazy fucker was bleeding from the wound in his shoulder, and dizzy from the battering he took, but he looked a hell of a lot better than Bo.

"Damn Tarp, you could have waited to kill him until after we talked to him." Trapper said, as they entered the room. "How the fuck are we going to find out where Donna is, if no one can talk? Why did hell did they start shooting at us anyway?

"Cool your jets. He ain't dead. I can hear him moaning. Once Tune gets him patched up, you can talk to him. I'm going out to check the vehicles."

Tune had found a rag and had the man lying flat on his back, with his left hand clamped atop the hole in his right shoulder. He was stable, but he kept his eyes on the two officers, looking for any chance to escape. His face was blanched, and his breathing agitated, as if his heart was hammering in his chest.

Trapper stood calmly, watching as Tree checked out Bo, with little hope that the man would be all right. The slightest tightening of his finger on the trigger of the Barretta pointing at the injured man's head was the only sign his casual demeanor hid the war going on inside Tree's head. Donna was one of the team, and while she might not be dead, he knew that given the choice, the proud Vietnam vet would have preferred to give it all, before allowing some dip shit pervert to sexually assault her. Tree would find out where his friend was, and what shape she was in, and then he would take care of any loose ends.

He watched Tune strap the big man's head and neck to a board with duct tape, trying to minimize the damage. Tune and Tarp had searched the building, finding no sign that Donna had ever been inside the shop. Tarp had gone out to investigate the two cars and the truck. He had the trunk on one car open and was moving toward the second.

Trapper walked over to a toolbox on a rolling stand and dug through the tools, finally coming up with a pair of stainless handcuffs with an unusual protective covering. He removed the key, unlocked them. and threw them to Tune with a smile.

Tune quirked his eyebrow, curious why a mechanic had owned furry pink handcuffs, but left that question for a later time. He slid the injured man's wrist into one cuff, clicked it close and passed the second cuff around a metal support post before he snapped it closed around the other wrist. He wasn't going anywhere.

"Hey, Trap! Need a little help out here."

Trapper heaved a loud sigh and walked over to the car Tarp was examining. He felt slightly uncomfortable digging through the vehicle in broad daylight. He also hated leaving Tree inside with the prisoners. Tune couldn't control him when he was 100percent, there was no way he could do it while injured.

Tree wanted answers. "Where's Donna?" he asked.

"I don't know, no bitch named Donna."

"Where can we find Kindrick?"

"Shit. I knew that little perv was gonna draw attention. No, he had to keep doing it."

"Doing what?"

"Dropping a drowsy Smurf."

"Huh?"

"Pulling a Cosby...a roofie cola... the little white pill in the drink that makes him look good."

"So that how he does it. He doctors the drink so that they don't know what's happening." Tree looked at the injured man. "If you have nothing to do with this Kin, why did you start shooting at us?"

"I think I can answer that," Trapper said as he entered the room. "We just popped the trunk of the cars outside. One is packed full of meth. Has to be at least ten pounds in there. I bet they are waiting for their connection to drive up."

"So, what should we do?" While Trapper was confident that the captive was cooperating, it was obvious it was under duress. He was heehawing around, giving as little information as possible. He insisted he didn't know who Donna was and had never seen her. Bo had been alone when he arrived. Either he really didn't know anything, or he was stalling for time, and that usually meant he was expecting the cavalry to arrive. Since no one had time to call for help, that meant it was a prearranged rendezvous. They needed to work fast.

Tree was expressing his sentiments to the prisoner, and he wasn't pulling any punches. "I want to talk to Kindrick. I would like to get to know him. Very much so. I want to get to know him more than I want to put a bullet into your head. But my patience is limited. Your friend needs to get to the hospital and every minute I waste with you puts him at greater risk."

"You wouldn't like him. Hell, Bo was his cousin, and he didn't like him. Pussy whipped little weasel would be better off with a bullet in his head."

"Enough," Tree snapped. "Where would he take Donna? We don't have time for this bullshit. I need to call an ambulance now or he ain't gonna make it."

"Tree! Out!" Trapper kept his eye on his second until he was through the door. "You might want to stop stalling and start cooperating. Tree is quite fond of Donna, so you better pray she's okay. They have been partners for years."

"Hell man, his partner is better off dead, then in her hands. I've seen her skin a deer, and it wasn't a pretty sight. I never thought I'd be scared of a damn woman."

"Her?" The sheriff had mentioned some-thing about the target's wife.

"Hell yeah. That crazy fucking ol' lady of his." The prisoner actually looked afraid for the first time since being captured.

"Wait, let me get this straight. Kin doesn't kill the women?"

"Hell no. He just wets his willie before he takes her home. It's that psycho bitch he's married to that scares the shit out of me." The injured man managed a short laugh. "She ain't just a woman. She full blood Cree. From Canada. There's nothing scarier than a native woman with a grudge against whitey. I can see it now. First, she will flay a few strips of skin away from her body, just to see her scream. Once she is satisfied by the amount of begging the woman has done, then she might cut her throat. I once saw her bury this bitch beside a fire ant hill. To get the ant's attention, she poured honey over her head, then poured a trail for them to follow. Imag-ine the pain she was in as those ants ate her alive, bite by bite until there's nothing left but bones."

The thought of an angry native American woman with a skinning knife might not have been enough to push the man over, but the added image of the fire ants was more than he could handle.

Tree stepped closer, moving into the room from the doorway. "Fuck her, she ain't getting you. You need to be worried about me. If Donna dies because you stalled and kept us here, I will make sure you experience exactly the same pain she felt."

"Relax, man, she's safe. Theres no way she's already dead. Margo wants the woman alert, so she knows exactly what's happening to her and why. They keep them locked in the well house until the roofie wears off. She should be safe until the sun comes up tomorrow.... maybe longer if they sleep in."

Trapper turned to Tune. "Let's go. I'll have the sheriff call for a bone wagon and some of his boys to take this bunch to the hospital. They might want to wait around for the buyer to show. Just to tie up loose ends."

"Wait, you ain't gonna leave me like this?" his eyes went to the door like he was scared someone might find him that way.

Tree looked him in the eyes. "You got two choices. You wait for the ambulance, or I shoot you. Choose. I don't have time to waste."

The icy glare left no doubt in the prisoner's mind. He lay back against the side of the toolbox. "Good luck with your raid."

Chapter Thirty

There was an old-fashioned clapboard Baptist Church about ten minutes down the highway along their route back to McDonough. Ben pulled around the main building into a secluded area of the parking lot so the team could go over the plan of attack.

After listening to all the options, Ben decided Tree would attempt to get Donna out before the rest of the team went in. There were at least two children in the house, and they hoped to take the two prime suspects without endangering the kids. Removing Donna from the equation was the easiest way to guarantee no one would be emotionally invested during the assault. Sending Tree meant no one would know he was there. No one could ghost like Tree.

The well house was a good fifty feet from the main building, but there was nothing around it to use as cover. Tree parked about two blocks past the driveway and walked back to the edge of the yard. There was no sign of any movement, but that didn't mean no one was around. There was also the possibility of dogs. He carried a special narco-pistol in case he had to disable any canines in a hurry. The contents wouldn't kill the animal, but it would send it to lullaby land in seconds.

Working against the clock, Tree crept along the old deer trail at a steady pace, moving with impressive silence for a man of his size. Normally, he would have spent a few minutes watching the wellhouse, to ensure Kin had set no type of guard on his newest acquisition. Tonight, time was of the essence, and he didn't have any to spare. To reach the door of the building, he would have to cross twenty feet of open space. Anyone watching from the house would have a clear shot once he began his approach. He hated the thought of running blindly across the open area, but to save Donna, he would have to confront and overcome those fears. He moved until he could not see the house for the well building. This would be the track he followed since the well house would also block him from view. Holding his .45 ready, he charged the across the clearing toward the back of the small block building.

So far, so good. Then he heard something moving and the rattle of metal against metal. Just as he feared, a large pit bull was chained in front of the building. It turned and rushed him as he stepped around the corner. He reacted on instinct, knowing he had to shut the dog up before he barked. The only option he had was to shove his left arm into the dog's mouth and fire the narco-gun into his body with his right. The hundred-pound dog's jaws clamped down on his forearm, sinking his razor-sharp teeth into the tender flesh, using his weight to tear into the muscle. The pain only lasted a few seconds before the drug took effect, but the warm blood flowing down his arm would make it hard to use that hand. Hopefully, he wouldn't need it. He pried open the dog's mouth with his boot knife, something he couldn't easily do if it was dead.

He froze, listening to hear if anyone had noticed the dog's attack. Tree could hear something moving around inside the building and hoped it was Donna. Recognizing the suspects love of big dogs, he hoped it wasn't a second version of the sleeping canine behind the building. Nothing. Not a sound. Great, that meant there was not likely to be another dog.

There was a steel bar across the door to prevent it from opening. Since anyone determined to get into the shack could have kicked their way through the rotting wood, he assumed it was to keep someone inside, not out.

He lifted the bar and slowly opened the door, keeping it between him and any unexpected occupants. Nothing except rats. There was a big one sitting on the top of a wooden cask just inside the door. He was probably the source of the skittering noise. After a moment, his eyes adjusted to the inadequate light, and he could see inside.

Twist lay unmoving on an old mattress, her expression blank, staring up toward the ceiling but not really seeing anything. Zip ties bound her hands and feet and a piece of duct tape covered her mouth, leaving her nose uncovered for air. There was a small amount of dried blood on her forehead and a spot on the mattress where a trickle had rolled down her chin before dropping onto the dirty cloth. When he'd stepped through the door into the wellhouse, he had been certain Twist was dead. He had fallen to his knees next to the blood -stained mattress, tears streaming down his face. It took several seconds for his brain to analyze and push out the info through the anguished haze. Dead people do not bleed. She was still alive. He put his hand in front of her mouth and smiled when he felt the warm air. She was breathing, which was great, but he had no way to judge her physical injuries, nor did he have time to waste making any type of examination.

Tree looked at the sleeping figure and realized his life would never be the same. So much had happened in such a short time. He fought to get his emotions under control. Twist had always claimed there was something about his eyes she loved, eyes the color of warm caramel, like a doe or a cow, a beautiful, soft brown that melted her heart. She would not recognize his eyes today. Anger made his eyes grow cold...dark... icy... black ice. Today, onyx wasn't dark enough to describe them. He'd stepped across the line between anger and insanity. First, he needed to take care of Twist.

His pocketknife sliced through the tough plastic ties with ease. For a moment, he worried she wasn't able to move, but after he pulled her to her feet she stood there, weaving slightly but making no complaints even though he could see tears forming in her eyes as the circulation was restored.

"It's okay Twist. I've got you. I'm taking you home."

Her only answer was a tight nod.

Mentally kicking himself for parking so far away, he swept her up into his arms and started walking back toward the tree line. There was still the possibility someone would look out the window and see him, but the chance grew smaller the farther he got away from the house along the overgrown trail.

Twist had wrapped her arms around his neck, clinging to him as if she was afraid, she would wake, and find herself back in the old block building. With each tiny whimper, his anger grew. By the time they reached the road, she had showed she wanted to try walking. He knew the tape was an aggravation, but she knew he needed to take his time removing it, or she could lose a lot of skin when it came off. It would have to wait until they were safely away from the shack.

He flipped his radio button and said, "We are clear. Target is all yours."

Once he confirmed Twist was able to

stand, he took her by the arm and led her to the car. With every step, she seemed to gain strength. Her eyes reflected her surprise at seeing the loaner instead of the team's SUV, but she seemed to realize it was another question best left for later. Tree pulled her into his arms, holding her against his chest as she cried. Wrapping his jacket around her shoulder seemed to help, but he was wasting precious time. Minutes he couldn't spare if the team hoped to pull this off with no one discovering she was gone. Tree's hands had shaken as he pushed the damp strands of her hair away from the seeping cut on her forehead. He dabbed at the blood on her face. Twist's eyes had opened as his fingers touched her face and she had moaned. The bitch had hit her more than once directly in the face. She might not have broken any bones, but one side of Twist's face was swollen and bruised, her lip was swollen, and she could use a stitch above her eyebrow. Her eye was already changing color, by tomorrow it would be black.

Naked except for his jacket, she perched on the edge of the seat as if she feared by sitting back, she might sink down into it and never escape. Gradually, her trembling decreased, and she calmed enough for Tree to look for a place to pull off the road and explain.

Before he said anything, he walked to the back of the car and removed a set of coveralls from the trunk. It was he'd been able to scrounge up from the team, but it was better than her arriving naked. She moved stiffly as he helped her into the oily one-piece jumpsuit but seemed happy to have it on. Since she was now out of any immediate danger, he took his time as he carefully removed the band of duct tape from her wrists and mouth.

"Sorry about the tape, but I couldn't risk you waking up and screaming before you realized it was me. I needed to get you to safety first."

Twist worked her jaw a bit, then smiled. "I was wondering what was taking you guys so long."

"Asshole left your clothes in the dumpster back at the Sleeping Lizard. Took you out in a drum case. Took us a while to locate you."

"Where am I?" She looked around, seeing nothing but trees and the dirt road.

"Henry County. Not far from McDonough. Maybe half an hour south of the airport." He looked into her eyes again and felt better. The light was coming back to her eyes, she would be okay. "If you're ready, we need to join the others."

She nodded, and they headed toward the church.

The paramedic was waiting when they arrived.

As expected, Detective Price insisted she needed to be taken to the hospital to get checked. She refused to go, insisting she wanted to stay with the team. It was the only place she felt safe.

The laceration needed stitches. Even half-conscious, Twist had fought the idea of going to the hospital' "Can't you apply a butterfly to close it until the team finishes the op?

"Sorry. Because of the angle, a butterfly will not hold it closed."

"Then stitch it shut."

"I can't give you a local until the medication they gave you is cleared from your system. They have to do tests at the hospital."

" Fuck. Just put in the stitches. I can handle it." She'd jumped once or twice while he was removing the dried blood from her face, but she hadn't said a thing until the ambulance had arrived. The paramedic added two stitches to close the cut over her eye.

Tree felt like someone punched him every time she winced. It had to be extremely painful without anesthetic, but Twist never complained. The Paramedic had cleaned her up as much as possible, but what he could do was limited by law.

Tree had no limits. "Get that thought out of your head. There's no way."

Twist frowned, but she was smart enough to know there was no way she could go with the team. She wasn't happy about Tree's request, but she agreed to wait at the church with the Henry County Sheriff.

The team was ready to move out as soon as the paramedic was through with Twist. He had been gone less than fifteen minutes, but the extra time had stretched the time to half an hour.

It was still quiet at the house. The Henry County officer watching the building had not noticed him go in or noticed him leaving with Donna. The sheriff was not happy with his officer but felt this was not the time to bring it up. He made a mental note to request funds for some additional training at the next budget meeting. This would be first on the list.

***

It was almost dawn when the team hit the house. Approaching the building was simple. With the dog knocked out, there was nothing to wake the sleeping occupants. But many people woke about this time to get their kids ready for school, so they were racing the clock.

The front door was not locked. Tree and Trapper moved into the living room. Once they had ascertained no one was sleeping on the couch, Tree walked to the back door and flipped the deadbolt. Trapper was waiting. Using techniques learned in the military, they worked their way from room to room, clearing each one as they approached the area where the two suspects were sleeping. They scouted the rooms the kids slept in, closed the door and wedged them shut from outside. If there was any resistance, this would keep the children inside the room and out of the line of fire. They were professionals who would not, by their own rules, rush into an unknown situation, even when they had been told the targets were an unsuspecting man and woman, who most likely did not know they were about to get arrested. That didn't mean they didn't keep a gun by the bed.

Trapper signaled he had glimpsed someone moving around in the room ahead. Both men carried silenced pistols with clips holding fifteen rounds. As far as they knew, there were only two adults inside the house. The team should have more than enough firepower to take them out and still have contingency coverage. They edged their way closer to the room, moving toward the opening from the side to prevent anyone from noticing their approach. At Trapper's signal, Tarp opened the door and entered the bathroom, guns held ready.

Hearing the slightest sound of movement, the man spun around in time to see a stranger wearing military combat gear pointing a gun directly at him. A tiny trail of urine sprayed the floor before he got his stream under control.

"What the fuck?" The man standing at the toilet looked like he was about to pass out. He fit the description of primary subject one.

"Keep your hands where they are and don't move." Tarp was disappointed the bastard had not tried to make a run for it.

"No problem." He went to tuck himself back into his briefs."

"Unless you want to lose that, I wouldn't suggest moving any more. Simply put, your ass belongs to me. Well, strictly speaking, it belongs to the APD, but my team usually goes along with whatever I decide."

"Can't I pull my briefs up?"

"Don't even think of moving. We're going to sit here and wait for Trapper and Tree to arrive with the lady of the house. No one is happy about what you and your wife did to Twist. He held out a pair of cuffs. Slip these over your wrists and then I might let you tuck. After you make yourself comfortable on the floor."

Taking the second primary target was even easier. She slept with a mask over her eyes. Trapper kept his gun on her as Tree reached for her arm. It was hanging off the side of the bed, and she was dead to the world. When she felt him grab her arm, she jumped and tried to jerk it away. Tree had no trouble holding on. As the sleep daze left her, she realized it was not Kin holding her arm. She screamed and lunged for the drawer of the nightstand. Tree jerked her back toward him. He bent her arm up behind her back and held it there with his left hand as he reached for her free arm with his right. The movement flipped her over onto her stomach. In a matter of seconds, he had her secured with a zip tie.

Trapper informed the waiting sheriff it was now safe to approach the building.

He marched her toward the front door. Henry County had a transport waiting, and they rolled up within seconds of Tree's "all clear." Tree needed to get her in the transport before she opened her mouth and made some kind of wise crack about Twist. If she did, he wasn't sure he could control his reaction. Tune was right behind him with Kin. They wanted them in separate transports. From this point on, they would not be allowed to communicate.

Once she was secured, Trapper checked the entire house once more, making sure the children were the only additional occupants. Both kids had slept through the entire raid. Because one was a teenager, they used zip ties to hold his wrists, but the little girl allowed to sit in the living room until the social worker arrived to take them into their care.

The entire operation had taken less than five minutes.

Once Henry County had arrived on the property, they brought in the APD special forensic team to sweep the home and the wellhouse. Within minutes, they had collected DNA that matched at least five of the victims in the activity files. The team had transported the two suspects to the Henry County jail to be processed. They would be transferred to APD custody within the next few days. It was time to go home.

No one complained when Trapper pulled the SUV out into traffic and headed north toward Atlanta.

Chapter Thirty-One

'Free!'

'They got the wrong man!'

'This Cats Grinning again!'

The media headlines blasted out the information that Ace Ryder, the lead singer for Cats Grinning, had been cleared of any involvement in the Fangirl murders. Many stations ran front-page stories touting the screw up. Others pointed out the way ADP had cleared six murders with this arrest. Either way, a serial killer was in jail and her partner, a serial rapist, was offering evidence hoping to avoid the electric chair.

Sales of Cats Grinning's recent release shot through the ceiling as jubilant fans and new listeners who had wrongfully trashed them bought everything available. Fifteen days after he had been arrested and extradited back to Georgia, Mason walked out the doors of the Atlanta jail and into a crowd of screaming fans who had faithfully protested his arrest every day for the last two weeks.

He blinked in the bright light and waved, then allowed the officers to escort him to the waiting transport.

Robby waited in his truck for him to work his way through the milling crowd. He hated Ace had been subjected to the humiliation of a public arrest, however, he realized that without the photos the two detectives might not have solved the string of murders. The one-hundred-foot trek to the car from the building had taken him almost fifteen minutes. Mason didn't care. He'd been surprised to see how many people had shown up to celebrate his release. Despite the warm welcome, he was happy when Robby pulled the Ford F-250 out of the lot and turned up Memorial Drive toward home.

Robby passed by the studio so he could get a look at the eight-foot-tall fence that had been completed while he was incarcerated. The yellow police tape was still up across the back loading dock and storage area.

"It still feels like a bad dream but seeing the fence and the tape makes it real. Of all the people to be a murderer, Kin would have been the last one on my list. It's hard for me to get my mind around the idea of killing eleven women.'

"He didn't actually kill them. It was his ol' lady that got off on torturing young, beautiful girls. She should have been put down like a rabid animal. What little I was able to get from Detective Sansom, Kin had been not always been so henpecked. About six years ago, he'd picked up a groupie after a show they played down in Macon. She'd given him more than a wild ride. And he'd taken it home to his wife. Instead of telling her about his STD, he went and got treatment for himself, thinking she was not infected since she never showed any signs of infection. It almost killed her. Only after infection was so severe the pain became unbearable, had the doctors realized she had been exposed. They treated her, but it had already damaged her insides. She had to have a hysterectomy. Physically, she recovered, but the doctors think the mental damage only increased as time passed.

That was her first victim. She had forced Kim to return to the club in Macon several times until the girl had shown up for a show. Then she had him roofie the girls' drink. No one thought anything about the drunken woman leaving with a couple. They found her bones buried out in the woods behind the house. Along with two others. Five more were found buried in the woods near the old garage. It seems that after he discovered his sister's new pastime, Bo got his own system going, figuring one more body, more or less wouldn't matter."

Ace shuddered. "I thought I knew him. Now I want that sonofabitch to hurt. I don't care if I go to jail for the rest of my life. I want his fucking head on a platter. There's got to be a way." Ace didn't care what it took. He would come up with the money.

"That won't change what's already happened. I know. I've already run every option through my mind."

"But why? Why would Kin do it? He always seemed so meek. I always thought he had been abused as a child or something."

"The police think it was guilt. He really loved her. Even after she changed, he tried to keep his marriage together."

"It's hard to believe no one noticed the first woman was missing. If they had, maybe the other ten would still be alive."

"Her parents lived in Florida, and she worked all the time. It wasn't until she missed calling on Mother's Day that her mother thought to check and see how she was doing. Her brother drove up from Daytona and discovered she had disappeared several months earlier. The apartments had stored her things, but someone else lived there. The last message they could find was a Facebook post saying she had met someone new, and they were going to Texas. We believe that Kin or Monica posted it using her phone. We think they used her key fob to find her car. One must have driven her car, and the other drove the truck with the victim."

"Damn. It sounds like some kind of low budget horror movie."

"I'm sure he got most of his idea from the movies. The car went into Lake Jackson, in an area that was not highly developed. The coroner thinks they kept her alive for three weeks. Once she tired of her plaything, Monica had Kin dump her just outside their property, in a rural farming area. The body wasn't discovered until hunting season opened and a hunter stumbled across the bones. No one connected her skeleton to the other missing women."

"At least I woke up, and my nightmare was over. I hope that in time, we can get back to normal. "

Robby laughed. "Don't plan on any long

trips. The phone hasn't stopped ringing since you were cleared. We are turning down offers because we are already booked into next year." He looked serious for a moment. "I know you need a little time to unwind, so I didn't book anything for the next six weeks."

Mason nodded. "Thanks. I need some time. Have you talked to Mikey? Any idea when he will come back to work?"

"The doctor released him last week. He's been practicing with the rest of the band while we waited to hear what was going to happen with you. They wouldn't tell us anything." He stopped talking or a minute. "Did they tell you anything about Tyce?"

"A little. Tim, the detective, mentioned he was upset after Bo was killed in the raid. Bo started shooting at the special swat team that went in. It turns out he was dealing crystal meth on the side. They found over two pounds in the trunk of his car. Since the car was registered in Tyce's name, they arrested him for distribution"

"Tyce? Meth?" Ace had trouble putting the two together.

"Yeah. They were cooking it in his uncle's old garage. Seem his uncle had been a player in the illicit drug market. The forensic team got lucky while they were digging the spent bullets out for evidence. Without prior knowledge of the room, it would have been almost impossible to locate it. The wily ol' coot had built a false wall in a storage room, then added a narrow staircase going down into an area of the basement that had been walled off with cement blocks. The room was only two feet wide and was about the same length as the basement. Along one wall was shelving. Every shelf contained plastic bins, labeled and stocked with a wide assortment of pharmaceutical products. Tim said DTF figured there had to be a couple of hundred grand in stock inside. Besides the vacuum sealed bags of marijuana, there was an as sortment of barbiturates and amphetamines in pill and capsule form. Four containers held acid, two held Ecstasy, and one was labeled with a name he didn't know. He even spotted a container of the little blue pills sought by so many of the middle-aged male customers."

"So Tyce was cooking bathtub meth?"

"No. But he owned part of the building, so he was included in the arrests. He claims his uncle didn't trust him. That he did not know the secret room was there."

"Well, it's over now. Maybe we can get our lives back to normal." Mason said the words, but he wondered how much he meant them. Lately, he wondered if he was getting too old for the music business. He would be thirty-two in a few months. The life had gotten old. It just wasn't fun anymore. He remembered the brief flash of hope he'd felt back in Biloxi when he thought he'd spotted Misty. After that wonderful night, he could not get her out of his mind. During the investigation he's learned Misty was friends with the young fan that had been killed, her sister was her roommate, and they lived a few miles from the studio. He'd been looking everywhere else.

Mason had made one last request of officer Sansom when he'd talked to the detective once they'd released him from custody. They'd agreed on a plan to get her to a neutral spot so he could talk to Misty. It was a long shot. One Sansom couldn't guarantee would work. But he said he would try.

Chapter Thirty-Two

The restaurant was a pleasant surprise. Someone had shelled out big bucks to transform the stately antebellum mansion into a stylish bar and upscale dining establishment. The person who decorated the three-story atrium had taken the surrounding area into consideration. The entire back of the building was glass and opened onto a terraced patio overlooking a crystal-clear lake. An enormous chandelier lit a towering great room that could easily hold three times the number of people currently inside. Two wings of additional dining rooms angled off to each side of the main service area.

The heavenly aroma of hickory smoked steaks from the kitchen wafted his way as Mason entered the room and his mouth started watering. It had been a long day and the two apple twists he'd grabbed that morning were a fast-fading memory. He was surprised to see how nervous he was. He hoped no one noticed how badly he was perspiring.

He'd left his cologne in his truck.

The hostess was giggling with a server when he approached the counter and said he was meeting someone. She smiled and looked at the seating chart, found the table with three people waiting on a fourth, and led him that way.

Mason was used to attracting attention. A suntan could never duplicate his exotic complexion, which was a mix four distinctly different grandparents. Photographers loved shooting his face and his body. He was often featured on the cover of music magazines. On stage he wore it loose, but tonight he wore his thick hair braided down his back in a single long tail. He was also clean shaven, but the distinctive hints of a five o'clock shadow were peeping through. Though he never understood until that night with Misty, he'd been told he had eyes you could drown in.

The outfit he was wearing was nothing like the black Harley tee and jeans he'd been wearing the last time he saw Misty. Instead, he'd swapped out his casual attire for a dress shirt and khakis. His white cotton shirt was unbuttoned about halfway down. The sleeves rolled tight against thick golden-bronze forearms drew attention to the tattoos covering his lower arms. He struggled not to grin when he saw her eyes drift up to check him out. The vee of his shirt allowed a hint of a six-pack she could glimpse whenever he moved. Unlike many of the men on the beaches back home, his lean body was sculpted by muscles earned through hard work, not metal weights. He hoped she remembered.

They were sitting at a table near the far back wall when he walked in. His first impulse was to run to her and beg for forgiveness. But that want going to happen. Groveling wouldn't help him explain it hadn't been his fault. In a crazy way, he was also a victim. Other than the blow to his pride, he had suffered no long-term damage during his brief incarceration. The time in the cell had showed him he never wanted to go back to jail again. Some lessons stuck with you.

He could see the surprise in her eyes as he walked up, and he wondered what Tim had said to get her to agree to meet with him. Clearly, she had been expecting someone else. Maybe she thought it was another cop?

When he slid into the chair beside her, he could feel her trembling. She didn't say anything, so he fought back the impulse to run and simply said, "Hope you haven't been waiting long."

"Not long at all," Tim said. He passed Mason a menu as if he did not know that Mason and Misty knew each other. "This beautiful lady is Lois, and her friend to your left is Misty."

Mason took his cue from Tim. "Lois, Misty, nice to meet you."

He turned to Tim and asked, "What you drinking?"

"Blackjack and Coke." The server was hovering nearby, so he motioned her over.

"Sounds good to me. Anyone need refills?" He was surprised when both women nodded. "Bring a full round for everyone."

The server hurried off to fill the order and Tim scrutinized the menu.

Misty decided this was the perfect time to go to the powder room. "Would you excuse me, I need to ..." she cut her eyes toward the Ladies sign.

Lois immediately motioned to Tim to let her out. "I think I'll join you."

Tim stood so she could slide out of her chair. The two women began walking toward the Ladies sign without saying another word.

Tim watched until they entered the bathroom and then he exhaled heavily. "Damn. That went better than I expected."

Mason laughed. "I kept my eyes on the knife the entire time. I kept imagining it buried in my shoulder, or worse, my jugular."

"Could she have been so drunk she doesn't remember you?"

"No. She knows exactly who I am. The only thing I can think of is, she doesn't think I remember her."

"What are you going to do?"

"Play dumb and see where it goes."

***

Misty collapsed as soon as she entered the restroom stall. Her face went into her hands, and she shuddered. How was she going to make it through a dinner with him? He didn't even remember who she was.

Lois stood by the door. After a few minutes, she asked, "Are you okay?"

"Hell no, I'm not okay. I'm having a nervous breakdown."

"I'm sorry. It didn't click into my mind to ask Tim who his friend was. I can ask Tim to take us home. I'll tell him I'm cramping. You don't need to suffer through dinner."

Did she want to go home? No. Despite everything she'd been through, she felt comfortable next to Mason. He had been through his own private hell. Being arrested for something he didn't do. Facing the photographers and the news media, then being thrown into jail. It had to be horrible. At least she didn't remember any of her nightmare. He had been awake through it all. "No. I'm fine. And I'm hungry. Mason can afford it, so let's enjoy our dinner."

"Alright. If that's what you want. The food smells fantastic."

Misty opened the door. "How bad is my makeup?"

"Theres a tiny bit of a raccoon eye, but it should come right off. I've got some concealer in my purse." She dug through the black bag and pulled out a small makeup bag. In less than a minute, you could not tell that Misty had been in tears.

"You look fine. Besides, I'm sure he's experienced plenty of mornings when the woman awakened looking nothing like she did when she fell asleep." Once she said it, Lois felt a twinge of guilt after seeing the flash of pain cross Misty's face. She might not want to admit it, but her girl had it bad. All she could do was wait and see what happened and be there if it didn't turn out the way she hoped.

Misty took a deep breath and smiled. "Let's go order something expensive."

***

Mason surprised them by having an assortment of appetizers waiting when they returned to the table. The server took their orders, as they shared the different treats he had ordered. Several of the starters were familiar, battered onions, bacon wrapped scallops, and crab stuffed mushrooms. She also liked the grilled lobster, shrimp and crab skewers, jalapeno, bacon and chives cheese balls and soft pretzel bites stuffed with melted queso. The salads were crisp, and you could tell they were made to order. Even the steaks were cooked to perfection. About halfway through the meal, Misty was pleasantly surprised when a five-piece band began playing instrumental dance music. Several couples immediately moved toward the dance floor. She saw Lois eyes light up, and she knew her best friend was eager to join the dancers swaying to the old-fashioned ballroom music. They had once gone to a club in Buckhead that specialized in the 1940s style, and Lois had loved it.

As if Tim could read her mind, he stood

and held his hand out for her. Lois grinned and allowed herself to be swept away into a classical waltz. Misty was surprised to see how smooth his footwork was. She had never pictured the by the book detective doing anything other than the typical hold and sway two-step taught in middle school.

"Shall we join them?" Mason was watching her intently, and she suddenly realized he knew exactly who she was. He also knew once he pulled her into his arms, she could not hide her body's response to his.

She took a deep breath and nodded.

He didn't bother hiding his smile as he took her hand and led her to the dance floor. Once they arrived, he pulled her into his arms. Misty stepped forward gracefully, following his lead as the song changed and he swept her into a swirl, before pulling her body closer into an intimate Latin rumba. If Tim was considered an excellent dancer, then Mason was far beyond an expert. She couldn't help comparing him to her ex-boyfriend. When Steven had taken her out, he always turned the dance into a contest of wills, forcing her to accept his song choices, even if she had expressed little interest in dancing to that song.

She had to admit she was disappointed when he led her back to the table at the end of the next song. Frustrated by her body's reaction to his presence, she finished her drink, then smiled when the server brought her another one. She concentrated on her dinner, not meeting his eyes while she sipped on her drink. Tim and Lois had returned to the dance floor, leaving her alone at the table with Mason.

She did not know why; maybe it was the silence. It was oppressive. She had to fight down the urge to say something, anything to fill in the emptiness. This man gave her the same feeling. Which didn't make a bit of sense. Finally, she gave up trying to avoid acknowledging the attraction and looked up. Her gaze locked with his soulful brown eyes, picked up the invisible gauntlet, and accepted the challenge.

That was all the invitation he needed.

The band began an intimate slow ballad, and the lights dimmed. He immediately pulled her tight against his body, allowing his hands to slip downward to cup her cheeks. They were pressed so closely together, she could feel every inch of his body, some parts more than others. His knee had slipped between her legs, forcing her to press against his loins. Her body's response was immediate. A warm flush swept over her as her senses awakened in anticipation. He could feel her muscles trembling as his hand traveled along her side, casually tracing the outline of her curves. With a sigh, she lay her head against his chest, relaxing into his arms.

He continued to gaze down into her eyes. Even in the shadows of the dimly lit dancefloor, he saw she smiled. She looked exquisite. Her beautiful hair, her high cheekbones, her flawless face. The perfection he fell in love with long ago. "You are... so beautiful."

She fought down a blush. "You're not too bad yourself, even if you are a bit of a player."

"Player? I've been called a lot of things by a lot of women, an ass, a bastard and once, a whore dog, but I think this is the first time anyone has ever called me a player. You must be mixing me up with another handsome singer."

"I could never get you mixed up with another man."

"Flattery will get you anything, but I guessed you already figured that out." His grin was devilish and full of insinuation.

"Uh huh...like I said. A master player, yet

you claim you are not very adept at the art of flirtation," she replied, squirming her way deeper into his arms.

"I guess I have been a player. At heart, I'm just a big kid. I've always been good at games. Flirting is just a game of words and innuendo." He leaned closer to and whispered in her ear. "This time I'm dead serious."

She gave him what she hoped was an angry glare. "Are you trying to seduce me?"

"Yes. Is it working?" He tried to keep his comments light and flirtatious. He could tell she wasn't as confident as she was pretending to be.

"Not really. My daddy told me not to play with fire," she quipped, throwing down her own challenge.

"Afraid you might get burned?" He ran the tip of his tongue across his top lip, and she shivered. Damn, he was hot as hell. When she realized she was unconsciously leaning forward, she had to force her eyes away from his mouth. For a second, she thought he would kiss her. She wanted him to kiss her, desired it, even craved it, with a raw desperation that threatened to overcome her body and soul. He knew it. And he made her wait.

Misty cut her eyes at him, and he winked, making her laugh. Damn him, she needed to get off the dance floor before she gave in to her inner demon. After this dinner, she would need a cold shower ...maybe two. Luckily, the band chose that moment to start up a faster, much bouncier song.

She laughed, trying to twirl around, and lost her balance.

Mason caught her before she fell. He swept her up in his arms and headed for the table.

"Wait, my shoe!" He stopped long enough to pick up the missing slipper, then returned to his previous plan, depositing both Misty and her wayward shoe on the waiting chair.

"I suppose a lot of women have fallen at your feet." She was feeling wonderful and didn't care what the other diners thought.

"Well, I don't think my feet were what they wore aiming for." He shifted his weight, trying to move his growing erection into a more comfortable position. He might pretend there was nothing there, but his body was saying something different. To say there were sparks between them was an understatement. The attraction was mutual and growing stronger. Last time he was too drunk to do anything more than fuck. The idea of finding out what buttons to push to make her scream his name was extremely seductive. He was saved from further mental debate by Tim's attempt to grab the check off the table.

Lois was giggling like a teenager. "Hope you don't mind. Tim and I are gonna take off."

"No. Go right ahead. I've already taken care of the check." He stopped Tim. "You're not going to drive, are you?"

"No. We came in a cab. We are leaving the same way." Lois was practically dragging him toward the exit.

Mason grinned as he signed the check and added a fantastic tip. Their server had been on top of everything. It had surprised him to see that both women had drunk five margaritas. It was a miracle they were walking, much less dancing.

With his arm around her at all times, he helped Misty to the car, going back inside to find the wayward slipper she'd lost once again. Instead of his usual truck, tonight he was driving a dark gray custom sedan, with a black leather interior and all the bells and whistles of a luxury car. Misty slid down into the buttery soft calfskin and turned so she could see him better. Suddenly nervous, she wet her lips, using the tip of her tongue to trace the outline. Mason noticed, he noticed everything about her. For a fleeting second, their gazes locked, and time stood still. Misty found it hard to breathe. She felt her nipples tightening, and he grinned. His knowing how he was affecting her just made it worse.

Mason shifted his weight, easing the pressure of his now tight khakis away from his rapidly hardening erection. All he could think about was how he wanted to take her home and fuck her until she was screaming out his name. But he didn't want to scare her away. Gently, he pulled her closer, cupping her face between his hands. He whispered her name, and she shivered. His face was so close she could feel his breath on her skin. She curved into his body, letting a tiny moan escape, and his loins tightened once again. She was so hot...and willing. Finally, when she was certain he was just playing games, his lips came down.

Chapter Thirty-Three

Mason wasn't sure if it was the alcohol or moonlight, but he knew he had to do it, even though it might scare her away. He was looking down into her face, his intense perusal moving gradually downward as he studied her eyes, her mouth, the soft pulse at the vee of her neck. He was suddenly overcome by the need to taste her lips again. Gently at first, he brushed across her lips, tasting the sweetness. It wasn't enough. He sought her mouth, his tongue probing, his teeth nibbling on the swollen flesh. He couldn't seem to get enough of her delicate rose lips. His mouth trailed kisses down her neck and across the curves of her breasts, sending delicious twinges throughout her core and causing her nipples to tighten and distend. His hands slid downward, cupping her ass as he pulled her close against him. Like a teenager at the drive in, he used his weight to push her back against the seat, immobilizing her by pressing his rock-hard body against hers. Her body's response was immediate. A warm flush swept over her as her senses awakened in anticipation. He could feel her muscles trembling as his hand traveled along her side, casually tracing the outline of her curves. He needed to get control of his emotions before he did something he would regret. Damn...he wanted this woman. He could not remember ever wanting to fuck someone so much in his life. No, not fuck her. He wanted to throw her on the bed and kiss every curve, every crevice, every little dip, and dimple. With a deep sign, Mason pushed away from the trembling woman who had just been in his arms.

"We have to get out of here before someone calls the police. All I need is more publicity." He cranked the car and pulled out into traffic, heading south down Peachtree Street. Driving the main route was all he could handle. There was no way he could remember the myriad of back streets that would allow him to cut across the city to his home. He knew he should ask her before heading that way, but he was afraid she might say no.

The look Misty had given him had been dark and skeptical. He realized she wasn't as drunk as he'd thought. This made him feel a little better. It wouldn't be the first time he'd taken advantage of a drunk woman, but right now, that was the last thing on his mind. Well… maybe not the last thing. She was sexy as hell and if he didn't get her hand off his dick, drunk or not, he may not be able to stop himself. There wasn't a snowball's chance in hell she was sober enough to understand why he pushed her away, but he had to try it if he wanted to get them home safely.

Misty could feel Mason's erection through his clothing. She had to fight the temptation to reach down and unbuckle his khaki's and take the solid length of him in her hands. Of course, it might cause him to wreck the car on the way home, but he could get another car. She knew her hand was driving him crazy. That's exactly why she left it there. She wanted him to feel some of the frustration she'd been feeling ever since he pulled her onto the dance floor. He had no idea she'd asked the server to leave out the Jack Daniels after her second drink. Every intense sensation she was experiencing was by her own choice. There was no question Mason wanted her, but she needed to know it was more than a fan girl fuck.

Misty didn't remember much of the drive to his home, only that his cock had grown rock hard under her hand, and much larger than she'd expected. That it had a similar effect on him became clear when he slammed the car into park outside the garage, flipped the key and pulled her into his arms with an urgency she'd not expected.

"Damn woman...you don't know wh... you're killing me." His mouth claimed hers, savoring the sweet taste of coca cola as he relished the pleasure of the kiss and the sultry promise of more to come. His hand swept up her back, teasing the nape of her neck before arching her back so his lips could nibble on the tender lobe of her ear. Once more his mouth returned to hers, his kiss deepening, urging on the slowly building fires. She leaned into him, thrusting her tongue against his, as they entwined in a seductive dance of animalistic hunger. He made a strangled groan, then swept her up into his arms. Somehow, he managed to get the door open and her into the house without breaking their bodies apart. It was all a blur; lips, hands, and rising passion, too long denied.

"I could never get you out of my mind. I dreamed about holding you in my arms again." Somehow, he needed to make her understand he'd been a complete jerk, and he was sorry. It wasn't going to be easy. He couldn't remember the last time he'd apologized to a woman...maybe his mother? He pushed his hair away from her face. "You don't know how much I want you," he whispered. "Tell me you want me, not Ace. Mason Reeves."

"Mason, I'...um.. I—" Her eyes locked on his and he could see the hunger reflected there. "Who's Ace Rivers?"

Triumph flared in his eyes. "Mine," his voice a primal growl as he reached for her, pulling her down to kiss her neck and throat. She was tired of waiting.

Her hands trembled as she unsnapped his khakis and slid them down his legs. He grinned and released the zipper that ran the length of her dress. It fell away, leaving nothing but a demi bra and her thong. She wanted to feel his naked skin against hers. She wanted him, all of him.

He used his hands to gently squeeze and caress her while he lavished her breasts with his tongue, making delicious jolts of pleasure dancing along her veins. She groaned out loud as his tongue traced the hollow between her breasts before returning to the flushed pink nipples. His tongue rolling the sensitive buds between his teeth enticing a sudden gasp with pleasure. Then he squirmed as Misty reached up to nibble on his earlobe, before stroking it with her tongue's tip. She whispered his name, her voice deep with lustful. Her seductive move caused him to moan deep in his throat, sending shivers racing throughout her body. Her partially opened mouth invited his tongue inside once more. His hands roamed her back and hips while his tongue took possession of the cavern of her mouth, thrusting his tongue against hers in an erotic rhythm all its own.

"Let me make love to you," he whispered. He pulled her down onto the carpet beside him. His dick was so hard he couldn't walk away if he tried. Then his teeth bit gently on her nipple, sending a wave of raw desire over her, flooding her body with a hunger she had never felt before. Her heart was beating much too fast. She needed to get her mind off the sensations flooding her system before she lost all control.

She twisted against him as his lips assaulted her breasts, his fingers stroking her flesh. "Mason, I need you now." She raised her hips to him, welcoming him, holding him tight as she felt him slide into her warm sheath and fill her body with the magic that was uniquely their own.

"Misty," he groaned as his head fell back, responding eagerly, hungrily. His hands roamed up and down her legs, then gripped them tight to hold her steady as he bag to move inside her. She pressed upward, urging him to thrust harder, holding him a willing captive as their bodies started moved together, in a demand to reclaim what was almost lost. She rolled her hips, eliciting a harsh gasp from him as he stroked her hunger toward its highest peak. He groaned her name, his breath coming faster as her hands, soft and silky smooth, explored him, roaming over his back and shoulders. Her breath slowed and matched each deliberate thrust, in as pulled away and out as he surged forward above her, hips rising and falling. She met him thrust for thrust, finding the rhythm she needed, each one deeper and stronger than the last. She opened her eyes and looked up at him. He couldn't help but look down at her with wonder as she gasped and ground herself even harder. He moved with her, feeling his passion growing, moving higher and higher, blocking everything except his growing love for her. And then there was no coherent thought. Just a blinding need to be consumed with a white-hot fire that was ready to explode. "Baby, come with me now!"

Misty cried out as a tide of pure pleasure rushed over her, each crashing wave pushing her higher and higher until any more pleasure would have brought tears to her eyes. Mason shuddered and gripped her hips as he erupted beneath her in a groan that was choked and desperate, joining her in a flood of ecstasy. She collapsed into his arms, and they held on to each other in the darkness, their bodies tensing and ebbing like the rhythm of the lapping ocean.

He rolled so that he held her head in his arms. His lips touched hers. "Promise you won't leave me," he whispered. "Let me make love to you forever."

He saw her smile in the darkness. She bent to kiss the corner of his mouth. "I'll give you a few years to convince me not to leave," she whispered. He let her sink down into his arms. She moved her cheek so she could rest it on his chest. Mason finally understood what he'd been searching for as he lay holding the woman he loved, listening to the rain fall, and looking at the softly glowing ivory towers in the distance.

One Last thing…

If you enjoyed this story, or any of my other books, I really would appreciate it if you could leave a review. I realize its a hassle, but it helps authors more than I can explain. It would take another book to list all the ways.

So Thank You in advance!
VC Sanford

Facebook - Bell, Book and Claw

Instagram @vcsanfordbooks

www.bellbookand claw.com

TikTik @bellbookandclaw

Bell, Book
and Claw
V.C. Sanford

MAKING
MEMORY
V.C. SANFORD